WHAT THE NIGHT TELLS THE DAY

What the Night Tells the Day

HECTOR BIANCIOTTI

TRANSLATED BY

LINDA COVERDALE

FROM THE FRENCH

THE NEW PRESS, NEW YORK

1995

LIBRARY OF CONGRESS CATALOGING-IN-PUBLICATION DATA

Bianciotti, Héctor, 1930–
   [Ce que la nuit raconte au jour. English]
   What the night tells the day / Hector Bianciotti; translated
by Linda Coverdale from the French.
   p. cm.
   ISBN 1-56584-240-5
   1. Bianciotti, Héctor, 1930– —Childhood and youth.
2. Authors, French—Argentina—Biography. 3. Argentina—
Social life and customs. 4. Authors, Argentine—20th
century—Biography. I. Coverdale, Linda. II. Title.
PQ3959.2.B53Z46413 1995
848—dc20
[B]   94-43354

ORIGINALLY PUBLISHED AS *Ce que la nuit raconte au jour*
IN 1992 BY ÉDITIONS GRASSET & FASQUELLE

PUBLISHED IN THE UNITED STATES BY THE NEW PRESS, NEW YORK
DISTRIBUTED BY W. W. NORTON & COMPANY, INC., NEW YORK, NY 10110

ESTABLISHED IN 1990 AS A MAJOR ALTERNATIVE TO THE LARGE,
COMMERCIAL PUBLISHING HOUSES, THE NEW PRESS IS THE FIRST
FULL-SCALE NONPROFIT AMERICAN BOOK PUBLISHER OUTSIDE OF
THE UNIVERSITY PRESSES. THE PRESS IS OPERATED EDITORIALLY
IN THE PUBLIC INTEREST, RATHER THAN FOR PRIVATE GAIN; IT
IS COMMITTED TO PUBLISHING IN INNOVATIVE WAYS WORKS
OF EDUCATIONAL, CULTURAL, AND COMMUNITY VALUE THAT,
DESPITE THEIR INTELLECTUAL MERITS, MIGHT NOT NORMALLY
BE "COMMERCIALLY" VIABLE. THE NEW PRESS'S EDITORIAL
OFFICES ARE LOCATED AT THE CITY UNIVERSITY OF NEW YORK.

BOOK DESIGN BY CHARLES NIX

PRODUCTION MANAGEMENT BY KIM WAYMER
PRINTED IN THE UNITED STATES OF AMERICA

95 96 97 98   9 8 7 6 5 4 3 2 1

FOREWORD
BY
OCTAVIO PAZ

ONCE PEOPLE WROTE ONLY IN THE LANGUAGE OF AN empire or a widely established religion: Latin, Sanskrit, Arabic. Nowadays, all languages – or almost all – are accompanied by a body of literature. This multiplicity of literatures entails the multiplication of translation, and these two facts accentuate the international character of the modern tradition: our classics are written in Italian, French, Russian, English, German, Spanish – in diverse European languages and a few Asian ones as well. A less frequent but equally characteristic phenomenon is the appearance of authors who do not write in their native tongues.

Both French and English literature may boast of several writers of foreign origin whose contribution is particularly rich: Conrad, Santayana, Nabokov, Ionescu, Cioran, Beckett... To this category belongs the Argentine author Hector Bianciotti. Although he has produced a number of highly regarded works in Latin American literature, he now writes exclusively in French. Let me add that his French is elegant, natural, free of archaism and familiarities of style, unaffected by either precosity or expressionism, a French that does not bear the stamp of any one region, but is rather the language of literary tradition. His prose is governed by a sense of proportion; it is clear without being obvious, and lively, but not overwrought. The author knows how to surprise us with an unexpected turn of phrase, a startling image, a soaring flight, a sudden twist – all so many intrusions, not of his Spanish nature, but of his genius. Bianciotti might say of his French prose what Santayana said of his own: "I write the least English of things in the most English of Englishes."

What the Night Tells the Day is the evocative title of Bianciotti's recently published memoirs of his youth, which he spent in the Argentine province and in Buenos Aires. Our past is so profoundly linked to our mother tongue that the resurrection of this past in a different language is both a discovery and a farewell: the encounter with the person we once were becomes a definitive separation. Gazing into the mirror of an unfamiliar language, the revived self identifies the image it sees, but does not recognize the voice it hears. Bianciotti's book relates how he slowly took leave of his native land and the boy he was; at the same time, the story foretells a decisive encounter: in abandoning his birthplace, the author somehow knew that he was drawing ever closer to his true self.

Indeed, the change of place and language gradually gives birth, not to another person, but to another writer. The resurrection of the past thus implies its alienation: the person I was does not understand my words, but I understand his. Far from abolishing communication, distance actually makes it possible: my former self speaks in me, and I translate this self into another language. Writing is a bridge that allows me to communicate with my past – and to exorcise it.

As its title indicates, Bianciotti's book is a story the author tells himself. The narration is not linear; just as in a novel, it moves forward, backward, begins again, goes off on a tangent, jumps around in time or space, imperturbably pursuing its winding course. Bianciotti proceeds by deft touches and sketches, preferring suggestion to explanation; he insinuates things instead of stating them baldly, and reduces each situation to a few essential elements. He does not describe; he evokes – he conjures. His art is closer to music than it is to painting.

The author uses all the resources of the novel, beginning with ambiguity – which is more than a resource: it is an attribute the novel shares with poetry, the defining characteristic of the literary imagination. Ambiguity allows us to perceive the double or triple nature of everything human; it is a literary procedure endowed with moral value as well, for it teaches us that nothing in man, from his reason to his sexuality, is simple.

Ambiguity eludes explanations. Bianciotti's intention is not to explain, except indirectly; he shows, or rather, he reveals. To him, understanding the world is not deciphering it, but accepting it. And he accepts it not through reason, but through his senses, or more exactly, through that strange alliance of intelligence and instinct that defines the poetic sensibility. It was not easy for him to accept reality; each acceptance began with a denial, and each break led in turn to a reconciliation followed by another, even more radical denial.

The first denial was that of physical space: the protagonist, the son of Italian immigrant farmers, contrasts the immense Argentine plain with his family home and its sprawling garden; later, he leaves the farmhouse for the town, then moves on to the capital, finally turning his back on that city to sail for Europe. He flees the stifling reality of Latin America, a sordid mixture of political oppression, injustice, and moral intolerance. These changes of place correspond to psychological changes, reflecting the rigor of that intimate exploration, the search for oneself.

Sexuality asserts itself according to the same law of division and acceptance: the solitary pleasure through which the adolescent tries to achieve a fleeting reunion with primitive nature, from which he was torn at birth; the gradual discovery of love in the person of a fellow seminarian, followed by a separation so wrenching that Bianciotti forgets even the youth's name; then heterosexual love, in the form of a passionate affair with a young woman that ends in another break-up.

The same process is repeated in the realm of ideas and beliefs. The family professes a fervid Catholicism, but the father is an atheist, which means that the childish religiosity of the protagonist is also a denial of the father. The adolescent Bianciotti renounces the ritualistic religion of his family, and this denial immediately becomes a new affirmation: the decision to enter the Church. Disappointed by religion, however, the young man abandons one faith to discover another: literature. The high priest of the new cult was named Paul Valéry. Faith in literature is a mixture of doubt and zeal, of daily joy and sorrow, of long struggles and brief flashes of inspiration. Bianciotti has always remained loyal to this faith.

All these denials and divisions are contained in the first: the rejection of the pampas. But how does one define the pampas? They are not the countryside, cultivated and transformed by settled farmers; neither are they the setting of History, like the plains of Central Asia, crisscrossed by nomadic peoples, by caravans and Buddhist pilgrims. The pampas are a locus of the indefinite and the indefinable: there, beginning and end, near and far, center and periphery, nature and culture cancel each other and dissolve. The unlimited combined with the undetermined: here is one of the poles of Bianciotti's novelistic memoirs.

The other pole is one of formal excess: the picturesque, the bizarre, the extravagant. A kind of hypertrophy of the formal impulse is manifested in figures such as the father's aunt, La Pinotta, a dreamer and vagabond, a feminine avatar of Don Quixote, wandering in rags along the dusty roads of the plain; Florencio, the suicidal acrobat; the priest captivated by village Lolitas: the lewd hunchback; the clairvoyant shuffling shiny marked cards, telling fortunes for those who have none; the Janus-faced characters, the villains suddenly moved by generosity...

Gradually, the meaning of all the painful separations, the reconciliations, and the fresh partings becomes clear. Bianciotti comes home to the Old World, searching for his roots, of course, but for something else as well, something no less precious. Between the limitless and the grotesque, the formless and the deformed, he seeks not a norm, but a form. Freedom is a thirst for incarnation, a quest for form. This is what the night tells the day.

WHAT THE NIGHT TELLS THE DAY

I

TODAY, MY OWN LIFE HAS COME LOOKING FOR ME. I have never felt much like thinking about my life, either past or future, still less like puzzling out the reasons behind this or that attitude or sudden change that might have surprised or intrigued those close to me. But together we have woven a tapestry, emphasizing or softening contours, heightening or toning down colors, weaving at the pleasure of the passing days, and with the approach of a winter that will never melt into spring, now that my term – however long a respite I may yet have – is coming to an end, I feel a longing to examine the hidden side of the material, the interlacing of its threads, some of them neatly tied off, others dangling unused, at loose ends.

No good fairies bent over my cradle, which I remember was very deep, with rough patches on its wooden surface.

When we are on the threshold of adolescence, uncertain whether to plod on or fly away, we believe that the decisive events in life will be heralded by fanfare, that glittering messengers of destiny will advance to greet us. With maturity, however, when memory strives to recapture the past, comes the dawning realization that the true harbingers of the future arrive on the sly, with the silent step of doves.

I am convinced that, as with all other things, we are born well before we come into this world, and that the paths we will take follow a prior design, a pattern that is already in our blood.

Of course, I can have retained no memory of this, but I do know that of all those endlessly renewed struggles, the most decisive battle, the one that would forever leave its mark, was fought by the infant lying in a cradle that resembled a miniature gondola, where his diminutive life was paralyzed by the swaddling clothes binding the tiny body from head to toe, following a custom intended to insure that the bones of his skeleton would grow straight and true – as my mother was to tell me solemnly one day, in a voice resonant with ancient wisdom.

To tell the truth, I still feel a certain raw connection with the horror of those early moments because I saw the same treatment inflicted on my little sister and witnessed the anguish, the rage, and the futile resistance (which must also have been mine) experienced by a consciousness doomed to oblivion and soon to be displaced by a self as yet unformed, but already beginning to take shape.

A carnal despair as different from lucid suffering as it was from soul-sickening grief; the impotent fury of an absolute rebel unable to loosen his bonds, struggling on behalf of his sheer animality, his only weapon a cry of outrage – *there* is the wellspring of the sudden gusts of terror that sweep through me, and the helpless desire to whimper, the phantom tears, and the stifled anger in my breast, an anger that explodes throughout my body. I awaken from these episodes as from a nightmare, and sometimes, at that very instant, nothing has happened: I cannot tell what has come over me, for I have skirted an abyss, an abyss that belongs to someone but is not completely mine, an inner arena where my demons fight among themselves.

I was, in the original, fresh sense of the metaphor, a bundle of nerves. And I tell myself that this must be why I continually feel driven to transgress, to race madly toward a shattering smash-up that would finally drain me of the violence I carry constantly within me, violence disciplined at this moment by the strokes of my pen. And for the same reason, I cling as tightly as I can to the system of precautions, manners, and courtesies perfected by men over the course of centuries to help keep themselves from one another's throats, a system in which I am willingly confined and *bound*. I fear myself. I obey myself.

2

My mother and older sisters worked from dawn to dusk on our farm, and when I was five my mother placed me in charge of my little sister Elida, who must have been a few months old at the time. Elida's temperament was calmer than mine, for despite the tight band around her – so artfully wound with reverse twists that it resembled a spear of barley, like the swaddling clothes in Nativities – she never complained as stridently as I had, or so I was told. She would sob now and again, and between sobs she would stare in puzzlement; she seemed to be trying to understand. One day, she turned her gaze on me, as though seeing me for the first time. She was drooling. Then, mindful of the reprimand I might be risking, I took her in my arms and laid the rigid envelope on our parents' unmade bed, over which hung the image of the Sacred Heart, with a blessed palm frond tucked into the frame and my father's black revolver hanging on a nail beside it. I smoothed out the bedclothes.

First, I tried to pull loose the tight-fitting band that had once been my own prison; it was made of a very thick piqué, frayed and threadbare in places. Then, probably the next day, I ventured to remove the safety pins that secured this meticulous wrapping in back. I stroked Elida's moist, tender arms, and she began to stir; she wriggled, babbled, fidgeted. I removed the linen square covering her diaper, which I would never have been able to put back on her, and for the first time I saw my sister's body: soft, plump, with red marks that slowly faded from the skin. And also for the first time, I saw something most unusual in the austere world of adult behavior: the brightness of a smile. Slowly, almost painfully, Elida opened her wrinkled hands, waved them suddenly, clutching at air, then studied them intently. She had just discovered her first toys, and gurgled with pleasure.

Simply to see her smile, I felt like dancing with Elida in my arms, the way Cecilia did with me to calm my fears at night. I would have danced to the sound of her cooing.

When she found us, my mother must have sensed our happiness, because I was not punished. And so the undressing ceremony before the tall mirrors on my mother's wardrobe – gleaming enigmatically in the semidarkness of the bedroom – became a ritual. The mirrors served as witnesses, and I felt what I would later recognize as the hope of surprising, in their depths, a specter beckoning me with its hand.

One afternoon overshadows all the rest. The little girl had grown but did not yet know how to walk. She was lying on the bed: chubby cheeks and belly, skin all rosy, warbling away. Her precocious game of coy evasions as yet consisted only of the invitation to rush directly to her side. I was fondling her dimpled arms and began to plant little kisses from wrist to armpit, lingering at the moist fold of the elbow. Nosing along her neck, I moved down to the tiny nipple, which I sucked. She wailed like a newborn baby, and my hand, as if remembering some ancient gesture, strayed about her curving belly a mite longer than it need have for an innocent caress. At times, seized with an irresistible desire to bite, I nibbled her thighs while tickling her nose and feet. Without knowing it, I was searching for the nodes of her sensuality, which I believe I detected through certain shudders, interruptions in her twittering, even her very gaze, which seemed to see something beyond me, something within herself. And I was learning, at an age when the imagination does not yet influence the senses, that no embrace will ever be close enough, and that we can never strain fiercely enough to make it so. I was beginning my apprenticeship in the despair felt by all who seek to enter, become part of, and disappear into the other.

If I were to live a hundred years, I would still see the empty sky and the branch swaying in the wind outside the small square window. I had looked up to make sure we were alone, and my lips still felt the soft, silky, and passionate kiss I had given her hidden femininity. This was a moment that, in passing, would manage not to prove fleeting.

Afterward, I can see only the disorder of the bedclothes, the open safety pins and the swaddling band strewn at the foot of the bed, my flushed face in the oval mirror of the wardrobe, and perhaps, inexpressible at the time, the perplexity of childhood slipping from pleasure into tears.

Have I learned all there is to know about mirrors? They always seem determined to conjure me into invisibility, showing me some stranger who invites me to follow him. In any case, it was in their presence that this feeling of guilt appeared, guilt that preceded – in the muddled passage of time – what is called the offense, just as obedience comes before the law, and in a way, creates it. And being certain of this does not alter remorse or change in any way the misadventures of existence. I do not know if everything is permitted in defense of one's life, but in one's defense against life – yes, everything.

3

PERÓN'S ASSUMPTION OF POWER WAS STILL FIFTEEN years away when I was born, in the month of March, on that Argentine plain I have tried to describe, or to exorcise, so many times. For a long while, all I knew of the world was a natural setting as grudging and severe as any on earth: the ground stretching out into infinity possesses none of the amenities suggested by the word *landscape*, for any curved lines the eye might have followed – aside from the elusive circumference where earth and sky draw their boundaries – have been banished from a surface so homogeneous that it seems to precede the Creation. Dawnn lays it bare, high noon annihilates it, and the wind sweeps out of its primordial lair to raise high curtains of dust that darken the sun before sifting slowly down like a fine, dry rain. Off in those regions, the center of the world shifts with each man who walks that earth, and all distances radiate from his footsteps. It was only gradually, by blindly piecing bits of information together, that I learned how to imagine the mountains, cities, or the sea I would sometimes hear mentioned by a grownup. That is why certain images dazzled or terrorized me, and why they endure indelibly inside me, alongside the reality that proved to be so different from my expectations.

4

MY MOTHER WAS THIRTY-FIVE WHEN I WAS BORN, AS she was, under the sign of Pisces. I have before my eyes a sheet of ruled paper, properly yellowed and torn at the folds, as befits documents found after someone has died. On this paper my mother wrote the date and hour of birth of each of her seven children, from Cecilia, born in 1915, to Elida, in 1936.

Why did she make this record? I can see her sitting at the mahogany desk, with its drawers to which my father alone had the keys. The pose is dignified but not solemn; her posture reflects, so to speak, the scrupulous modesty that characterized her behavior. Reserved, expressing joy with only a smile, and unhappiness simply through an attentive gravity, she must have drawn up her list with the same seriousness she applied to her everyday tasks, displaying no particular emotion. Her handwriting shows application and aspires – one can see this in the capital letters – to the elegance of calligraphy.

I take pleasure in the illusion that she wrote these things down for the scribe who would one day devote himself to prospecting his own memory, busily seeking traces of his past without suspecting that his mother had already appointed him guardian of the dead. Of our own dead, who lie deeper within us than anywhere else (unless they have been forgotten) and who must be protected, named, recalled in all their absurd ordinariness, until their ashes glow red in a few moments' remembrance.

5

As I SAID, MY CRADLE WAS A DEEP ONE, AND FROM it I scanned my first images, all striped by the small, grooved bars of the cradle's sides, except for the aerial vision of the faces bending over me, and the muffled, jerky flight of a bat my mother chased with a broom. My parents' bedroom had no windows. I slept there until my fourth year.

I was no longer imprisoned by a swaddling band, and one night I must have been awakened by a noise, or by the light from the girls' bedroom; the half-open door allowed me to glimpse something I had never seen before: a foot wearing a patent-leather pump decorated with a large, glittering buckle, and a flared skirt of a soft, soft pink that probably seemed even rosier in the yellow lamplight.

If I were to try to reproduce a conversation from long ago, or simply a sentence, the phrasing or the words might not be the same, but people sometimes confirm the truth of images recalled from my earliest childhood and are astonished that I remember them.

So it was with the paste buckle on the shoe and the skirt hem falling in folds about the ankle. It was the first time I had seen a shiny object, quivering with light, and I wanted it immediately for myself, in my cradle, in my nest, for I had the soul of a magpie. And also for the first time, there was the color pink, no longer the ephemeral rose of the sky at sunset, but something tamed, conquered, within reach.

The world had suddenly swung ajar, charging the hopeless *plainness* of the open plain with mystery; an accident had occurred, and the child recognized a marvel that belonged to him, just as the light on the morning of his creation from a handful of dust belonged to Adam: struck by beauty or love, any man (and a little boy even more) becomes once again, for an instant, Adam in Paradise.

In those faraway regions where the land never tires of supplying vast distances, a memory, an anecdote, or a muddled evocation of cities would now and then inspire the intimate dream of a beauty existing elsewhere – and in ruins, of course, as though the survivors of some Atlantis were counterfeiting a world of vanished wonders.

My eldest sister was taking a correspondence course in dressmaking, and for the final examination before obtaining her diploma, she had been required to sew an evening gown with a tight bodice and close-fitting skirt that flared at the knees – a gown cut from georgette, the most difficult of all materials to work with, she told me later, this woman who has always earned her living as a seamstress. In addition to the diploma, which raised her standing among the other families in the area (who would become her first customers), her skill earned her a letter of congratulations, and as a reward, the pair of pumps.

The improbable and all the more eagerly anticipated occasion to wear this finery presented itself the evening my brothers escorted Cecilia to one of our local balls, a dance like the ones I would later see in our own home, after we had moved as tenants to a larger farm: celebrations of an engagement, a birth, a successful harvest, or a hog-killing, when pigs were slaughtered and processed into varied bounty with the help of neighbors – if one may even use that word for people who needed binoculars to see the nearest house.

In the summer, out on the patio of beaten earth, or in the open, corrugated iron shed in the winter, when the sacks of wheat piled in pyramids had been cleared away, to the sounds of an accordion, and sometimes of a bandonion, a few percussion instruments, and a guitar (if a Creole had accidentally found favor in the eyes of these Piedmontese, who went so far as to shun the only Calabrian family in the area because they were from the south of the Italian peninsula) – out on the patio or in the shed, then, where water had been sprinkled to lay the dust during the week before the gathering, the young people from the neighboring farms would dance, somewhat awkwardly, as their mothers looked on, seated in a circle around the dance floor, their hands folded as though holding a lapful of memories, every maternal eye measuring the precise distance between the partners, alert to any nascent romance or offense to propriety. I remember the last dancers of one summer night; stars tumbling all the way to the horizon; a cozy sky of fireflies up in the trees...but the music has faded away.

On the evening when I awoke in my cradle to that dazzling vision of the paste buckle and the swirl of pink, I knew only one thing: Cecilia was abandoning me. I can still feel the grooves in the bars to which I clung so tightly, and I wished that they would hurt my hands even more. I must have burst into tears, shrieked my head off, cried my heart out, really bawled – and then suddenly have understood that I had won, because I calmed down.

And now Cecilia picks me up; she has red lips and a fragrance I have never smelled on her before. I see us in the wardrobe mirror, where her skirt puffs out so far it escapes the frame: Cecilia slowly twirls around in one spot, dandling me in her arms, humming a melody that floats off on high notes, and, to my delight, she strokes my cheeks, but not to caress me, only to dry my tears, to keep them from smearing her makeup. I snuggle in her arms, with my head on her shoulder, and at each half-turn I look up to glimpse my reflection, the pink of her skirt in the mirror, our shadow moving across the wall and up onto the ceiling. From nothing more than sheer longing, I would have given anything for a caress. Where I was born, neither children nor adults took pleasure in touching one another. And so, all that remains from my infancy is my big sister's hand upon my tear-stained cheeks as we move off into the distance in the mirror, a wraithlike whirling of pink disappearing beneath the silky slumber that envelops me.

6

ONCE I HAD LEARNED TO WALK, I TROTTED CONSTANTLY about the patio, a stretch of ground enclosed by a chicken-wire fence through which campanulas had twined in places, and season after season, year after year, we waited in vain for bluish purple blooms like the ones that flourished for my Great-Aunt Pinotta, bellflowers to which I placed my ear in hopes of hearing music, for although they were small, they seemed to me just like the trumpet of the phonograph that occupied a place of honor in my great-aunt's bedroom.

Our house? Five rooms of brick (including the floor) arranged around a kind of gallery. My father had built our home with his own hands, on the site once occupied by one of those mud hovels with thatched roofs abandoned by the Creoles as immigrants moved into the area.

The water pump was protected from the elements by the overhang of the roof. I liked to set one foot on the edge of the tank, which formed a cement platform, and let myself fall forward, leaning one hand on the post supporting the roof. I would play with my shadow in the sunshine, sending it tapering out into nothing by leaning forward, only to snap it back toward me as I balanced back and forth on the edge of the pump basin, like a pair of scissors plying its blades.

I was to experience the primordial terror of my life there, dangling between the tank and the post.

On the brick floor, beneath the spread of my legs, a yellow snake with black markings rises cobralike into the air. The only forms of animal life I know about are ants, birds, and livestock; this apparition, this *absolute*, paralyzes my entire being. I must have uttered some cry, because my mother appears instantly at the kitchen door, snatches up the braided leather whip kept hanging there on a nail in case of God-knows-what dangers, and strikes the snake, which recoils and darts off despite its wound – but my mother strides after it, and with a fierce strength that I have seen only in my father until this moment, she whips that writhing creature, and as I watch, she steps back, swings the whip handle like a club, and crushes the serpent's head before grinding it into the dust with her foot, doubtless to cast off her own fear.

There will always be a black-and-yellow snake rearing up in my memory, ready to strike, only to be itself struck down by my mother.

While all this was going on, Great-Aunt Pinotta, standing in her gaudily painted, jingling cariole, drove her fleet chestnut mare (the only creature in the world she ever cared for properly, according to her relatives) like a whirlwind into my nightmare and simply blew it away. I remember her eyes riveted on the ground, and her rags flapping out like wings when she raised her arms heavenward and shouted, "The 'leopardina'!" And I recall her hearty, toothless laugh as she picked up the carcass, twisting it deftly about her arm like a bracelet before tossing it into her cariole. I would later see the snakeskin, which she had tanned herself, hanging at the head of her bed, between Christ and the Madonna.

I have tried a hundred times to exorcise the dread I felt at seeing that snake irrupt from an unknown universe, with its fugitive and inexorable choreography utterly unlike anything I had ever known. I was at the age when a child tries to master the names of things, and my ignorance was tested at every turn. I would later vainly peruse cosmogonies in which the serpent figured as the bearer of the world and guarantor of its stability; I took no comfort in such things, as I could not fathom the creature's deification or even begin to imagine anyone not feeling an immediate revulsion, a sensation of skin-crawling sliminess at the sight of it. There was also the scandal of its duplicitous simplicity, beneath which lurked an infinite wealth of possibilities, all of them connected with death.

My childhood was transfixed by the traumatic revelation of the "leopardina," an event so charged with power that it enslaved me through sheer terror and instantaneous loathing – an event that is with me still. When I think about it, I cannot help believing that even though I had never gazed upon the figure of the snake in limbo, it must nevertheless have been engraved on my mind – even before my birth – as the very emblem of evil. In no other way can I explain the unfathomable effect of a form endowed with such concentrated energy and adorned, besides, with hieroglyphs as sumptuous as those of butterfly wings or the milky lightning that streaks through agates.

All the same, I have entirely given up seeking solace in scholarly texts, where I gleaned other representations of snakes that melded with the first one, multiplying it into an intolerable, seething mass that constantly vanishes only to reappear. I recall one very old work, the *Hamartigenia,* or *The Origin of Sin,* by Aurelius Prudentius Clemens of Zaragoza, translated by Remy de Gourmont, in which the author, who moves in an entirely predictable fashion from vice to viper, offers a description of the latter's sexual behavior that is certainly fantastic, but that also reveals a captivating precision, despite its exaggeration. "At the first rush of sexual excitement, the obscene female provokes the male, opening her mouth wide as if to

engulf him; the male introduces into her throat his triple-tongued head, and, all aflame, shoots out his kisses, ejaculating through this oral coitus the venom of generation. Wounded by the violence of sensual pleasure, the impregnated female breaks this pact of love, cuts the male's throat with her fangs, and swallows the sperm diffused within his saliva."

7

HOW FAR THOSE EARLIEST YEARS ARE FROM MY SEARCHING gaze! The heart of a child floats on the eddies of the past, already a prey to feelings that never linger long enough, however, to leave their mark, moving from sorrow to joy without transition, and from laughter to tears. Those scenes that have found a niche within my memory are bright spots scattered through a void of darkness, and the discovery of a color is associated with most of them, even with another memory I have of suffocation, which – unlike the swaddling clothes around my body – was only the slight squeezing of a slender band, similar to an engagement ring, that had been slipped onto the third finger of my left hand.

Whenever anyone would present her with a recollection, my mother – who had a feeling for the value of these modest treasures and was doubtless acutely mindful of their fragility – would hasten to place it in its proper setting, polishing it until the precise date was reestablished and the memory was clearly outlined in its true light (with a precision the memorialist would honor without embellishment) and restored, for an instant, to life.

When I spoke to her one day about that terrifying episode

with the little ring, she told me that it had once been the custom among country people to give very young children a piece of jewelry: for boys, a ring; for girls, a thin chain with a medal blessed by the Holy Father. My ring had been a present from my father, which surprised me, given the nature of the Piedmontese, who boast at every opportunity of their extreme frugality, recounting endless stories about people leading lives of plenty – cosseted, entertained, waited on hand and foot – and who are plunged one day into the miseries of Job. But in remembering the arduous world of that immense plain, where the begetting of children was tantamount to procuring one's own labor force, I also recalled the hunter I had encountered in some great saga who bands a falcon, ensuring that from then on the bird would hunt only for him, and thus I paid tribute to the father whom I had not loved.

And my mother: Had I loved her? Driven by life, we strive relentlessly to escape our parents, so that the heart – and this we realize only at their deaths – always lags behind.

As my mother continued her seamless recital of the tale, we came to the only episode I still recalled and recognized: There is a candlestick on the chest of drawers, and my mother is dressing me while my father urges her to hurry; I am crying, but the orange color of the knitted outfit I am to wear intrigues and distracts me. I had not yet ever seen an orange.

In the middle of the night, they take me to the doctor in the nearest village. The ring has become simply a wire strangling my swollen finger, and my entire being is concentrated in that finger, that tiny part of my body.

Pain typically divides you from yourself, which is why a hard knock on the knee will immediately displace the pain of heartbreak, sending the beloved's face spinning into oblivion. After all, as with the sufferings of love, there is almost never a connection between the severity of the distress and the severity of the injury.

I remember the bumpy ride in the break driven by my father, cracking the whip, and then the office of Dr. Tissera, a dark, handsome man with a mustache. He selected instruments from a case where each one sat in its own special recess: a pair of tweezers with hooks, a tiny saw, and pincers. I still recall how they reminded me of the tools my father wielded so impressively at his forge, the golden flames that shot out when he opened the furnace, and the red glow of the plowshare laid on the anvil, where, to the rhythmic beat of the hammer, the blade would slowly cool to blue.

While the doctor was preparing to remove the ring, he tried to amuse me with cajolery that must have calmed my distress and even won me over, because I still remember his face. My father announced that he was counting on me to act like a man. I don't see my mother in this tableau, which has closed in around my finger, but I sense that she was near. And just before the doctor slipped the tweezer hook under the ring, my attention was directed to a picture whose surface was painted a very dark blue, with a pointed white object sitting lopsidedly in the middle. They took the painting down from the wall so that I might see all the details: I could make out a tiny man in shirt sleeves waving a handkerchief. It was a picture of the sea, which was as boundless as the plain, they said, but there was no land, only water, and the little man was traveling in a carriage without wheels or horses, a break driven by the wind.

As the unfamiliar words and explanations made my ignorance seem more and more complex, the idea of an immense expanse of blue entered my imagination, if I am to believe my father, who afterwards and throughout his life, supposedly, related that while gazing at the picture, I had said the word "alfalfa." He had shown me our field of alfalfa in full bloom, its purple, cloverlike flowers rippling in the breeze. I do not know if I was able to picture what the sea was like, but for a few seconds I was the man in danger who looks out upon the scene and signals in despair to the little boy: pain and fear were now elsewhere, outside of my body.

A minute click brought me back to reality as the doctor finally snapped the ring, removing it from the deeply furrowed swelling. I will never wear rings: my fingers are claustrophobic. And although I love to see them flashing on women's hands, I feel distrustful of them, even hostile, for they will long outlive the hands they ornament, hands they have guarded, armed, rendered untouchable.

But I have only to behold the rolling waves of the ocean, a sailboat heeling over, and I can see that painting once again and, framed by its gilded boundaries, the infinity of sky and water it contains.

Why do innocuous facts or things glimpsed in a dream imprint themselves on us forever, while events of capital importance are lost and the heroes of our lives vanish into the wings? And to think that memory is the very fabric of my present, that what I remember makes me what I am!

The seascape that so enchanted me in Dr. Tissera's office is with me still, whereas I could make nothing of his patient description of the roiling waters and the pitching of the ship. I tell myself that knowledge precedes language, even calls it into being. I have known how distressing it is to speak in ignorance and to experience the panic of feeling imprisoned inside myself for lack of words.

8

IN THOSE WIDE OPEN SPACES OUT ON THE EARTH'S BARE crust, no one looked at the sunsets, or the moon hanging from its astral pole, or the night sky that sometimes spilled its cargo of stars clear to the horizon – except to predict the weather. Beauty, if it was perceived at all, was considered merely a caprice at the heart of the necessity for survival, the relentless struggle for subsistence. People took no delight in art because they were ignorant of its metamorphic powers. The aesthetic emotion provided by nature depends upon its evocation by man; one admires not a god but the creation of a likeness that has been touched by the grace one might have merited oneself. And so, it was La Pinotta, as she was always called (the article preceding her given name made her, if not unique, at least singular, a kind of monster), who was responsible for my awakening to beauty.

A deep wrinkle cut across her forehead between her stiffly bristling hair and her bushy eyebrows, which jutted out like awnings from her weathered face. Right up against her girlish nose nestled a pair of owl's eyes, one of which, although milky, seemed to see me better than its companion, because it was always that filmy one I looked at.

The threadbare garments wrapped around her neck enveloped her from head to waist, where they spread scarflike over her skirts, which were a verdigrised black. I was filled with reverent terror by this palimpsest of billowing petticoats, which she was constantly lifting and letting fall again as she stealthily concealed some valuable pilferage, and when she pulled me close to her, clamping my head against her knee, I stiffened with dread at the idea of being thrust into that heap of rags and lost forever. I feel this same anguish whenever I am at the edge of a wood or the mouth of a cave: my mind seems to shut down, leaving me panicky and helpless.

Of all the images bequeathed to me by La Pinotta Tarquino – such was the surname of the husband, who decided to hang himself the day after their wedding – my favorite is the sight of her standing in her cariole, hurtling across the fields, her rags flapping about her as she dwindles into the distance. As I see her in my mind's eye, the wind lends drama to her streaming tatters, the trappings of a messenger flying in fateful haste. The most precious happiness I ever received from her, however, was music, and so the afternoon of the *ranchera* and *La Traviata* must take precedence.

The first image that comes to mind is that of my great-aunt sopping up sauce with large slices of bread, wiping the plate on her lap with the soft crumb of each piece. We had not informed her of our visit beforehand – how could we? – since good manners required solely that visitors avoid arriving during the hour before mealtime, but La Pinotta lived alone and followed her own schedule.

After cleaning her plate, La Pinotta bustled off to her cluttered bedroom while we waited in the gallery; she had gone to fetch her phonograph, and I suppose that was why my eldest sister, who so loved to dance, had brought me with her.

Since our house constituted the norm, in my eyes, I was surprised to find no water pump in this one. My great-aunt showed me the well, and lifting me up in a cloud of musky underarm odor, she plopped me down on the brick lip of the well. Pushing aside the rusty iron cover, she urged me to look at my reflection in the dark water and whispered that her oldest friend lived there, the indispensable tortoise, which was supposed to purify the water, according to a Creole legend of uncertain origin.

La Pinotta possessed two phonograph records discovered, who knows how, in the course of her bartering out in the wilderness, when she would take advantage of a poor harvest or an epidemic among the livestock to carry off the overseas mementos of unfortunate immigrants: the crown of waxen orange flowers worn by the successive brides in one family, a garishly colored crockery fruit dish, the occasional small piece of jewelry, a trunk, a grandmother's rocking chair or her trousseau, her only dowry, which had been kept intact at the bottom of a chest, where the meticulous needlework had turned as yellow as the bones of the embroideress in her tomb. And so, having invented the pigsty and the secondhand business out in that solitary wasteland, where she occasionally hired out her services mending clothes, La Pinotta lived amid a constant hauling about of bric-a-brac, always in the process of moving house, but never leaving her scrap of property, where a Creole tenant farmer grew corn. And as soon as the ears were as big as her thumb, she would remove a leaf or two from their involucres and dry them, thus amassing in the end a fine stack she would sell to her sharecropper for cigarette papers.

One of the recordings was of Argentine dance music that has since fallen almost completely out of favor: the *ranchera,* the Creole waltz, the *milonga;* the other record contained highlights from *La Traviata.* It was only long after the phonograph and its records had become relics that I learned how such recordings were made. I have never heard an Argentine mention the *ranchera,* which had only a brief vogue; sometimes I hum La Pinotta's, and then I have the fleeting and rather melancholy impression that I am the last person alive who knows it.

La Traviata? I had not understood that a voice was carrying the melody. These sounds pitched so high, wafting far away, toward the sun, vanishing there only to burst from the shadows close by – I tried in vain to imitate them, and they still affect me. My older sister's humming had not given me a sense of what music was, but whether *ranchera* or *Traviata,* it will always seem to me like a world within the world, a visitation of greatness from elsewhere, the irruption of a kind of grace into reality. As a child, I thought of music as a light similar to the divine beam that pierced the clouds in the frontispiece of my mother's Book of Hours.

La Pinotta...People said she was as cunning as a procuress and dishonest to the core – and of course, shady intrigues of all kinds were her business and her pleasure, but if anyone dared challenge her on this in public, she defended her fraudulent dealings with such a lofty air that the audacious accuser and any witnesses won over to his cause would give in to her, their sarcasm slowly ceding ground to a timid respect. She would not even deign to scold the poor fool. She simply took advantage of the fact that Hell was on her side.

Although she bristled with foul-mouthed abuse and nastiness, one yet sensed in her, at times, great powers of forgiveness. She forgave the plain its harshness; she forgave fate for having decreed she should die on that plain in poverty; she forgave Heaven for everything else.

From time to time she would relax, suddenly let herself go,

because her campanulas were in flower or huge dark clouds had passed before the sun, like the hood my father would pull up on our break, to protect us from sunstroke. Did these moments of relaxation hint that a day would come when age and reason would bring her to repentance? A certain lassitude would seep through her limbs, but without lulling to sleep the concentration of energy and guile that remained her peculiar treasure and that would shortly revitalize her body, setting her back on her feet with a sparkle in her eye – as it did that afternoon, with the music playing, when she abruptly kicked off her espadrilles and, moved by the voice drifting ever farther off over the fields toward the sun, she began to spin around and around, humming like a wasp, to the sound of the waltz that accompanies the most beautifully plaintive music of *La Traviata*. Why are the saddest songs sung to joyous rhythms? The voice implores, intoning its *lamento*, growing fainter in endless farewells, while the precise throbbing of the dance stubbornly continues in three-quarter time, as life pursues its merry round.

I remember La Pinotta's dirt-encrusted foot pushing off from the heel at each spin, keeping time with the music, her skirts and shawls whirling up and away from her body. I glimpsed her crooked legs and her rag-picker's purse hanging from the garter that held up her knitted stockings in the wintertime. And when the music of that voice rose up so high that it was lost in the sunshine, I remember the dancer stopping short, then running ecstatically out into the fields, stirred by pleasure from the depths of her soul.

Then I recall nothing more until our trip home in the carriage. The clouds were growing sleek as the day drew to a close. And the happiness of the music, already in the past, had become tinged with sadness.

Since I remember the *ranchera*, I assume that I went often to La Pinotta's house, but the first time remains the only one for me. I would see her again – before she disappeared for a lapse of five years – during our move to a larger farm, when the house was in such an uproar that I was put in her care. She took me to the shantytown surrounding the village of Luque, where I witnessed, at sundown, a service at which my she-devil was the celebrant and some wretched Creoles formed the congregation, handing their pitiful coins over to her in the hovel of the "saint."

I hesitate at the threshold, reluctant to cross this floor of beaten earth to find a place among the people kneeling at the bed, which is illuminated by a small window that frames the fading red of the western sky, without first trying to gather together whatever memories I still have of an event that involved the two of us but that I experienced all alone, when I was almost five years old and still living in the house where I was born, the house my family was about to leave.

9

MY FATHER YEARNED AFTER CULTURE, WHICH IS WHY HE sent his sons to boarding school – usually to one run by the Salesian fathers in Villa del Rosario or even in Córdoba – once the boys had learned the rudiments of spelling, arithmetic, geography, and Spanish-American history from the schoolmaster (or, more often, the schoolmistress) who lodged with one or another of the local farmers.

This stay in town would last between two and three years, depending on the profits from the wheat harvest, which could be wiped out by a single ill-timed rainstorm. As for his daughters, it seemed to my father quite enough that they should know how to read and write, and if they were also skilled in cookery and sewing, able to do everything from making his trousers to knitting his socks, then he allowed them to devote themselves to their embroidery on Sunday afternoons.

My father was the only farmer in the region to subscribe to a major newspaper, *La Prensa*. He believed it was essential to keep well informed about world affairs and would glow with pride whenever his children fought over the supplements in the daily paper. And his satisfaction – which he savored in private, for lack of anyone to share it with – reached its highest point when Armando, his second son, made friends at boarding school with the son of a lawyer who was regularly and favorably mentioned in the pages of *La Prensa*, a man who had proven his courage by speaking out in court against the "Black Hand," a miserable association of Sicilian thugs who specialized in extorting money from the Piedmontese.

Accordingly, when Tomasito Carrara came to spend a few days on the farm, no effort was spared to put a respectable face on our poverty.

Had I ever seen an automobile? When the stranger's black cabriolet with its gleaming chrome pulled up between the two trees that alone adorned the strip of ground in front of our house, it was almost like La Pinotta's music – something from out of this world. And when I saw the young man whom the grown-ups were welcoming in awkward embarrassment, my mother and sisters hanging back shyly, I was struck with timid amazement: he became my idol on the spot.

From that period of my life I can remember neither my mother's face nor my father's, nor, with the exception of Cecilia's, can I remember the faces of any of my brothers and sisters, whereas I can feel the atmosphere that radiated from each of them, and sometimes I have a sense of their bearing. But when I think of La Pinotta and Tomasito Carrara, how I wish I could show them the image I still have of them!

Tomasito Carrara was the very first person to show me just how different people can be beneath their common humanity. He possessed such charm that he was able, quite unintentionally, to captivate everyone around him, and he had a gentle strength, an ease of manner that made him unique, particularly in our company, for we always seemed uncomfortable with our bodies, and even when seated would shift our rear ends on our chairs as if trying to settle all our limbs in the right place.

We put an extra leaf in the table and brought out our good tablecloths: the cross-stitched cloth, the scalloped one, and on the last day of the visit, the drawn-thread cloth that my maternal grandmother had begun sewing in the Piedmont and that my mother had finished, using it for the first time on her wedding day. In honor of our visitor, I saw my mother drink a glass of water tinted pink with wine at supper time.

The women of the house bustled joyously about, constantly vying with each other in culinary skill and imagination, and in the evenings they abandoned their espadrilles for low-heeled shoes. Never had there been such a flourishing of hand mirrors, and never had our family displayed such awkwardness at the dinner table when it came time to unfold the napkin, a thing we never used. We kept an eye on the stranger, who kept his on my father, trying to imitate his manners and movements, and failing in spite of his careful efforts, for from birth he had belonged in a different element, in a light that came neither from the sun nor from lamps. Once – I must have been hovering around him during the dessert – he put his arm around me and hugged me to his chest. The gesture was one of sweetness and delicate strength: no abruptness, rudeness, or pretense, but a kind of skillful distribution of his energy in affection, never condescending to coddling or coaxing.

Tomasito Carrara: I suddenly see him again, in a short-sleeved shirt and trousers as white as sheets; he wears sandals; he tosses his hair, which is quite short at the nape but frizzes luxuriantly on the top of his head, falling symmetrically from a perfectly straight part to frame his temples in curls. We are getting everything ready for the tennis match that will almost cost me my life. Our guest has offered to initiate my brothers into the game, one spoken of as if it were an art rather than a sport, and discussed in quite specific terms, as when a reporter would put the finishing touch on his panegyric by comparing the player in question to some famous dancer.

Like traveling actors setting up a stage with a few planks and a dozen nails, we lay out a kind of tennis court on the strip of ground next to the black expanse of charred stubble-field that has been burned over after the harvest.

Assigning tasks to everyone, my father undertakes to mark the court by planting stakes at the four corners, as well as halfway along the sidelines to hold the net the girls have made by sewing gunny sacks together by hand. My brothers have cut some racquets out of plywood, after tracing the outline of Tomasito's with red chalk.

We are all sitting in a line, my mother, my sisters, and I, in front of the wire fence around the patio, while my father paces around the court, checking to see that the stakes are solidly anchored in the hard-packed soil; he seems to be familiar with the rules of the game, and affects the air of authority of a stern referee, an authority that I, for one, am not prepared to accept. He must be thinking how puzzled the young locals will be when his children, in turn, try to introduce them to this rich man's sport.

My brothers are facing Tomasito Carrara. I can see once again my brothers' long, ungainly strides, like snippets from a damaged film – particularly Armando's lurching as he smacks the ball heartily into the fields, so eager is he to show that he has already understood his friend's instructions. Incapable, however, of mastering the game all in one go, he imitates the other man's position: knees bent, legs apart, almost crouching, head swaying evenly from side to side, watching for the return of the ball with the nervous alertness of a goalie.

I can also see the little white sphere hanging motionless for a moment at the summit of its arc before descending to be gathered in by Tomasito, who leaps up from the ground – his body twisting with the flamelike torsion of those depicted rising from the dead in my mother's Book of Hours – and stops the ball cold. And now my brothers begin warming to the game, drawing on a strength that comes more from their desire to rise to the stranger's level of play than from their untrained muscles. Is he only pretending, out of pure politeness? The young man who had seemed so superior, at times even imperious, showing faint signs of impatience at his students' clumsiness, is letting shots well within his reach go by, losing on purpose. And now the beautiful architecture of his body is collapsing, and he flails about disjointedly, like the others.

Suddenly, I am struck by a racquet, full on the forehead. With the index finger of my left hand, I sometimes slide the skin over the gently curving bone, as I am doing at this moment, exploring the double scar that has almost faded away with time, touching the narrow fissure that has, on the contrary, enlarged with the growth of the frontal plate. Family history has it that I did not faint, nor did I cry when the wound was disinfected with alcohol, and that up until the departure of Tomasito Carrara, I displayed a courage not unmixed with affliction (to ensure that he would keep lavishing attention on me).

The child's infatuation with the stranger exceeded all bounds on the day he was invited to sit beside the young man in the car for an outing to Luque. He watched his mother and sisters waving their timid hands, playing at farewells; then there was nothing besides the future of the dusty road and the longing to remain forever ensconced in this car that was carrying him away. He had no idea that when he awakened the next day, the car would no longer be parked, as it had been on previous mornings, beneath the roof of the open shed where the wheat was stored, and that he would never again in his life see Tomasito or hear any news of him, except that of his death.

The hearts of children can also break from love, and no one could ever console them where they go to hide in themselves when *that* hurts them, when *that* happens to them out of the blue, with the rumbling flashes and disasters of a thunderstorm. They burrow into their secret, like an ailing little animal that goes to ground, without words to express their sorrow, wounded for life.

IO

La Pinotta Tarquino – whom I did not address as "Great-Aunt," since she was larger than life and well beyond any family relationship – was taking me, as I was saying, to the shanty-town around Luque, to the "saint's" hovel. I would gain some idea of the ceremony I witnessed there, speechless and amazed, only long afterward, when I questioned my mother, persuading her to tell me (somewhat uneasily) about what she considered to be La Pinotta's sacrilegious activities. Be that as it may, what I saw affected my ignorance so strongly (and – I think I can say this – my soul as well) that I consider the event to be a revelation and even an act of grace: to a certain extent, and in a different mode, I will have spent my entire life seeking simply to reproduce it.

The "saint's" mother was not a dwarf, but her frame was so small and her skin so tightly drawn over it that her sharp little face reminded me, in the dim light, of an animal's muzzle. In addition, she trotted ceaselessly about like a nervous mouse, and I remember that as soon as we had crossed the threshold and started making our way through the assembled devotees, La Pinotta began bossing this woman around relentlessly, as though leading her about on a leash.

The raking light of the setting sun poured through the little window, mottling the semidarkness, tracing the folds of the mosquito net enveloping a camp bed where the form of the "saint" rose and fell with sibilant inspirations and expirations so feeble that each one seemed to be her last. Now and then a faint cry escaped her, followed by a soft muttering that must have arisen from some great inner consolation. It was difficult

to see her face, and became even more so when the mother
lighted the candles on either side of the bed, because the gauze
of the mosquito net turned opaque in their glow, but then the
shaft of light from the setting sun struck the netting, and stifled
exclamations stirred the crowd: through the tattered veil could
be seen the head of the sleeping woman, resting on a pile of pillows, wearing a close-fitting cap anchored by a crown of chiffon
or crepe-paper roses like the ones my sisters made to honor our
family dead on All Saints' Day. Her thick lips opened and
closed as her eyebrows puckered into points and then relaxed
again with the rhythm of her breathing. And when the "saint"
had brought her hands together over her breast, in response to
some prearranged signal she may have obeyed from simple
reflex, La Pinotta stepped like a high priestess from the silent
shadows into the blaze of the sunset, which, growing ever
brighter, surrounded her with a halo of red and gold. Stretching
out one hand, gathering up an armful of her ragged garments,
she launched into her sermon. Her voice sounded completely
different to my ears. I did not understand a thing she said, and I
remember her words as a kind of cantilena. Many years later,
however, when she replayed that scene at my request during a
visit to our new farm, I learned that she had recited to her Creoles the story of Saint Rose of Lima, the Peruvian of Spanish
extraction who became the first Christian in the New World to
be elevated to sainthood. She died at the age of thirty-one in
1617, and was canonized – with admirable symmetry – in 1671.
She would converse with her guardian angel or sing duets with
a song thrush while she sewed dresses or cultivated flowers for
the benefit of the Indians. At the moment of her death, the sky
was covered with roses, and a shower of petals fell over Peru.

La Pinotta paused occasionally and listened, gauging the
effect of her words, seeking in the eyes of the faithful some
answering sign of assent; she spied upon them, hoping to catch
them unawares, and when she urged them to pray, holding her
arms out in front of her, you would have thought she was holding her own soul in her hands. Years later, in a concert hall, I

would be reminded of her gestures when the orchestra conductor swept his hands through the air to drive the sound higher, ever higher, until in a single wave it reached its apogee and was there abruptly cut off, allowing silence to sing at the very limit of hearing, in the same way that La Pinotta's outstretched hands seemed to command the miracle of the erubescent sun then sinking on the horizon, its last rays piercing the shadows of the room to set the ragged mosquito net on fire for one brief second. Then the mouse, who had remained at the head of the bed, furtively pulled a string, dropping a sudden shower of wild-flowers upon the breast of the "saint," briefly interrupting her snores.

The sun's last burst of light had given way to an almost lunar clarity that quickly faded, and the mud walls, their coat of whitewash long gone, absorbed the shadows cast upon them by the faithful who, guided by the mouse, filed past the "saint's" resting place as though it were an altar, kissing the foot of the bed and the crucifix that passed from hand to hand until it arrived in mine; terrorized, I hastily returned it to the mother of the sleeping idiot. Despite being as weary as a pytoness after pronouncing her oracle, La Pinotta barred the crowd's way at the door like a majestic grandmother, holding out her alms purse.

I constantly feel the hovering possibility of *feeling* in a different way. Of course, the person who experiences things is not the same one who remembers them. I suspect the present of nourishing the memory more than memory nourishes it; things have imprinted themselves on us without our noticing them at the time, and their reviviscence transforms them into magnets for all sorts of relics and impressions that come to cling there like shellfish on a rock. But the magnet sometimes rejects what has drawn near it on the strength of some affinity with this fragment of the past. As on the day, for example, when I read these last lines of a sonnet: "As pompous as a melodrama's throne / The fragrant Bed, unmade, in shadows bloomed." I saw again, as the five-year-old must have seen her, the "saint" on her camp bed. But the hovel was too cramped and its ceiling too low to welcome the sumptuous theater evoked in those two musical lines by Verlaine.

Even more than the comparison linking the bed to a throne, the word *melodrama* awakened a retrospective echo: a kind of Ur-theater had been created by La Pinotta's plaintive recital, the intent and silent audience, and the striking (albeit impoverished) setting, where even the sun was only a stage light off in the flies. Light playing along the folds of a backdrop and the hypnotic power that intonation can lend to words are enough to make us believe in oceans and battles and faraway places. But the crown of chiffon roses circling the forehead of the obese idiot child, her bellow of alarm when the mother let go of the handful of small coins La Pinotta had deigned to grant her, the pathetic rite, and those credulous souls are all destined to be forgotten.

If these things should perish with me, at least you and I will have spent a moment reflecting on them together.

II

THE FIRST DISTINCT MEMORY OF MY MOTHER'S FACE? Her sudden reflection in the wardrobe mirrors that evening when she abruptly turned down the lamp: ordering me in a low voice to be quiet and stay still, she cautiously brought out from behind the chest of drawers the long rifle I considered, along with the revolver, an attribute of my father. I would never again see such anxiety in my mother's eyes, such an expression of alarm. The watery surface of the mirrors lit up at her approach, reflecting not so much her features as the clear, pale light of her face.

We spent the first night on the new farm all alone, she and I. Ever since sundown, we had been holed up in her room, where the chest of drawers, the wardrobe with its folding door, the night table, the big brass bed with its tall head and foot pieces painted to resemble wood, the revolver hanging from its nail, and the Sacred Heart of Jesus with its blessed palm duplicated exactly, but in roomier surroundings, my parents' bedroom in our former house. We had just caught the sound of a motor: cars were slow and noisy at that time, out in our area, and not many farmers owned one. Automobiles belonged to the owners of those properties, to the world of cities, or else to the unpredictable Black Hand. In the endless night, the mere chugging of a car was enough to give alarm: lamps were extinguished, and men took up positions, weapons in hand, behind shuttered windows.

This car stopped on the road, well beyond the line of poplars that screened the house from passersby. We didn't hear any doors slam, but we could see the beams of flashlights signaling through the leaves before the night closed in on us again, and silence. It was then that I glimpsed my mother's face, just before she turned down the lamp, leaving only a faint gleam, like that from glowing coals, by which we could just make each other out in the darkness. Then, with the rifle slung over her shoulder, the way my father carried it to go hunting, she checked to make sure the door was tightly bolted. I was huddled quietly on the bed, clutching the footboard, while my mother stood with her finger on the trigger, pointing the barrel toward the rafters with her left hand, listening to the silence, trying to identify the noises we paid no attention to during the busy daylight hours.

What did she hear? She blew down the glass tube of the lamp and fumbled for me in the dark, to reassure me. We heard cautious footsteps, barely audible but soon more hurried, and then rustling sounds and whispers. Once again, as with the "leopardina," I felt *that:* fear, and an impulse to flee that was struck, at its very height, by paralysis.

For the rest of her life, it seems, my mother would tell how our teeth began to chatter when we heard those men gathering just outside the window. A shaft of white light came through the shutter slats, piercing straight into the room, then slanting, wandering, sweeping across the mirrors that might have betrayed us. On the edge of terror, I was aware of two parallel sensations unfolding inside me, pulling me apart: I could see my face disfigured by fright, and although I recognized myself, I refused the horror that image was trying to transmit to me, and I managed to see the figure in the mirror as someone else, a frightened child who no longer dared even to fling himself down on the mattress and hide behind the footboard. He was the one in danger; he was the one who risked being kidnapped or killed by the Black Hand. A kind of joy surged through me, but at so deep a level that it could not ease the torment of the reflection watching me. Then the room was left once more in utter darkness. We heard conspiratorial whispering; the sudden barking of a dog tightened into shrill yelps, clearly caused by a kick to the animal's ribs. We had never had a dog, so it must have belonged to the former tenants.

The footsteps on the terrace grew bolder; were the men going away? They went around the house once more and returned. The light crept back into the room through the shutters. The lugubrious barking began again, farther off, somewhere in the clump of trees at the end of the farmyard, and this time there was a brief struggle: shouting, growling, the sound of blows and thrashing branches; we could hear the animal whimpering, and then, at the end, an atrocious howl cut off by astonished silence, which quickly exploded into hideous laughter.

We stayed for a long while without moving. The car engine started with a cough, and setting down the rifle, my mother took my hand to lead me into the next room, where the windows looked out toward the road. She opened a shutter slightly, and we watched the headlights of the car as it turned around behind the row of poplars.

I will always be waiting for someone to take me by the hand and lead me through the darkness.

There is in fear a complicity more immediate than any agreement or understanding, even a carnal one; this complicity stabs like a needle as it courses through the body, seeming to freeze the blood and all thought in its passage. We try in vain to describe it, to find some other definition besides that of "the feeling experienced in the presence of danger"; no matter how old we are, we always become children again, back in a time before words. Fear? Sometimes it makes the words *mother* or *father* spring to the lips; it depends. As for myself, there is nothing that does not frighten me.

My father arrived the next morning, well before dawn, and when he awakened us, I felt quite proud of the fear my mother and I had shared. And at first light, I ran out to explore this new territory, so rich, so varied, so elusive in its confusion of trees, sheds, and silos, and it was at the end of the first yard, amid the thick foliage of the fig trees, that fear caught up with me, rooting me to the ground and freezing a scream in my throat. The night was just rolling up its last shadows, uncovering the land, and in the morning twilight I had unknowingly bumped my forehead into the paws of the dog. It was hanging from a branch, stiffened by death, with its tongue sticking out crookedly, its neck twisted, its fangs bared threateningly, and a bloody cross cut into the soft fur of its belly, carved by the bottle shard glinting in the grass. Gaunt, mud-splattered, covered with contusions, as though a squad of torturers had vented their rage on the animal by pounding and ripping it, the dog hung with a splinter of wood planted in its heart and the grimace of death drying in its jaws.

Other animals – cats, a puppy – have died curled up in my arms. Aside from the eyes, whose depths can lose their light long before the heart has ceased laboring, their faces remain unchanged; but when the purring or the death rattle has been stifled by the last heartbeat, there is a transfiguration, and each time I have found myself holding a strangely old little body.

And now my mother calls my name, to the north, to the south, her voice echoing inside the house and along the gallery, and I cannot answer her, for I still cannot move. The summer-scorched grass crackles beneath her espadrilles; I wish that my grief were as deep as my disgust. She catches sight of me and calls to ask the reason for my silence, but as she draws nearer, her reproachful voice breaks off abruptly, and in a useless gesture, she slips her hand over my eyes. Pushing me along in front of her, we set off to find my father. Her voice has failed her, too.

My father's, however, reaches us loud and clear through the gaps in the partly unhinged door of the shed where all the farming machinery and harnesses are stored in a jumble with the break, the sulkies, and the stores of sausages packed in lard. At the top of a ladder, busily driving pegs into the wall with great hammer blows, he pours out his monologue, although this word hardly ever suits the flood of crisscrossing challenges and retorts through which my father gives rein to his native intransigence. For as long as I can remember, he cultivated the genre, and I was – mostly during the years I spent on the farm – the fascinated and rather frightened witness of his soliloquies.

First the vehicle shed, and then the open storage sheds, which were larger and more resonant, provided the theater where he was both actor and spectator; as soon as he entered them, scythe or ax in hand (the tools he most enjoyed using), he seemed to glimpse in the half light a throng of skittering, rustling antagonists, all plotting against him. (And what was I doing there, on top of the sacks of wheat he and my brothers piled up so skillfully? I simply liked to climb them.)

Always bustling about in a state of almost ungovernable excitement, he would quickly strike up a discussion with the shadows, and once they had settled firmly on a subject, his anger would get the better of him, cresting in an exhaustive torrent of insults, injuries, outrages, and astonishments, as he thundered in the name of justice against the arguments bedeviling him. He upbraided his audience, shouted, hurled excommunications left and right; sometimes he would break off, struck by the way his fulminations echoed off the corrugated-iron roof, or by the wind yammering cheekily along the grooves.

At times the show ended in an uproar when the participants in the dispute all turned out to be equally hostile toward one another, and then my father (or one of his opponents) would try to end the debate by imposing on the group some sort of judgment without rhyme or reason – and without appeal. So saying, he would throw back his shoulders, preparing to leave behind his august solitude, so crowded with phantoms and the chatter of inner voices, and, abruptly hitching up his pants, he would return to earth.

Judging by the ample sweep of his pantomime outlined against the horizon, there was another theater where he felt completely at ease: out in the fields on blustery days, with the untrammeled wind of the plains that rippled through the grain and tangled the alfalfa. Our tragic actor would return home from his walks exhausted, as if after giving an inspired performance. The farmhands or family members careless enough to meet up with the tireless speechifier tried to dodge him and continue respectfully – or thankfully – on their way, but if the pretense failed and my father was startled into interrupting his soliloquy, his face would pale as he emerged from whatever limbo he had reached, one eye glowering, the other still back in the beyond. He never tried to laugh off such episodes, and although we did not discuss this among ourselves at all, we knew not to be surprised at his penchant for ranting.

I do not think I am guilty of exaggeration in the preceding lines; like my father, I also talk to myself, especially in the street, and although I try to keep from gesticulating as I speak, too often my hands get carried away. The streets are my fields, and the relentless roar of the traffic is my wind from back home.

A year before the death of my father, whom I was seeing again for the first time in fifteen years, I was disconcerted to discover a resemblance between us, a common habit of interpolating incidental clauses in a narrative, that made me his counterpart: to a certain extent, we were, at that moment of realization, the same person. But it is not yet time for me to recall that revelation. To find my way there, I must set down in black and white the many pages that have written themselves within me, and cross the three and a half decades separating that distant moment from the child left speechless by the sight of the butchered dog.

After a moment's hesitation, my mother plucked up enough courage to push open the rickety door of the shed where my father, perched on the ladder, was haranguing illusions, and I followed her inside.

When he saw the dog, my father did what he always did whenever something shocking happened: he swallowed his indignation and put on his stoic mask. He attributed the crime, and specifically the affront, to the Calabrese, who had always envied him, he said, and who in this case were furious that he, not them, had taken over the farming lease on what was our new home. This outrage smacking of malefice would provide him, however – to the huge relief of his family and hired hands, who would temporarily be supplanted as the targets of his ravings – with the plot of a drama that this actor would play and replay, tinkering with it constantly, for a very long time.

Actually, in other respects, these southern Italian immigrants were no hindrance to the Piedmontese colony, because although they were kept at a distance and rendered invisible by the contempt in which they were held, they were nevertheless our rivals and had to be shown that we were their betters in every respect. That was why the Piedmontese tenant farmers, in particular those whose land was adjacent to theirs, took special care with their fields, from the straightness of the furrows, and the sowing conducted according to a kind of divination by inspired meteorologists, to the hanging of lanterns from a bar across the front of the combine so that the harvest need not be interrupted by nightfall and the grain might be taken at the peak of its maturity.

One evening, my eldest brother, Francisco, allowed me to sit next to him in the cabin of the combine, where the kernels of wheat fell in a continuous cascade into sacks that he swiftly sewed up as soon as they were full. I can still feel that flood of grain in the palms of my hands and smell the billowing scent of a dust even finer than powder.

What seed does this wheat sow in me? Why does the memory of it soothe my heart? No one can ever take away from me the certainty that this streaming grain, held – for an instant – in my hand, belonged to me. I felt the weight of it, just as I would like to feel the weight of my life, beyond the confines of existence and fate, in a kind of absolute purity.

12

IF A TRAVELER FROM THE TOWNS, OR, RATHER, FROM THE green pampas roamed by grazing stock, ever came to the farm that had just become our new home, he must have thought that only a somewhat deranged mind could have conceived the idea of creating, in the heart of a landscape so hostile to great hopes, one of those *estancias* where purebred horses and cattle imported from Europe vouched for the proprietor's nobility. As evidence, this traveler need only have considered the concrete trough lying between the paddocks and the pastures, a kind of swimming pool once intended to ensure the cleanliness of thoroughbred animals and which at our arrival contained a puddle of stagnant rainwater much appreciated by mosquitoes. The visitor might also have noticed the dilapidation of the stalls from a former stable that had been converted into a series of sheds. As he approached the house, the stranger would certainly have been struck by the variety of trees, most of which were unknown in the region, and the smell of the eucalyptus would have welcomed him graciously. Then, as the tall brick building began to appear through the foliage, he would have felt the sadness inspired by all glorious projects that have fallen into ruin. A trained eye, in any case, would have appreciated what the child exploring his new territory could not possibly notice right away: faint traces of a park, half concealed by broken-down and trampled fences, posts held upright by their spans of barbed wire, and constructions of boards and sheet metal sheltering the washhouse and concealing the latrines.

In fact, even the house – a rather imposing building designed for a different kind of life, and for people other than farm workers – showed signs of ambitious plans that had come to grief. The bathroom, for example, where no one ever took a bath because there was no running water; or the gallery with the checkerboard floor in black and red, completed on one side by assorted lozenges of different sizes and colors, with cement patches here and there filling the inevitable gaps. There was an attempt at a mosaic made out of other lozenges; it represented a woman's face, which I studied, intrigued by her goddesslike air. Except for my parents' bedroom, which had boards that smelled of Javelle water, the flooring in all the rooms was of trusty brick, and judging by the rust-colored grit we swept up daily, the broom was harder on the floors than were the comings and goings of the household.

Quickly losing interest in the hapless dog, the child rambled all over the property, where the planned orderliness of the vegetation had lapsed over the years into an overgrown jumble, with rows of trees wandering off into impassable thickets of rushes, shrubs galore, and clumps of giant thistles obstructing every view. The boy inspected the "paradise" trees covered with clusters of bluish flowers like lilac blossoms; he looked over the acacias, the ash and plane trees, the clumps of tamarisks with their frothy pink flowers and lacy shadows; he examined the fruit trees – pear, apple, mulberry – which, just like the grapevine, bore only sour, rock-hard fruits, doubtless because they had not been properly pruned. For a long time the child would know nothing more about fruit than the general shape of certain kinds and their tendency to be more or less brownish.

Attracted by a bush adorned with mauve and white bind-weeds, the boy ventured into the brambles, careless of scratches: one more step and the little flowers would be within reach – and he was stopped short by a bright eye in the dense brush, a glance that vanished in a silvery streak, leaving only a rippling ribbon of grass.

The boy did not see the iguana, but he felt within himself the swiftness of its flight and, rising from his still shallow depths, the gliding unreality of the black-and-yellow snake, coiling and uncoiling, rearing up beneath his legs, suspended, pointed, ready to attack. Choking with fear, the child raced blindly away and entered the garden, where the dream of the unknown builder was still intelligible: the central path was flanked by neat flower beds edged with brick, each bed the mirror image of its double across the way, displaying the same plants, the same blossoms, from threatening yucca to timid phlox, from roses and laurels to irises, dahlias, and gillyflow-ers. The sole exception was a cactus, about a meter high, that destroyed the symmetry of the garden, unless it served to reveal it. This cactus would later bloom for us, but only once.

13

No matter how far I follow this thread of ink, memory will still lead me astray, by reserving for events a fate disproportionate to their importance. The sound of footsteps fading in the night, the shadow of a flight of birds over a meadow, a crumpled letter in a gutter, the gait of a passing woman, flames hissing amid the crackle of burning logs: these things become invulnerable to time, while oblivion swallows up so many things that were ourselves, as if their very intensity had blinded us to them, so that they end as idols of the depths, like statues lying at the bottom of a bay, disguised from the deep-sea diver by silt or the magnificence of madrepores.

I try in vain to recall the first time I made love; or that perplexing moment when, letter by letter, and syllable by syllable, I read my first words.

Other events live on in memory, however, saved by my senses of smell and hearing, perhaps. I am thinking of the afternoon when Florencio, the cowherd, taught me during siesta time how to clamber up on the old mare, a red bay we named "Filly" because she was quite short in the legs. Still, she wasn't any kind of pony, not even an Argentine one, and when I recall her size, her big belly, and her elongated head with its drooping chin, I would be hard put to think of an uglier horse. We left her mane and tail long, which simply added to her unsightliness – in the same way, if you think about it, as a too-youthful hairstyle mocks the ravages of time in a face gone puffy and sagging with age. I would describe Filly's trot, however, as "rippling," like the touch of a pianist who plays each note distinctly without destroying the impression of legato.

Clutching the mane with the left hand, and being careful not to lean too hard on the animal's neck, you had to hoist yourself up in one go and land already astride, holding the reins in your other hand. Florencio assumed that I would know immediately how to use the reins one-handed to guide Filly in the right direction.

Florencio was a boy of about fifteen, dark, with a prominent forehead and small, delicate features made striking by a single quirk: no matter what expression he wore, even when he scowled, one side of his upper lip never joined in, as though it were sculpted in stone, or dead. What ancestral mood had stamped his face so permanently? Once I ran a finger over the impassive part of his mouth, the way a lover will outline the contour of the lips after a kiss. That made him smile but never changed the look in his eyes, a quick, set look, indifferent to the immense distances all around him, a look that seemed, like his lip, to be keeping something back.

Jerking on the muddled reins, squeezing with my legs and tapping my heels at her groin, I tried to get Filly to take the path leading to the open plain, but she simply swung her head from side to side, baffled by the conflicting signals from the bit. Seeing how clumsily I was dealing with her confusion, Florencio jumped up behind me, leaping straight into the air after crouching only slightly with his feet together, not leaning on the horse at all, simply gathering himself into a single coil of energy surging up from his knees and out even to his fingertips.

We were riding bareback, and although Florencio sat so that his torso was not touching my back, his arms went around me to hold the reins, his trousers rubbed against my bare legs, and when Filly broke into a trot, I could feel the soft friction of the horse's coat beneath my thighs and the cowherd's sour breath along my neck.

Then, as we left the woods behind us and came out into the open country, Florencio set Filly into a gallop, tickling her groin with the toe of his espadrilles, and whipping at the air to urge her on. He grabbed me and held on so tightly that I felt I was a part of him, of his self-assurance, his ardor, felt that I was nested inside him, and his expert hands taught mine how to use the crossed reins.

We went on, and on, ever faster, as though Filly were trying to break free of the plain, but suddenly I felt the wind at my back: everything in Florencio was subsiding, exhausted by his vehemence, and sensing this, our gallant steed became bewildered, slackening her headlong pace.

And so they began, the days smelling of grass and the horse: blissful, at first, then hellish – and now, today, the only memory of Argentina that fills me with nostalgia.

14

Among the feelings of remorse that never lose their sting, the most tenacious have to do with animals. In the long run, the offenses I have committed toward my own kind cause me only a kind of discomfort; even if you don't really mean it, you can say you are sorry to people – but not to animals. I'm thinking of the ovenbird's nest that Florencio shattered to satisfy my curiosity. The *hornero* is a little architect that lives only on the plains of South America.

What was he thinking behind that bulging forehead, beneath that thicket of hair (from which head lice periodically emerged, only to be startled by the light)? I imagine him existing in the state of beatitude attributed to animals, never unsettled by hope or dispirited by longing, but I realize that my imagination is doing him an injustice, since he taught me the names of birds, even of some he had never seen, like the royal parrot of Brazil.

Amid the great throng of sparrows, Florencio could distinguish species and varieties simply from the fluttering of their wings. He often crouched up in a tree, chewing on a twig, alertly scanning the branches. Finding a red dot in the opaque foliage of an ash tree (a cardinal) or a pensive bit of yellow (the canary perched on the wire guiding the convolvulus across the garden) filled him with a joy he could barely express. I remember the gleaming shadow of thrushes, and the blackbirds' whistle he imitated so well that he could disrupt their evening conference; I remember the plover, standing on a single leg out in the fields or by the edge of a path as though studying some proposal laid out on the horizon; I remember the only hum-

mingbird to visit us in the spring, a flurry of feathers pinwheel-
ing around a slender beak, a marvel Florencio tried in vain to
catch; and I remember thinking of Florencio on the only two
occasions when I ever heard a nightingale, both times in the
same patch of Corsican maquis. A quarter of a century separates those two nights, which are as one. Besides, the song of
the nightingale has continued to belong, for me, to poetry rather
than to nature, and when I heard this song, as though by divine
dispensation, I was not sure whether I was listening to the bird
singing then and there, or far back in time, when Theocritus
heard a nightingale close by, and perhaps that is how it was for
Virgil as well.

In fact, the birds still cheep, twitter, warble, and sometimes,
modestly, they sing for me, way back in my childhood home,
when earth and sky mingle in the attentive twilight, and night
sets down its vast illuminated birdcage. Did I listen so closely
to the birds that now I will always be able to hear them? That
was Florencio's doing. Who can say when and in what way a
person becomes part of someone else's destiny, blindly playing
a role he knows nothing whatever about?

As though a whirlwind were sweeping them up from the
fields, they came from all around, filling the air, bickering and
teasing, arguing over the space they needed for their swoops
and turns, and their chirping gaily shredded the serenity of the
evening. The poultry returned to the double row of compart-
ments in the henhouse, where they nestled only in the top row,
heeding an ancestral fear of skunks. The pigeons, with their
slate-blue eyelids and iridescent breasts, lined up on the
eaves, and as the peeping of the swallows died away, a tremu-
lous cooing was heard – but only now can I offer this metaphor –
like a violin bow prolonging a sustained note into silence.

The *hornero* was a rare bird in those parts; I vaguely recall a
sparrowlike creature, reddish-brown with a white throat, but I
could easily draw the outside of its oven-shaped nest, and the
inside of it as well, which Florencio showed me by topping the
little house's dome with his knife. I also recall a few of the bird's

traits and habits the cowherd taught me: its wings are weak, and its flight, short; sedentary by nature, it prefers to live in bushes and thickets – not in family groups or with a flock, but with its mate, and so is never alone. An *hornero* is always two, male and female working together to build their nest. I have seen them bringing daubs of clay as big as peach pits mixed with tiny sticks, winging along like those chubby, laughing cherubs homing in on the Virgin to place the heavy crown they bear upon her head. In two days, they build on bare branches, cemetery crosses, poles, or fences a dwelling that can last for years and is fought over by swallows and parakeets after its owners abandon it. The entrance is twice as high as it is wide; the structure consists of a wall that curves around and in upon itself to form two chambers, a vestibule and a "sitting room."

Wishing to make me jealous, perhaps, Florencio insisted that where he came from, on the plains of the Gran Chaco, a different variety of *hornero* used thorny twigs to build nests that were half a meter high on giant cacti, and sometimes on branches that dipped and swayed in the wind.

I can still hear the grating of the knife blade slicing off the rounded top of the nest Florencio had torn from a fork in the branches of a shrub; I see the design of the shelter, and, on a mattress of grass, four white russet-speckled eggs.

Memory long ago turned its back on the world of childhood and, in a word, my native land; I found it hard to live in that past, and so I forgot the *hornero* and my wonderment at its nest. These returned, along with the precise moment when Florencio revealed the secret of the nest to me, only in 1977, on the day that Roger Caillois was telling me about his philosophy of nature. He had been showing me his extensive rock collection, and he handed me a stone that, when held against a light, revealed within its milky opacity the outline of an equilateral triangle. Gazing at what I consider to be the most perfect geometrical figure, and one traced here by no human hand, I asked him if his mind was not tempted by the idea of the existence of God. He burst out laughing – although the word *burst* does not suit his thoughtful ways – and behind the thick lenses of his glasses, his eyes never stopped twinkling. Everything that, to me, might help make plausible a Creator only seemed to him one more proof of His nonexistence: the relationship between the forms offered by inert matter and the inventions of man made God superfluous in his eyes.

There was a slight pause, and then, going over to his side of the question, I brought grist to his mill by recalling the nest of the *hornero,* a subject that delighted Caillois, who had spent the war years over there, across the ocean. Having traveled all around the country, he was familiar with the bird and its talents. I was distressed to hear him speak of mere masonry in connection with a work of architecture.

He murmured, as if to himself (trying out a turn of phrase), something about the complicity between the two realms; then, with the look of having discovered one of those analogies he so cherished, he announced that, as a matter of fact, the rotundity of the nest was a latent representation of the dome, its form constituting a presentiment of the cupola, or perhaps a yearning after it.

15

IT WAS NEITHER THAT DAY NOR THE FOLLOWING ONE THAT Florencio performed a ritual as yet unknown to me, but which – aware from the start that it was absolutely forbidden – I would soon be celebrating in turn, quickly acquiring an expertise so precocious that it now amazes me. But memory has drawn these two afternoons closer together, perhaps because both events took place in the same spot: the angle formed by two sheds, where clumps of nettles grew amid the tall grass of the meadows. Or perhaps because they both equally evoke above all the idea of unctuousness, of viscosity, of stickiness.

If I think of the nest, I see the little eggs that Florencio smashed against a post, and slowly dripping threads of reddish slime; when I recall the initiation scene, there is Florencio, wiping his gummy hands on couch grass.

He was sitting on the ground, leaning back against a wall of corrugated iron, which at a certain point began to vibrate; no expression, no other movement of his body accompanied the regular back-and-forth motion of his hand around a skinny rod. Florencio made me a party to his activity only when he broke his concentration for a moment to glance obliquely at me as his pleasure mounted. I thought of the milk that squirted from the cows' udders between my sisters' fingers. He buttoned himself up, staring at the nettles he had flowered, and went off to saddle Colorado, without a word, as if I did not exist. I felt feverish, ill, but this feeling was outside my body, in a way, a suffering that enveloped me entirely and then, when my little sex grew hard, I was so afraid, and yet content as well: a beast was awakening in me, one with which I would spend my life.

That thing between the legs – the object of so many jokes and nicknames that I pretended to understand by laughing along with the adults – had suddenly become charged with mystery. What completely unsuspected desires had Florencio awakened in me? By looking on, my body had experienced an insidious mutation. Does the ape live on in man? I was aping Florencio. We spend one part of our lives imitating others, and the rest imitating ourselves.

Soon more than skilled in the art of masturbation (handy enough, in any case, so that at the age of seven, during my first confession, the old priest – whose leathery palm gently pressed my still chubby face against his knees as I knelt before him – sat back with consternation in his protruding eyes, which were of a very light blue threaded with scarlet, and shaking a reproving finger, he told me sternly never to lie again) and tireless in its practice, I enjoyed myself prodigiously, falling asleep over my appetite and upon awakening, rejoining myself through this same hunger.

Even so, I did not acquire a real awareness of the body, or of its resources. It takes so long to become familiar with one's sensual nodes and the irradiation of pleasure that the beauty of adolescence has already begun to fade by the time the adept has finally mastered the keyboard of sensations.

Colorado and his rider were disappearing in a brief cloud of dust on the horizon when I came – and something fell in the blind center of my body, as though this very body had hurled itself from the supreme sphere of desire. It would take me a long time to learn how to hold back desire, to suspend it over a void, letting it fall and be snatched back until finally allowed to pierce through the flesh, which then lets go, subsiding into a longing for oblivion. For as long as I lived in the country, I had to be content with this tireless gift of myself to myself. And I spent my hours in patient touch-ups.

One day, my mother caught me; she must have been waiting for her chance, probably made wary for some time by my prolonged absences, since she and my sisters were used to my constant company. At the washing tub, I had been waiting for the second rinsing, when it was my job (a task I had specifically requested) to immerse the round sachet that released a cloud of bluing into the clean water. After the linens were rinsed, my sisters would hang the large sheets on a line that stretched from tree to tree across a little field adjoining the garden: an entire theater of whiteness rippling in the wind, favoring my comings and goings. Before I ever encountered the very idea of a theater and its characters, my eyes were ready and waiting for them.

In the kitchen, I greedily watched the preparation of certain dishes, fascinated by the skill with which my mother wrapped blanched cabbage leaves around tiny meatballs, packing them snugly into a frying pan to brown over a low flame on the stove. My sister Elvira was the official maker of raviolis, which had to rest until the next day, sprinkled with flour and covered with a dish towel, a family tradition that ensured just the right firmness for proper cooking. When I came in from outside – and everything was outside, except for the house and the clumps of trees – I could tell from a distance who was cooking, my mother or one of my sisters, because each of them had her own little ways, and their creations had their own special aromas.

But where did I go when I was not in their company?

On the day my mother caught me attending to myself, to that part of myself that had gotten the better of all the rest, I was in a kind of closet behind the girls' room, crouching among the four wide-open doors of two cupboards set face to face. I don't remember what she said when she scolded me; her reprimand was brief and without explanation, as when she would look up from her chores to find me playing with something she had forbidden me to touch.

I must have heard her footsteps, because suddenly I was holding a heavy book snatched up in a hurry, at random, a book so heavy that I wound up falling over, out into the open. Even though I managed to stammer, "In a village of La Mancha...," she was not fooled. The *Quixote*, which nobody ever read, was one of the few books we owned; I remember *Maria*, by Jorge Isaacs – I often reread the last chapter, for the pleasure of shedding tears; *Amalia*, by José Mármol, the first blind librarian in Buenos Aires; and *Quatrevingt-Treize*, by Victor Hugo.

I barely caught a glimpse of my mother's face, where her irritation showed only in a slight narrowing of the eyes. I was to follow her: she needed my help in the kitchen garden. Having issued an interdict in her own fashion, perhaps she felt that her duty had been done. As for me, blame reinforced the innate idea I had of the offense, without diminishing either my ardor or my eagerness to manipulate it, alternately stimulating and quenching my desire. From secretive I became dissembling, and since guards merely stimulate a prisoner's ingenuity, I greatly pleased my father by offering to look after the livestock, which would free Florencio from some of his labors and gradually eliminate the need for his presence on the farm.

That was how I became a cowherd.

16

I LED THE COWS TO NATURAL PASTURES AS WELL AS to fields of rich alfalfa, of which they were so fond I had to limit their grazing time to keep them from getting dangerous indigestion. More than once I have seen my father, surrounded by the family and farmhands, plunge a blade deeply into the flank of a heifer, dexterously enlarge the opening between the ribs, and draw out the knife with a great flourish to arouse the admiration of his audience the way an actor lays on the grandiloquence at the end of a tirade to stir up some applause. Soon, a dense green chyme would erupt from the wound, and the animal would be saved.

In my daily attempts to haul myself up onto Filly's back unaided, wriggling my belly against her glossy coat, I would occasionally feel a glimmer of the pleasure my hand gave me. From then on, as soon as I was far enough away from prying eyes, I would lie down on Filly, grasping her mane, and slide backward until I felt the roundness of her rump; then, still holding on to her mane, I would pull myself back up to her neck, and start the whole operation over, again and again.

There is nothing more peaceful than a herd of fat milch cows grazing in a field; ours were almost all white with big red spots, and they are gathered, in my memory, around their bull, a shorthorn I never fail to think of whenever I hear the word *massive*. Gentle, broad-backed, stocky, he seemed built all in one piece, without a neck, so that his head, with its filed horns, was attached directly to his breast, and he was so heavy that it was hard to imagine him suddenly rearing to cover one of his harem. He was like a creature fashioned by the gods: ancient, eternal.

On the back of my mare, my *frisson* would come from farther away, and reach me as though in stages, coursing slowly from my nape to my heels. At sundown, the herd would amble home. All those afternoons melt into a single one. I must have perfected my new method of pleasuring myself because it simply ravished me, distracting me from reality. What was that firestorm of clouds festooned with gold, high overhead, that great bird with flaming wings, carrying off the world in its flight, driving the sun down into the plain? Earth and sky were reversed, and the heavens lapsed suddenly into silence.

Time had passed. The cows were coming into the yard where they would spend the night; some of them were already lying down, chewing their cuds. In the bull's sad eyes, I could see my reflection as I slid down from my mount, and then my mother loomed before me, holding my father's large binoculars. She told me threateningly that I was to stop such behavior immediately, and when a pleading note crept into her voice for a moment, undermining her severity, she raised her hand to me. Like a spring, mine shot up to the same height – and when I think that she remembered this gesture for the rest of her life, and told herself, at that very moment, that she had already lost me....

The appearance of Florencio put an end to this scene, but in a way, I remained frozen in the shame and scandal of that hand lifted against my mother. That was the day I paid the terrible price exacted by remorse. Besides, my mother's sternness was calculated, so to speak, a thing quite contrary to her nature, all the more so on these two occasions when the cause of it remained unmentioned, and only much later did I understand that it was meant above all to protect me from my father's reaction, should he himself happen to catch me at my pastimes.

Florencio's presence, the servile, ingratiating, and at the same time confident way he came over to us, the look with which my mother dismissed him – all this was more than enough to suggest to me that he was well and truly the reason I had come under surveillance. My suspicions were confirmed by his eagerness to help me whenever I had any problem with the livestock, and especially by the complicity he now sought with pretended casualness – after having more or less lost interest in me – by jumping up behind me on the mare as if by magic, with one of his aerial leaps. There he might pull me with one arm as though to make me fall, but a decided squeeze from his legs would keep me on the horse, at his mercy.

Although he opened the floodgates of my sensuality, neither his face nor his body held the slightest attraction for me. On the other hand, his treachery did not displease me. I saw in it a lack of ambition, and it gave me a kind of pride: betrayed, I felt more free, although I did not understand why. By falling so far, my betrayer raised me up.

When did I first become obsessed with another body? If I am bold enough to venture into those shadowy areas, I will later relate how, during a nap, while I was feigning sleep, I watched my eldest brother lying on his belly, toiling over an imaginary lover, and how I was able – thanks to the sudden appearance, fated on my behalf, of a spider – to gaze on the splendor of his nudity.

The sexual awakening and first experiences I have related occupied a great deal of my time between my seventh and tenth years. Except for the two occasions when my mother caught me, I received no further warnings.

17

I WAS OFTEN SCOLDED BUT NEVER PHYSICALLY PUNISHED. What happened when my father wanted to strap me one day? I got away from him. This irascible man must have lost his temper particularly quickly, because there was no "before" to his outburst. One hand gripped the collar of my shirt, which I was unbuttoning while he unbuckled his wide leather belt and struggled to pull it through the belt loops of his trousers. I left him holding my shirt, and sped off.

Night had come by the time I stopped running, out in the open fields. I felt a wild, absurd need to flee the darkness, and was filled with a sudden despair: there was nothing in this blackness to help me orient myself, and when I glimpsed lights moving in the distance, and heard voices calling, deflected by the breeze, I lay down in the alfalfa. They were looking for me. It was half fear and half pride that kept me from answering, although I used the occasional beam from their flashlights, as they explored the woods and the out-buildings of the farm, to slip closer to the house; somewhat reassured, but with tears in my eyes, I resolved to master my fear and not give a single sign of life. At times the lights would stop, then vanish, swing around, and the horizon glittered with floating fireflies.

I find it hard to write these lines. I find it hard to relive that night; I loathe the stubborn little boy who makes me ridiculous forever. It's too bad for him that they have stopped searching, and that the lonely night has lapsed into indifference! Now that he knows where he is, and how far away he is from the property – which is surrounded by dense stands of trees that make the darkness even thicker – he is painfully disconcerted when no one calls his name anymore. He has been reduced to sharing in the endless patience of the earth. They have abandoned him. They do not care about him, and he feels so very small and unimportant. Shame and humiliation come and go, attacking his pride; determined to save face at one moment, tearful the next, he resolves not to make any gesture of conciliation to his family, a vow made all the more emphatic by the smoky odor of grilled meat wafting to his nostrils with the tantalizing promise of other tasty dishes prepared by his mother and sisters.

He will stay where he is, a heroic figure, albeit with no one to admire him. He does not even realize that his legs are growing restless, preparing to challenge that overweening foolishness upstairs, barricaded behind the forehead, where he thinks he can do whatever he wants; and the legs rally all the other parts of the body to their cause, so that together they contract, trying to expel this stupidity, this effrontery, and now there is nothing left for him to do but follow them – his legs, his entrails, his chest – for they have hold of him, while he has only his pigheadedness. In the end they take him back to the house, but only by dragging each step out of him, because he is as recalcitrant as a deserter under arrest who somehow thinks, upstairs, behind that forehead, that he can still protect his dignity. A continuous argument has sprung up between himself and his legs, a heated discussion that constantly threatens to stop him in his tracks. As they approach the first trees, his stubborn legs become suspicious for some reason and decide to accept a fair compromise: the child will not give in, cannot be made to enter the house, and will proceed no farther than the stable. Ah, how good those cowpats smell, in the comforting warmth of sleeping beasts....

He sits down on one of the tree stumps used as milking stools, and fear surges through him again. Making up after a quarrel requires taking a good look at oneself, setting reason aside, and agreeing to wallow in the delights of forgiveness, that delicate poetic gesture that will never reverse any past deed. In later years, whenever I would give in to some violent impulse, and then be filled with regret, the problem would turn out to be the unforeseeable reconciliation, the return home to the other person – for one does not always find Penelope waiting there.

Sitting among the animals as they dream, perhaps, of meadows, the child does not think of these things that have not yet been revealed to him by words. But in some strange way, he feels them, and this is how it will always be in the future: he will be ashamed, not of whatever he may have said or done, but of the overwrought aspect of his behavior, a kind of pathetic excess.

His father is not one to tolerate the insolence that everyone else takes in good part or even applauds. Like all children, the boy forms his own opinions, but his father must be persuaded that this son's judgment is informed by alertness, observation, and a bit of reflection, on which point he is not mistaken: I practiced my impertinence on him at an early age, essentially by pointing out his faults and mannerisms, which I would attribute, with a great show of indignation, to someone else, when he could not possibly fail to recognize himself.

He will never conquer the child in the stable, who drowses in a sticky mess of feelings and sensations and thus fails to notice the glimmer of light coming toward him, or at least not soon enough to slip away. When the shadowy form raises the lamp, he looks up into the face of his mother. She says nothing, simply stands gazing at him with those calm eyes of hers, as though she were trying not to smile. She has not given in, has not abandoned her child; she has probably managed to strike a bargain with his father – to let bygones be bygones, with no more said about the matter. And now, while the rest of the household sinks deeply into their well-earned rest, she has come to meet him, bringing to him everything of herself it is within her power to bring.

How could the child refuse this gift, the sole gift that matters, which she is offering to him? Between the house, his only world, and himself, there is now just this one link, this look, this wealth of trusting love. And what does he do, the fool, the idiot, when she looks into his eyes and begins to beckon him after her, tilting her head invitingly to one side? He recoils, stares down at the ground, then straightens up, fearing that she has left. She is still there. But what is that bundle she holds with one hand against her breast? She gestures again, inviting him to come home. And he lowers his head. Then she holds out the blanket she has brought him, and, turning up the lamp, she moves resolutely toward the door. He leaps up; she stops. He joins her, but stays one step behind.

Why does he feel that burning ache in his heart, that violent desire to rush into his mother's arms?

He already knows this, knows it only too well: in his family a child is protected but kept at a distance, never fondled or caressed. And so the stirring he feels in his soul for the woman who walks ahead of him must be choked back, deeply repressed, imprisoned within his head.

18

EVEN THOUGH I WAS A COWHERD, FOR A WHILE MY view of the plain remained more or less "frontal." After that first ride with Florencio, I did not push Filly too hard and was content with her even trot and canter. Since I did not venture very far afield, the house, the fences and farmyards, and most of all, the groves of trees spared me any perception of the geographical emptiness in which I lived, and saved me from the lasting anguish it provokes, until the day I was sent to carry breakfast to my brothers and the peons who had been up before dawn, drowsing in the seat of a plow or harrow, which were still pulled by horses in those days. As they were sometimes out at the far boundaries of our property, and the big bottles of café au lait in their quilted cozies had to be delivered while still hot, I was allowed to ride Colorado, who passed for a racehorse out in our parts.

For one whole winter I watched the night rising up off the horizon like a tent being folded back; I saw the last stars melting into the light spreading out from everywhere; I saw the sun showing the red tip of its nose, and sometimes I imagined it climbing out of a dungeon, afraid of the overwhelming vastness all around, that emptiness the sun would gradually round off in its course and divide, impartially, into equal halves. And in this revelation I saw for the first time the sweep of the earth before man: all

around my horse the land stretched into the distance, before my
eyes, on each side, and from then on, there was that same flat
abyss at my back. What spot on the horizon could hold the
promise of escape? How could I ever reach *elsewhere*? I was in
the very heart of elsewhere, and there was no beyond to it: one
cannot leave behind what is without compass or measure. In
those childhood mornings, galloping along on Colorado, I saw
the ground unrolling before me and the sky in endless retreat,
and becoming conscious of my captivity, I felt a growing, almost
unbearable demand for some limit, a boundary, even an obstacle. The wind blew from one infinity to another.

The plain, so real and yet as though invisible, has been the
fundamental experience of my life: there one is extraneous to
nature, a nature so monotonous it becomes almost supernat-
ural, which hardly suits the human race. There is no sign of the
future; only the all-encompassing present exists, despite the
rising and setting of the sun. What a relief it was when the bell
tower of the sky would ring out in a storm, throwing its din to
the four corners of the earth!

I think of Colorado, back then, over there; I don't see myself
on his back as he races with the wind, across this endless stage;
I think of people who have nothing to gain but their death, and
whose ashes have become part of this boundless land where
nothing ever becomes destiny.

The sky, so distant, so colorless, could grow dark during a
dry spell, at a time of the year when thousands of acres of soil
lay plowed and raked, ready for sowing; the gusting wind would
rage across the furrows until it had wiped them from the fields.
The sun became a moon glimpsed behind scudding clouds.
This air-borne earth was invincible: I felt it in the back of my
throat, between my teeth, in my hair – and what do I do nowadays when I happen to cross the Jardins du Luxembourg or the
gardens of the Palais Royal? I stick to the strip of bare pavement in the middle of the gravel walks to avoid hearing the
crunch underfoot that takes me back there, to those dust storms
and the curse of that drifting, endless grit.

The sky could also darken for reasons having nothing to do with the weather: awakened somewhere in the world at the approach of spring, migratory locusts would arrive by the hundreds of thousands of billions, in a dense brown cloud, settling thickly on the greenest fields to satisfy their hunger. In serried ranks, and with exemplary discipline, they would devour all vegetation in their path with application and art, an inexorable army abandoning in its wake a countryside as bare as a closely shorn sheep.

An entire year's work would thus become, in a few hours, a thing of the past, stripped of color and leaf, blackening our tomorrows with a finality even more solemn than when the November rains would blight the wheat in mid-harvest. I may have seen this massive swarm of locusts only once, but I witnessed their onslaught and the utter disaster they left behind, and that is why something in me continues to suspect there is vindictiveness in those powers the mind places above the laws of nature. I remember the mighty oath my father uttered when he discovered a locust in the wheat field as he was checking a head of grain – a harbinger of the horde to come.

Since life loves to juxtapose, between two monotonies, events that seem to reveal fate, or even to make us bow before it, the apocalypse was preceded by a scene that in itself would justify to me the meaning of the expression, "the age of reason": that moment when immediate perception gives way to a serious apprenticeship of life.

My mother had been instructing me in religious matters for several weeks, coaching me with the help of a booklet containing the Decalogue, the seven sacraments, the Pater Noster, the Credo, the Confiteor, and the Ave to prepare me for my First Communion. This was to take place on Assumption, during the festivities honoring Mary, the patron saint of Las Junturas, the village to which we now belonged, in a way, since our move to the new farm. Tradition stubbornly held that two rivers had formerly joined at the site of the village, although they had since vanished, probably to help unclutter the scenery.

We would sit down in the gallery. My mother would untie her apron and tidy the waves in her hair with a comb set with tiny paste jewels. Her manner did not change in any way, but its simplicity took on a particular dignity. We were isolated together, far from everything, protected by a transparent bubble secreted by our intimacy, and which no one else could enter. I think I understood how precious those afternoons were and savored their sweetness. My mother would talk about God, confiding in me; she seemed almost about to smile, and her candid brow would grow even clearer, free from any trace of the shadows that sometimes veiled her serenity.

A scrupulous perfectionist, even in the slightest things, she insisted on the absolute correctness of the answers I was learning by heart, and did not allow me to change so much as a pause for breath in my repeated replies. As it was simply not in her nature to explain what was beyond her comprehension, she did not try to back up the mysteries she was passing on to me with any formal reasoning. We were in a different world, and during these catechism sessions, we both probably formed mental images of the angels, Heaven, and Hell. Were our ideas so very different?

That day, the spectator who suddenly appeared did not share our peaceful mood: my father came and sat a few steps away, studying the sky, as though waiting for us to finish our chin-wagging, as he called it, before telling us why he had come. My mother, who had slowed her recital at his approach, now calmly closed the catechism booklet and turned toward him, but he was already getting to his feet, and taking me by the hand – an unusual gesture – he led me away, without saying a word to my mother.

19

THIS MUST HAVE BEEN AROUND MID-OCTOBER, BECAUSE the endless expanse of green wheat rustled noisily, bristling with grain. And the harvest would be a rich one, judging by how proudly my father surveyed his fields before turning to look at me in a way I had never seen before.

He has let go of my hand; he draws closer to me; looming up against the sky, with his hat set perfectly straight across the middle of his forehead, he looks like a scarecrow that has come fiercely to life behind the rags and painted mask, its blue eyes gleaming darkly. Gazing up at him, I see him grow, become omnipotent; without moving his body, he turns his hatchet face to one side, the profile sharply etched above his shoulder, and taking the land to witness, he pronounces the fatal words: "Neither God nor the Devil exists; everything ends in the boneyard."

Even if I had never heard his voice except on that one occasion, I would still remember it after half a century, with every inflection, stern and yet pensive as well. Although there is no way for me to remember what I thought his words meant, I like to suppose that the perplexity I naturally felt at the metaphor of the boneyard affected me more than his peremptory negation itself. I had not yet seen a cemetery, but I do know that on that first of November when I was taken there, my father's figure of speech suddenly came to me as I watched my mother decorating a tomb with roses and arums made out of crepe paper by my sisters. And I know that I understood, or began to understand, that there were other ways of referring to things than by their names. That was why I fell in love with literature.

But at the moment when an abyss was perhaps opening all around me, at the moment when my father, as though sweeping a rag across a blackboard, was erasing my Heaven and Hell of colored chalk, his fingers, testing the maturity of a head of wheat, closed over a big locust.

Breathless, shrunken, miserable, he scans the heavens, and knowing already that there will be nothing he can do, he flails his arms helplessly, spitting out curses and groans of impotence. I have no idea what is happening and am absolutely bewildered. What is that swarming in the air? It rises and falls, swelling like a whirlwind loaded with dust.

Did the miscreant wonder if this might be a punishment from on high? Was my father familiar with this line from the Gospels, which I am certain he would have relished saying? "Woe unto him, through whom offenses come."

Soon there is nothing overhead but the great wave of insects, like an awning whipped by the wind, tearing loose to spread out over the ground. Now there is not one patch of green that is not fringed with locusts, not one path that does not ripple like a conveyor belt. The destruction is meticulously thorough, for the slow tide, crackling and grinding, works its way through everything, leaving nothing behind.

They crunch and hiss and squish under our espadrilles. My father, in a state of absolute collapse and defeat, looks at me suddenly; something is churning deep inside him, and I am only a few feet away: there is nothing between me and his rage. I stand facing him. How close did I come to making a murderer of him? But all at once something snaps in him, and I count for nothing in his distress.

Back at the house, the women have brought out flame throwers in an attempt to save the garden, at least. My father mocks them, with the evil smile that heralds his nastiest taunts, but then, as though finding an outlet for his fury, he grabs the flame thrower my mother has been using with such coolness and discipline and begins torching the walks between the flower beds.

There is no other stench like it, not even the acrid reek of dead animals teeming with maggots – I have seen such carcasses baking in the sun, crawling with fat flies with bronze wings. An impossible fetor of burning vomit drifts upward into the dying light. Pestilential fumes seep into the bedrooms, feeding our nightmares for weeks.

Many years later, while reading, I come across a quotation from the Old Testament: "For the locusts covered the face of the whole earth, so that the land was darkened; and they did eat every herb of the land, and all the fruit of the trees which the hail had left: and there remained not any green thing in the trees, or in the herbs of the field, through all the land of Egypt."

Everything came back to me immediately: the booklet in my mother's hands and myself on a little chair by her side; my hand in my father's inhospitable grasp; the premature death of God, and then the first locust, the sky darkening with the sooty cloud of insects, their voracious and determined assault, the flame throwers, the stink, and the family's sorrow at the supper table that evening.

The adults must have thought about the lost year's work, and the endless patience that would be required of everyone now; they knew that the most stringent austerity would be necessary for a long time. The boys, their hearts doubtless bruised by memories of their first nocturnal escapades, were well aware that these excursions in the car, while rare enough before, would now be forbidden by their father – although, to tell the truth, even when things were going well, they had to plan their requests carefully, waiting for just the right moment before asking to borrow the big Chevrolet, that symbol of undeniable prosperity and even of social advancement in a region whose rural character remained, for all that, unchanging.

Such happy incongruities did sometimes exist in our isolation, the crumbs of a distant splendor, sparkling meteorites fallen from that world of cities – which I could no more imagine than I could mountains or the sea, but which I coveted all the same. Sometimes, approaching a mirror at the end of a corridor, one glimpses the tree, the sun, the donkey one sees every day, but these things now seem immortalized, as though they already belonged to another universe. That is how I saw the Chevrolet, the newspaper *La Prensa*, my sisters' women's magazines, the dressmaker's dummy (that idol), the cassimere fabric of my father's one suit, the English tea only my mother drank (at three in the afternoon, with lemon), and then reading and the radio and listening to the serials, that private ceremony in which the scattered signs I have just recalled took on the quality of gifts sent on ahead by a world that was out there waiting for me.

20

IN MEMORY, THE CHILD SCRIBBLING AWAY IN A SCHOOL-boy's notebook – not very different, after all, from the one in which I write these words and perform the same task, playing the same game – moves almost immediately into the romantic universe of Max du Veuzit, Matilde Serao, and Delly; I believe I was particularly moved by the stories that most closely resembled the tale of Cinderella, but without the intervention, thank God, of Perrault's fairy godmother or the Grimms' little bird. I have always felt an innate aversion to the marvelous. After all, was I so unfamiliar with the story of the orphan girl? I carried that story inside me. I am convinced that writers only put into words – using circumstantial features suited to their times – the few secret schemata on which our legends and lives are based.

If there is one scene that stands out from my early reading, it is definitely the one where the beautiful heiress, who is waltzing in the arms of the poor young man, notices that although he is properly attired in evening dress, he is wearing everyday shoes with crepe-rubber soles. Her suitor understands the meaning of his beloved's look of surprise, and I remember his embarrassment.

Out of defiance, I would never weep in front of adults, but I cried easily over the humiliations of fictional characters; later on, and even now, only happy endings would have the power to move me to tears.

At what moment did I cross through to the other side of the imagination, where one sees reality – that reality to which one will never return unchanged – as if through a windowpane iridescent with reflections? Like all children, I played with words, telling myself stories that became true as I made them up; I formed my consciousness with musing and invention, and it was my very lack of self-knowledge that made my stories somewhat shaky. On the other hand, as soon as I discovered novels, I felt as though I were pushing through a door and closing it behind me: I stole into their settings and shut myself up in them. When family life tore me from my reading, I lived in dissimulation, waiting for nighttime and the moment when, buried beneath the sheets (which my mother warmed in autumn with an iron filled with charcoal embers), I would follow the tormented story of some aristocratic lady in love with her tenant farmer, or the dreams of passion, ecstasy, joy – and elegant manners – of Emma Rouault, "the adulteress," according to the title of an old South American translation of Flaubert's novel, and God knows what metamorphosis the rest of the book endured. I never tired of their company, and perhaps, by postponing sleep this way, I began my initiation into insomnia, that other endless plain.

My father would have been glad to learn that another great mind, Immanuel Kant, maintained that the reading of novels weakens the memory and that, in any case, when a child reads them, he refashions them in his own way. Kant took this as proof of the genre's uselessness, and my father would have appreciated this contempt for the novel: he allowed us to read them only on Sundays or when it rained – and even then, the rain had to be turned to some advantage, an occasion for the whole family to gather in the gallery, where, sitting in a row, we looked as though we were admiring a bountiful gift from the heavens (if the weather had been droughty), or witnessing, if harvest time was approaching, the greatest tragedy on the face of the planet.

Be that as it may, on these occasions my father, stimulated by the presence of an audience, would give rein to his repressed tirades, stopping the rush of his warnings and reproaches only when he felt his irritation begin to flag. Sometimes, when he had run out of targets for his wrath, he would break off in the middle of a sentence, already on the verge of shouting, and then my mother, anxious, I think, to relieve the chagrin of an actor left high and dry by a lapse of memory and made ridiculous at the very height of his grandiloquence, would rise and go see to her cooking. My father would fall silent, withdraw into himself, and gaze pensively into the distance as if thinking deep thoughts. In his silence, he must have understood that despite his threats and sermons, it was not he who ruled the household but our mother, with her gentle strength, sustaining us all with her patience.

Because we lived in a world both limitless and constricted, our lives, which lacked so much life, became intense, and the slightest incident figured as a thing of great moment.

But I am going to tell you about one happy rainy afternoon.

21

AS IN ONE OF THOSE PAINTINGS REPRESENTING THE WAYS and customs of a particular milieu at a specific time, so cherished by historians and those for whom the anecdotal aspects of a work count for more than harmony of form and color, memory has here reassembled a few trivial details of our life back home.

Anyone studying a genre painting of our household would

notice an activity reserved for Sunday or a rainy day, one of those rituals of cleanliness often neglected by men who spend most of their waking hours out in the fields and are then too tired to wash up at bedtime – unless constant labor, from dawn to dusk, might be said to encourage a relaxed and even friendly attitude toward dirt. I remember the thin, powdery crust that shadowed the contours of our feet and climbed up the Achilles' tendons, making them seem more prominent.

The washing of the feet: I can still see us, my father and brothers and myself, sitting on low chairs with our trouser legs rolled up (except for me, because I am still in short pants), passing a piece of soap and a towel back and forth, soaking our feet in basins while the women bustle around with the hot water. As for my sisters, who have been waiting for the rain to fill their water jugs, because our groundwater is too alkaline and ferruginous to use on their hair, they set down enameled bowls with raised designs of flowers I love to feel with my fingertips, and they voluptuously shampoo their hair, which a permanent wave has set into a mass of small curls the village hairdresser calls the "sweetheart" look. I wished that I could have been curly-topped like them, and to tell the truth, every hour of every day I have regretted, and will my whole life long, not having been born with lovely locks. I have never stopped longing for a nice, thick, well-behaved head of hair.

Then my brothers would play cards, getting up a modest game of *truco* with the peons, for which our father would give permission only after the usual admonitions and solemn injunctions against playing for even the slightest amount of money. So in spite of their conspiratorial airs, our cardsharps had to play for chick-peas.

When he gave permission for this sort of thing, my father churned out all kinds of proverbs illustrating his moral position on the matter, even including concrete examples gleaned from experience over the years, and one of these concerned one don Benito, who became, in time, a figure somewhat larger than life. We all knew him: a beggar who would turn up at the house about every three months and who was assured of a respectful, even almost reverential welcome.

Don Benito, one of the most prosperous merchants for twenty leagues around, had been reduced to poverty by his passion for gambling, and sent wandering on dusty roads, endlessly criss-crossing the province, living on charity. I do not understand why my father insisted that this beggar should preside over our dinner table (and at our mother's place, while he himself sat facing don Benito at the other end) and then provided no better sleeping quarters for his guest than the buggy shed, which smelled strongly of rancid sweat, horses, and the greased leather of their harnesses.

But on this afternoon that my memory has pieced together, our father must simply have granted permission for the card game without any preamble or parables, because don Benito is seated among us in the gallery. Although he appears to be clean, he is all one color, the color of dust: face, hands, clothes. His complexion is pasty. He has on stout boots with compli-cated lacing at the instep, and over his baggy pants and a kind of flannel nightshirt he wears a raggedy garment, draped slant-wise so that it looks more like a toga than a poncho. His deep-set eyes have seen everything under the sun, and nothing disturbs his equanimity. Where does it come from, this deep serenity? He seems lost in the distance, at one with what he sees: the falling rain, the misty foliage – but as soon as my father speaks to him, his mind returns to the edge of the present and he listens attentively to his host.

Off in my corner, I am whipping fresh cream in a big earthen-ware bowl, waiting for the moment when don Benito will stand up. I love to watch him walk: he has a limp, and each halting step throws his torso back majestically.

When don Benito answers, my father is puzzled for a moment, and even though he has not understood his guest's reply at all, he pretends to be thinking it over, nodding his head and making faint lowing sounds that convey neither assent nor disagreement.

Does don Benito belong to the open-air theater of La Pinotta? In some degree, because, like her, he does not resemble us; but they do not appear together on the same stage. He only plays "heavy father" roles: his voice, although stern, remains confiding, and he speaks with assurance, as though he had long since settled upon the truth of the matter, once and for all. One senses that he is untouched by ugliness or pain, that he defies them, and beneath his gentleness there is a strength that compels our respect. He has found his place in the world: the open road. He is seen as a man who has lived out his life and who is now preparing himself for the silence that lies ahead. All that pale brown color – it's as though it were politely concealing the light that burns within him.

On this afternoon, the land is grateful for the falling rain, and the wanderer is sheltered beneath the roof of people who have often welcomed him. Fragile, eternal, he is as ancient as a statue.

Today, his features are less distinct to me; his profile and silhouette are what I see most clearly, and these resurfaced a few years ago, as if glimpsed through shifting clouds, while I was watching a Joseph Losey film – at the moment, in fact, during the stationary long shot at the very end of *Secret Ceremony,* when Elizabeth Taylor, lying on an iron bedstead in a sordid room, tries to take heart by telling herself the story of a mouse that has fallen into a deep bowl of milk: unable to climb up the side, the mouse spends the night swimming patiently, stubbornly, around and around, and in the morning finds itself perched on a lump of butter.

It was not don Benito who first emerged from the churning images but the bowl of cream on my lap, and the smell of "gounfiuns," the humblest of cookies, little rectangles of dough flavored with a bit of lemon peel, which my mother would make last for weeks, for her three o'clock tea. My sisters would cook them on pleasant rainy days. They puffed up like apple fritters in the smoking oil, which is where their name comes from in Piedmontese. Like some children, certain memories like to gather together their most insignificant toys.

The only noise that breaks the silence is the abrupt exclamation of one of the men as he triumphantly slams a card down on the table. I am whipping the cream, which is growing stiffer, producing a bright yellow butter; Cecilia is frying gounfiuns; my father and the tramp are sitting together; now the sound of chopping is heard from the kitchen, where my mother is mincing meat and parsley to make stuffed cabbage, another dish we sometimes had on a leisurely rainy day. And then, as if curtains of mist have parted on the horizon, Colorado trots into view, dragging his reins, his shod hoofs making no sound in the downpour.

My father leaps to his feet, glaring questioningly at the cardplayers, who drop their cards and sit open-mouthed, not knowing what to say. One of the peons runs toward Colorado, who waits motionless beneath the torrent, and another farmhand stammers out that Florencio had packed up his belongings that morning. Then my father flies into a rage, even though he has been threatening for months (especially since I began taking over the cowherd's work) to fire Florencio, who would never stand up for himself and simply stared back at his master in expressionless silence. My father accuses him of ingratitude and betrayal, of having stolen Colorado – isn't the fact that he never asked for his back wages proof enough? A wily thief, as arrogant as an Indian, worse than the Creoles, those wretched good-for-nothings....

At a little sign from don Benito, he falls silent, suddenly tired, his anger fading into a twitching of the lips, and then his face uncrumples: he is smiling. My father's smile reveals a set of sharp-looking teeth, and I cannot tell you how much it frightened me. It was as if a demon were grinning through a mask.

It is quiet once more, a quiet reinforced by my mother's appearance in the kitchen doorway. We listen to don Benito. That very morning, he had met the boy on the road to Villa del Rosario but had not recognized him until the fugitive slowed his horse to a walk and spoke to him; one freezing winter's night, in the buggy shed, that voice had offered him a blanket.

Florencio slept with the peons; he told me they would draw their camp beds close and huddle together for warmth. Would we believe it? The boy had dismounted, knelt before the old man, and asked for his blessing.

Don Benito coughs softly, or perhaps it is a little laugh. They say that if the angels were to laugh at a single thing in this world, their eternal coherence would oblige them to laugh at everything.

Now it is raining less heavily, and the sunlight behind the uniform expanse of clouds gives the sky a pearly glow. Fat raindrops gather in the hollow of fig leaves and fall heavily into puddles with a faint smacking sound.

Don Benito's narrative has changed Florencio into Paul prostrate on the road to Damascus. (The story of the saint's conversion was a favorite of my mother's, and I loved the engraving illustrating the episode in her Book of Hours because it showed a rearing horse.)

Judging from the murmuring and mumbling, I am not the only one feeling guilty; true, I do feel something like remorse, but also a sense of deliverance at the disappearance of an embarrassing witness, who had initiated me, moreover, into the life I led in secret with that first companion, my body. A fissure had opened between me and myself, which would only grow wider from then on.

Although my father represents nobility of character in the eyes of the farmhands, who do not much care for Florencio, this nobility changes sides after don Benito's revelation.

The sky is still overcast, and the faint red gleam on the horizon will soon fade as day gives way to night. Outside in that infinite landscape, only time is left, without center or direction. It engulfs us; we are bathed in it, and perhaps our souls can grasp, without our conscious knowledge, the immensity of the silence, and beyond it, the distant hum of another universe. All around us the captive odor of the earth rises into the air. And we are quiet. Everything that exists becomes, in abeyance, the thought of what exists.

One last memory of this day's end: the lamp my mother lights in the dining room, which casts an oblique glow touching only the temple and cheekbone of don Benito, the way a nearby candle will gleam upon those studious saints in paintings.

Off in the duck pond, the frogs have ushered in the night with the lively stridency their croaking acquires after a good long rainfall. We would have heard this sound, of course, but without really listening to it. I cannot think of anything else to add. Except that Florencio's departure led to a feeling of freedom that lasted only until his story came to a close, two months later, on the day celebrating the Dormition of the Virgin, as the procession in honor of the village's patroness was returning to the church.

22

IT IS OFTEN DIFFICULT TO KNOW WHAT WE ARE DEALING with in the twists and turns of memory. Standing before a forgotten door, you see your hand already reaching for the knob, and fearing that memory may overwhelm you, you hesitate; your hand falters...Sometimes there is no one behind the door.

I remember Colorado in the downpour that day, dragging the reins (along with my father's presumptions concerning Florencio), and now another memory catches up with me: Colorado arriving with the reins of his bridle flying loose, that time when I was leaving school with other children and Colorado simply took off, leading the other riders a merry chase and hurling me into a ditch at the first turn.

I was allowed to ride Colorado as I pleased only when our foolhardy teacher for the year was lodged at a farm more than two leagues from ours. (Schoolmaster or schoolmistress, none of them ever returned after their first experience of the region.) The girls would go there by sulky, and the boys on horseback. We had no other means of receiving an education, so these men and women from the city would try to pass on to us a few scraps of knowledge and even a rudimentary appreciation of beauty.

The sudden appearance of Colorado without his rider threw the household into an uproar. I was brought back in the carriage by the girls, who spoke up for me, and my protestations of innocence were finally accepted. The next day, however, don Varela, the teacher, made an example of me: he kept me after school for a quarter of an hour all week long as punishment for encouraging my classmates to race their horses.

Don Varela's injustice toward me hurt more deeply than I can say, because it put an end to an intimacy that had sprung up between me and this old man who cared for things that in the eyes of parents, then and always, serve no purpose – things he took the trouble to teach us, like drawing and poetry. I recall the giraffe drawn from his description: the neck left the page, the head appeared on the next one, and the spots went from mauve to garnet red on an orange background. As for verse, I still feel the emotion of the first rhyme: what could be more magical than this rhythmic, musical phenomenon that bestows upon an ordinary thought the gift of seeming inevitable, changing perplexity into both certainty and delight?

After he had punished me, however, what pleasure I took in catching his mistakes, how quick I was to contradict him, to confuse him whenever his faulty memory gave me a chance! I owe my first literary humiliation and happiness to this same man, along with a twinge of remorse. It is now, as I write, that this feeling awakens in me, dimly, as if detached from the words spoken to cause trouble for don Varela, but still bitter and unfading.

The farm where he taught school was quite rustic, and like my earliest childhood home, without a single tree. That landscape is such a part of me, and I can see it so well: nothing but earth... And in a windowless room, a motley collection of benches, some planks stretched across piles of bricks to make a desk, the teacher's straw-bottomed chair, and, behind everything, the grayish blackboard on the wall. Leaning on the back of the chair, don Varela: gray double-breasted suit (which he never unbuttoned, even when sitting down), spotless shirt, polka-dot bow tie, wavy hair parted impeccably over a flabby face. His eyes were those of a man who cherished no illusions; his voice was pleasantly sonorous, his gestures brisk, and his bearing reflected a studied elegance, like that of actors who must put on a style they do not naturally possess. Perhaps he dreamed of being a different man before a different audience, and the care he took with his appearance may have been a way not to give in to despair.

On one of those days, then, when he has launched into a repetition of the same lecture he has just finished giving, I hear my voice anticipating his words, carrying on the lesson for a moment after he has stopped in mid-sentence to stare at me with a horrified look in his eye. I no longer remember if there was any reaction from the rest of the students, nor can I recall either the names or faces of any of them. In striking don Varela's most vulnerable point, I have wounded him so deeply that it frightens me.

Perhaps he moved on to another subject; I cannot hear him. Darkness has enveloped the scene, blotting out the benches, the peeling walls, surrounding the two of us, and now I will always be alone with him in that circle of shadows, where he has turned away his face.

23

THE NEWSPAPER MY FATHER PROUDLY URGED US TO read to expand our horizons, the monthly magazine my sisters claimed enriched their study of fashion and dressmaking, and the discovery of rhymes were enough for a time to affect profoundly the dimension and meaning of my days. I even came to think of myself as the exclusive inhabitant of a world I imagined to be like a room with a locked door to which I alone possessed the key, the pleasure that I enjoyed there surpassing in persistence, if not in intensity, the rewards of my more carnal enthusiasms. The virtual existence we all remember with regret throughout our lives, as though we had once taken a wrong turn at a crossroads long ago, ran intimately parallel to my life in that closed room, and contained the other side of reality as far as my mind's eye could see.

In the end – I say "in the end" because I did not love him – some of my father's concerns for his children, which weighed on us like a loan to be repaid a hundredfold, left an indelible impression on us. Where did he get his almost superstitious veneration for culture when he himself could barely read and write? He even boasted, at times, that he quit his country school after only thirteen days; furious at the way the teacher was mistreating one of the youngest pupils, he threw his ink pot against the wall, walked out, and never went back.

I have never struck anyone, but my hands itch from all the slaps I held back. That ink pot my father hurled as a child (an exploit he glorified and tacitly held up to us as an example) – I can feel its faceted roundness in my palm, and my fingers tingle with eagerness to throw it.

Raised in fear of not speaking the language properly in a country where it was not enough to be born there in order to belong, to fit in, I was always conscious, for as far back as I can remember, of each word being shaped by my lips. My father had come to Argentina as a young child, and my mother was born shortly after her family's arrival there, so both of them grew up in the immigrant community and they suffered, as adolescents, from not being able to express themselves easily in the language of the country – a land where, until not too long ago, some doors were still closed to a person saddled with an Italian surname. That was why my parents had the foresight to require that their children speak only Spanish in a region where the Piedmontese dialect was deeply rooted. My mother and father spoke this dialect to each other, doubtless to safeguard their secrets, so that for me the mother – or father – tongue, around which the soul takes shape, will always be the forbidden language.

We children understood this dialect that pronounced *s* as *sh,* producing those hushing sounds in the mouth of La Pinotta, and we could have imitated that buzzing through which the adults communicated their private thoughts, although I do not believe I ever tried it. Feeling no love for the land and therefore none for the farmer's life on it, I wanted no part of the Piedmontese dialect, which quickly became to my ears no more than a vague hum that intrigued me only by its characteristic nasal twang and a few closed vowels, *u* and *e.*

Encouraged by quite modest scholarly achievements, I endeavored to excel in the language of others, of don Varela and the people photographed in my sisters' magazines, whose poses and expressions did not belong to anyone I knew. The words "high society" were used to describe these exotic creatures, just as a certain form of theater was referred to as "high comedy." I used to spread these magazines out on our big dining-room table.

Soon overly fascinated by the printed word, I found that reading was not enough: I would become a writer – ah, what a writer a child could be, and how supreme his achievement, if he carried within himself some innate and unshakable syntax, an armature to support the modeling of his dreams!

I would have liked to write sad stories, but I did not even know how to construct a sentence. I lived in a state of urgency – I might even say, of imminence – devoting myself in vain to writing. I became all puffed up, fabricated sham creations, already falling into that trap of vanity whereby the obsession with the printed page outruns the pace of reverie, and words must lag behind.

And so, remembering the little book of dictation exercises with which my mother had taught me to read – a book so old it was falling apart, a book no one could possibly be familiar with – I chose the abridged version of *Puss in Boots*, doubtless because of the magic boots that enable him to conquer great distances and flee far away. I recopied it word for word; I don't think I changed even one, but I may have switched a few paragraphs around, to cover my tracks. I signed it, the way you affix to your own life the seal that will mark it forever. I sent it off to my sisters' magazine, and the wait began.

Rosalinda arrived wrapped in a band of kraft paper that my sisters slid off with the precise, careful movements of lace makers, to avoid tearing the pages. They unrolled it, then rerolled it in the opposite direction a few times so that it would lie flat, finally opening it with a kind of impatient delight, their heads touching as they bent over it, with mine craning over theirs. I had been on tenterhooks ever since sending off *Puss in Boots*.

My mother was the one who saw it first. Did she remember that book of exercises? She did not mention it. Everyone slowly gathered around her in disbelief, and my father could not contain his emotion on seeing our family name in print. I stood a little off to one side, enjoying their wonderment and the respect they showed me. Unwilling to depart from his habitual severity, my father reminded me not to neglect my arithmetic. Later, I was finally able to go off by myself with the magazine, and I read and reread *Puss in Boots* until it became my own invention.

The next day – had my father gone to the village? – we were each given a peach at dinner, a big, yellow peach from Rio Negro, a province famous for its fruit production. We all compared our peaches, delaying for as long as possible the moment of eating them. My father reproached my mother for peeling hers, claiming that she was losing the most precious vitamins that way. I peeled mine.

24

THE WAR HAD JUST BROKEN OUT IN EUROPE, SO I must have been going on nine when my father bought a wireless set, all gleaming fretwork on the imitation wood front, with a nubby fabric in back covering the mysterious inner workings of the thing. I remember my father removing a brick from the dining-room floor in order to stick the sharp end of a conducting wire into the earth (I think that is called a "ground connection") to improve the strength and clarity of the sound.

After dinner, the men would sit in a circle around the radio, listening to the news, as though they were carrying out a duty. In the meantime, the women would clear the table, and for a while the clatter of dishes would be heard from the kitchen. They would join us in time for the musical serial and sit bent over their embroidery or mending; the plot of this program was a pretext for displaying the talents of performers more experienced in singing than in acting. Then my father – in the same way that he might speak with measured slowness to give the impression he was thinking something over – would leave the circle of chairs, and with much frowning and a particularly solemn air, take a seat at the far end of the dining table. There he would unfold the map of Europe, on which, with the help of a fat two-color pencil, he marked the positions of the armies; red for the Germans, blue for the Allies, and the smiles he reserved for the advances of the former and the retreats of the latter were as different as satisfaction is from sarcasm.

My parents did not care for music at all, but we children all loved folk music. The tango was everyone's favorite except mine: I preferred the bolero, especially when sung by Elvira Ríos, a sort of Mexican Zarah Leander. Because her voice was so deep and resonant, the gossip sheets claimed she was a man, even that she was an "intercontinental banker." I find the chest voice seductive in a woman, but it strikes me as comical in a man.

Occasionally – not without some reluctance and a desertion or two – we listened to a pianist of improbable ethnic background, shown in photographs wearing a turban with its folds secured by an enormous cabochon. He played his own compositions, his hands constantly gliding from one end of the keyboard to the other lest we forget his title, "emperor of the arpeggio."

I do not know whether the uncanny range of Ima Sumac's voice (which tore my father from his customary show of indifference) had anything to do with the afternoon when I was alone in the house and turned on the radio. A program of classical music was announced. I didn't know what that expression meant – didn't even know the meaning of the word *classical*. I listened attentively, until the moment when the break carrying the family home from the village came rattling back into the courtyard.

I had been profoundly bored, but that did not keep me from watching for my next chance to disobey my father, who allowed the radio to be enjoyed only by the family group. I decided that if the adults around me did not listen to that kind of music, it must be of a better quality than what we listened to after dinner. I was a child snob.

I finally acquired a taste for this universe of evanescent sound that I never succeeded in memorizing, that escaped me as it possessed me, and that had no need of me to exist. Once, a piece played on the piano moved me deeply, as if it were awakening some anguish in me or restoring a lost happiness. Since the theme was repeated several times, I managed to retain it, and in an effort to memorize it, I hummed it all day long, and even in bed before I went to sleep, but sleep erased it. When I awoke, no trace remained of the invisible bird I had held captive for a few hours.

Thus reality became illusion, and this last, a world to which I might escape. At the age of discoveries, I greedily refused to miss a thing.

I should add that so few things passed within my reach that well before I had grasped enough of them to satisfy my desire, I was no longer fully present wherever I happened to be in reality. To some degree, an instinctive attraction (where had this come from?) to the intangible, a passionate complicity with the imagination, had made me the victim of a deep-seated inner discord, the source of an almost painful anxiety. But it was at the heart of this discord that I began to grow, all by myself.

25

THE DAY FINALLY CAME WHEN MY FATHER TOOK US TO the village to see a movie. At the time, I felt even more staggered than I had been by poetry or music.

It was summertime. Whatever seats could be found had been arranged on open ground near the church, where boys from the neighboring districts used to play soccer on Sundays. Something white – a tablecloth, my mother insisted – had been stretched between the goal posts, where I once saw one of my brothers act as goalkeeper, capering about like a clumsy monkey.

I remember a long wait shot through with sparrows; cows lazily cropping the couch grass at the edge of the field; a sunset that seemed to take forever; the shaft of white light that cut through the air over our heads, after dark.

Only two scenes from *Wuthering Heights* still linger in my memory. First, Catherine, her shoulders bare in a dress with a large hoop skirt, waiting impatiently on the terrace of an imposing mansion; behind her, silhouetted against the windows, shadows twirl to the muffled sound of music. Then, Heathcliff, the bastard, striding through the crowd of waltzing couples, who fall back on either side to form a double row of faces glaring disdainfully. A few seconds, in all: the woman in love, tormented by anxiety, and the lowly commoner defying the society that rejects him. But that evening, it was as though I were witnessing a blaze of moonlight, as though I had reached the boundary between the two worlds to which I belonged: the precarious one of reality, and the other, where I escaped geography to build adventurous castles in the air.

My reading of the paternal newspaper became a constant scrutiny of the entertainment pages. I can still see certain advertisements and photographs: I guessed the importance of the film or the stars from the position of the ad on the page. Besides the famous names, I remember so many of the others — here is one I saved, like a talisman: Andrea Leeds. Whatever happened to her? Why does no one ever mention her? To me she will always be sleekly beautiful, with a smile playing about her lips as she gazes into the eyes of Richard Greene.

Soon, having managed to get his hands on a few movie magazines, the cowherd led his charges across the pastures, distressed to learn that Frances Farmer was losing points at the box office because of a malicious bit of gossip, or to discover the photograph of Isa Miranda stuck down at the bottom of the page.

Did I go into a trance, following my cows at the end of the day, when I slid back and forth in ecstasy on the back of the old mare? On such occasions, the engraving of God the Father sending shafts of light through roiling clouds, as depicted in my mother's Book of Hours, would come to life before the setting sun, and His voice would sound like the rumble of an approaching storm. But I would emerge from these raptures as quickly as pleasure slips away and is lost. Such transports lasted for a long time, however, after I began projecting onto the purple radiance of the sky the form of a woman shining with an even stronger light: it was Marlene, sheathed in a glimmering of stars, one knee bent, her hand on that cocked hip.

As the sun sank to the horizon, imagination touched up the picture, erasing it abruptly, beginning it once more, again and again, and my idols portrayed the characters of Max du Veuzit, Matilde Serao, Delly; Andrea Leeds was Emma Rouault. Once, at nightfall, while I wasn't paying attention, the herd scattered and was already wandering off in all directions when I suddenly saw my father standing in front of my horse, as still and straight as a poker, stone-faced, with a look in his blue eyes that cut right through me. And as I returned to my senses, he seemed to grow taller and taller.

26

WE HAD HAD NO DEFINITE NEWS OF FLORENCIO SINCE don Benito's story of his evangelical encounter with the runaway. Judging from the rumors that spread through the region now and again – he had been seen in Luque, then in Villa del Rosario, next in Río Segundo – he continued to travel farther away from us, and I imagined him leaving the farm in these constantly progressing stages, finding himself one day at the gates of the city of Córdoba, and – who knows? – leaving the province at last, on the road to Buenos Aires.

In the middle of August – a month that for many connotes a time of fruition and harvest, but which marks the heart of winter down there – on the festival of Assumption, all the families in our area went to Las Junturas to attend morning mass, watch the procession in the afternoon, and go to the dance held in a barn decorated with garlands and Chinese lanterns.

We left early, the boys in a sulky, I with my mother and sisters in our first car, driven by my father. We were all in our Sunday best; my sisters gingerly held on their laps the silk dresses they were saving for the ball.

Between the ceremony and the celebration, we also went to some christening parties, visited friends, and walked around the public square in spite of the cold weather. Young women complimented each other effusively on their dresses, the most fashionable of which had been mail-ordered from the big department stores in the capital. One of the most popular had a name more appropriate for a hospital, La Piedad; another was Gath y Chaves, which did not do business with the general public, and where only the Molnar brood, the richest family in the region, could boast of buying their clothes. Their house had imposing frontages on all four sides and was my idea of Paradise.

After mass, people would linger in front of the church, in that area between the portal and the street that I would call the parvis if it were not for my memory of its dusty bareness. Afterward everyone went off to eat lunch, some as guests in the homes of friends in the village, others sitting in their carriages or on benches in the town square. White tablecloths were carefully unfolded and wicker baskets plundered of their festive contents.

In preparation for the procession, the streets running into the square were closed, and people soon began to gather there expectantly.

Girls paraded along, walking arm in arm, while boys walked by in the opposite direction, calling compliments to the girls, who giggled and nudged one another with their elbows. Engaged couples also strolled together with arms intertwined, off in a world of their own, but preceded by a child whose job it was to make sure there were no unseemly displays of affection. I was set to keep an eye on my eldest sister; she was not in my good graces at the time, and her fiancé received lots of little kicks on the ankles. As the crowd grew, it split into groups; the young people would strut about, laughing and showing off, and then scatter with shrieks and squeals. Sometimes everyone would stop to listen to a sudden gust of music from the bando-nion wheezing on the threshold of a grocery that also sold refreshments, and the delighted audience would applaud wildly. But anyone glancing down the streets closed off by bar-riers would see cows in the distance, because everyday reality was still there, a hundred meters away: that endless, feature-less plain. So you had to avoid looking at it, you had to keep strolling around the square, and laughing, and exchanging the same tired remarks amid the rustling and medicinal odors of the eucalyptus trees, until the harsh clanging of the steeple bell called everyone together, transforming the merrymakers in a twinkling into solemn churchgoers who looked as if they had just been given new souls.

They all seemed liberated from their lives and labors. The hubbub of voices was stilled; even the wind died down for a moment and was forgotten. The women checked their toques, pulled their shawls closer, rearranged the folds of their mantil-las. The church doors opened, and to the strains of the harmo-nium, the little old priest emerged from the shadowy light sprinkled with candle flames, wearing a frayed golden cope borrowed from the parish of Villa del Rosario. Behind him appeared the Virgin, swaying aloft on a stretcher shouldered by some of the faithful and studded with tiny light bulbs that paled in the daylight.

Making their way through the crowd, the village's leading citizens took their places immediately behind the stretcher and just ahead of their own offspring, who got to play the part of altar boys in cassock and surplice, to my immense chagrin.

The throng of country people now moved politely out of the

way, with an affability they showed only on occasions such as this, and since they loved a nice straight furrow, they gradually cleared an orderly pathway. Then the elderly priest gave the signal to start. Anyone glancing back to the end of the procession at that moment would have seen an ill-sorted couple falling into step there: don Benito and the village whore, with her eyes cast down and not a trace of makeup on her face, who on that day was greeted with a nod by anyone who happened to pass her on the street.

The cortege went all around the square, as the music of the harmonium gave way to that of accordions, which would be playing at the dance that night. The same song was repeated throughout the procession, and although it was true that the singing was off-key, the harmony of the faithful in devotion made up for the music, except when the parade drew near the grocery-café, where the customers ostentatiously turned their backs on us to listen to a lively tango from the bandonion. Were reproving looks cast their way? Well, there was always someone ready to counter with a dance step or two out on the sidewalk. As small as it was, the village could boast of four or five freethinkers.

On the day we had news of Florencio, a brisk wind sent the Virgin's veil streaming off to one side and billowed under her robe, occasionally lifting it up altogether, revealing for all to see that aside from the head and hands, her body was only a wire frame concealed by clothes. That seemed pitiful and obscene to me; my sisters' solid and chaste dress dummy would have been more suitable for the Mother of God. Buffeted head-on by the wind at first, then from the side, and finally from behind, the procession returned to its point of departure and halted there with cries of outrage and fear: atop the cornice of the church, Florencio was parading his scrawny body clothed in rags along the sky.

Straining every fiber of his being to the bursting point, he executed the jump – feet together, arms clamped against his sides – he had used to leap onto Filly's back with me. And there he is, straddling the concrete cross, where, leaning one hand on the summit, he flings his body backward, only to reappear immediately, setting his feet on the arms of the cross. That wooden face of his, so impassive and enigmatic, now seems to gleam with satisfied treachery.

Slowly he draws himself up, holding his arms wide open, a living cross taking possession of all that sky. He disappears around one end of the cornice and pops out at the other end in a flash; he walks mincingly along the very edge of it, but that is no longer enough. Even if his audience does not dare express its pleasure, it would never forgive him for stopping there: it propels him, demands everything, and right away, and above all, it wants the impossible. He gives it to them.

Suddenly the crowd surges backward. Has he disappeared into the gathering dusk? My father pulls me roughly away.

We go home, my father, mother, and I, huddled in the sulky. I am more annoyed than upset.

My brothers and sisters are staying behind to attend the dance – they must, my father has told my eldest brother, to ward off the spitefulness of those who were trying to pump him for information about Florencio. He even lets my brother have the car.

I am sorry to miss the dance, the fluttering garlands, the Chinese lanterns, and the accordionists, who would have been joined by the freethinkers' bandonion.

But when my mother recalls, as though in prayer, the way the little old priest had draped his golden cope over Florencio's body, I burst into tears.

27

THE MANNEQUIN AROUND WHICH MY ONLY CHILDHOOD
games would center must have arrived at the farm when I was
quite young, since the large rectangular box it came in did not
make me think of a coffin. I was ten years old when I saw my
first one of those, La Pinotta's, which reminded me of the big
package and brought the analogy to life, if I may put it that way.

From the moment it was unwrapped and set upright, this
one-legged divinity made of cloth stuffed with sawdust cap-
tured my allegiance, and much more so than had the Sacred
Heart of Jesus behind its pane of glass glinting with reflections.
In some magical way, I sensed that the mannequin was completely absorbed in the thought of a single word, capable of
resting its trunk on that tripod throughout all eternity, alive, but
with another life, without days or nights, without seeing or
hearing or feeling anything, except perhaps a muffled cottony
throbbing within its breast. Having neither past nor future,
expectation did not enter into its nature. Neither lover nor
mother, it was the Idea, exacting the tribute of adoration while
offering its royal opulence to endless pinpricks.

Beheaded, she yet looked me up and down with her absent
eyes, and in the middle of the night, searching for them in the
shadows from my bed, I would have sworn that they glowed.
Despite her mutilations, which must have seemed sacred to
me, and despite her idol's chastity, she was nonetheless the first
mature nude figure I had ever contemplated – for on the day
when I saw my eldest brother's naked body, it was entirely soul-
less, and therefore formless, its lines consumed by the heat of
his passion.

I remember the time one of my sisters, kneeling on the floor in front of the mannequin, began to turn the knob hidden beneath the hips, raising the bust and with it the dress on which she was pinning up the hem. I felt as though she were committing a sacrilege. And I remember the first silks, the raspy crinkle of muslin, the rustle of the newspaper I used to invent my own patterns, and I remember the time I gave the mannequin a face, fixing upon its neck a fan made from a stick and an oval of red paper, which I then surrounded with pleats to grand effect. I had barely placed the mannequin in front of the mirror when it became terrifying: gazing at its image, it eluded me. And I caught sight of myself, my head just up to its shoulder, looking at it with eyes from another face.

When I think back on this now, and on many other things touched by the cold breath of madness – that draft creeping under the door – I am astonished that I ever left the dark prairies of childhood to slip away into the normal world.

Below its three folding doors, my mother's mirrored wardrobe had a drawer as wide as the wardrobe itself, a drawer that was always kept locked. For a long time my curiosity went unsatisfied because no one would open this drawer for me, but I finally determined which were the right keys among the heavy bunch belonging to my father, and promptly discovered a funereal marvel that horrified me at first, probably because my sense of transgression heightened the dramatic effect of the sight that met my eyes: a long gown of black brocade, a lusterless and gleaming labyrinth that lay upon a foaming mass of white, the boned collar flattened by the ritual crown of waxen orange blossoms.

Today, when I think of that recumbent figure without face or hands, I tell myself that, like my first coffin – a cardboard box – my first dead person was only an image: metaphors sometimes precede the terms underlying them.

During one of those Sunday afternoon naps when our sleepers sank to the bottom of their fatigue, abandoning fields, chores, the house itself, I managed to steal away the dark treasure and carry it off to the sewing room. The mannequin would never again be decked out so sumptuously, as if it had come all the way from the capital just to wear my mother's wedding dress. At the time, wedding gowns were made of beautiful black material, in anticipation of the inevitable periods of mourning to come. They were trimmed with ruffles on the cuffs and the front of the bodice, however, and ornamented with tiny buttons as white as the tulle that floated like a cloud over everything, the delicate, gauzy net that so well deserves its name: "illusion." Illusion. What couturier thought to call it that? The dressmaker's apprentices stop plying their needles for an instant; I can see them looking up in delight, and hear their youthful laughter.

I swept the room, placed my sisters' sewing things out of sight behind the pink gingham screen, and, leaving only the Singer sewing machine in place (the one handsome piece of furniture in the house), I set the mannequin directly across from the door. I dressed it; the high collar perfectly fitted the severed neck. Perched upon a broom handle slipped down the back of the dress, the bridal wreath swam on its sea of tulle foam, which cascaded endlessly down upon the carefully arranged train.

At the first sign that the sleepers were returning from their deep-sea slumbers, I summoned my mother and sisters, throwing open the folding door when they appeared in answer to my call. There will always be someone around to invent theater.

They exclaim, they scold me, they marvel, they congratulate me, they close the door and talk in low voices. And the mannequin draws itself up, untouchable, as though it were only just managing to hold back, as though it were planning to walk, to lead a rebellion, and even more: to ride the crest of a tidal wave of the dead. It does not need us to exist; it is what it is, sure of its destiny, conspiring with majestic powers beyond our ken. What does it care for what we feel about it? It has no more interest in us than would a colony of ants. But, suddenly, the main character in this scene, the one who determines the center of the action, the mother, steps back into the shadows, her hands clasped at her waist: the mother, her face lit up by a smile and as quickly veiled by sadness, who gives a short laugh that is nearly a sob, like a string set vibrating and almost immediately stilled. We sense that she is being drawn back into the past and is struggling to resist this fierce current, to remain present, here, with us. She does not fool us, however, when she tries to put a good face on things by going over to the mannequin and arranging the folds of the skirt into pleats.

She is completely imbued with the whiteness of the "illusion" that was once a promise of happiness and is now an ache in her heart. The morning roses were blighted by a dusty wind long ago, elsewhere, over there, where the future began to dwindle away. We are far from one another, wandering down our separate corridors of time, when suddenly our mother recovers her composure and I see her reach behind the boned collar, feeling under the knot of ribbons for the hook that she quickly unfastens, and the gown crumples to the floor, restoring the mannequin to its upholstered nudity, a ridiculous sight beneath the wreath of orange blossoms and the cascade of tulle – an obscene nakedness, just as our mother must have felt hers to be, conquered, consumed, and consummated by our father on their wedding night.

28

OUR SUNDAY NAPS? THE EFFRONTERY OF WATCHING the grown-ups sleeping; the awareness of betraying them: I have, on that score, betrayed a great deal. I found it moving to contemplate the sleepers' poses. Some tensions melted away; some struggles were waged more fiercely than ever. My mother seemed sad in her sleep, with her arms draped across her breast as though she were hugging herself. Lying on his back at her side, my father seemed as solemn as a figure on a tomb. He would have been proud of this.

In the girls' bedroom, in a faint scent of Coty rice powder, the sleepers set their bodies free. I remember Cecilia, her animal softness, her arms wrapped around the bolster, one hand cupping her ear – Cecilia, whom I suspected of dreaming about her fiancé from the city.

In the boys' room, I do not contemplate, I spy. Tiptoeing with words, I reach the incandescent center of my life, the place where I would always land, pushed by the image of my eldest brother lying prone on the bed that sags beneath his weight, rocking on its four iron feet, creaking cautiously at first, soon loudly, rhythmically, despite the hands gripping the bed frame.

Everything contributes to the preservation of an enduring memory: the heat of summer; the dim light striped with shadows by the bars of the high window, half opened onto the garden; the humming of the bees in their hives, which were installed by one of my brothers who had taken up apiculture and which a storm will soon carry off along with their improbable honey; finally, the narrow mirror on the wardrobe in which, while pretending to sleep, I can see my eldest brother better than if I were to lie turned toward him. Ever since childhood I have preferred the image to the reality, to the point that if I happen to see the objects in a room reflected in a mirror off to one side, then that second version of what I see appears more intensely delineated and more revealing of the secret heart of things, a cunning essence invisible to the naked eye.

The mirrored wardrobe containing my brothers' few good clothes had an inside drawer that concealed, as I well knew, the paraphernalia of my eldest brother's initial forays into manhood. Once a month, with paternal permission and perhaps even encouragement, he would patronize one or another of the rare prostitutes in the area. In this respect, they were like idiots: every village had only one of each. These women lived apart and received their clients only after nightfall, so that their neighbors, quite happy to be able to ignore their profession, treated them politely by day.

In the drawer – which will remain for me a kind of tabernacle annexed by the Devil – my brother had stashed an automatic pistol, two or three unwrapped condoms, a pile of pretty hand-kerchiefs, and a toy that was supposed to be macabre: a coffin about eight inches long, the cover of which was on a spring, so that it rose at the same time as the enormous pink penis of a gentleman in a three-piece suit whose eyes, although tiny, were on minuscule swivels, like the eyes of my little sister's doll, which I had baptized Deanna, in honor of Deanna Durbin.

With one hand, my eldest brother peels off his undershirt, and with the other, pinned under his belly, he unbuttons his fly.

Quite unintentionally, I mentally undress passersby, whether I find them attractive or not; I take the clothes off everyone I meet, but I usually get them dressed again very quickly. And have I learned a single thing from this involuntary habit? Very few men and women are aware of their own sensuality; there are even some who do not seem to live in their bodies, and I am astonished that certain people have children.

I am not moved by the body of my brother, whom I do not love, after all, because my father shows a marked preference for his eldest son, constantly holding him up as a shining example, rewarding him – and only him – with a bit of money if the harvest has been good. Was he praising his son's exceptional abilities, or was he trying to oblige him to develop such talents, the way we oblige those we love to live up to our image of them?

Beyond the window bars, the brutal light of summer, the bustling hum of bees; and in the bedroom, our siesta, the auspicious, shadowy light, and me, swept from head to toe by a desire taking my body beyond all bounds, and soon a kind of despair seizes me, as nothing seems connected to any feeling whatsoever but is instead in league with my brother's straining figure as he contracts, thrusts, pinning a dream to the mattress.

He is in a world of his own, oblivious now to the squeaking of the bed springs; his mouth is wet, slightly twisted, and he is panting, and just when he is on the very edge of happiness...like a lightning bolt in the night sky, down from the darkness of the ceiling beams drops a big hairy spider to land, quivering and venomous, upon his back.

A sudden leap, and he stands scowling in his contorted nakedness. His pants have slipped down, hobbling his legs.

Had he really believed I was sleeping? As soon as he sees he was mistaken, he pretends to ignore me, and releasing his penis, which he had been holding clamped against his thigh, he smacks the revolting spider with an espadrille, crushing it in the hollow of the bed.

That is what I was driven to, goaded on by desire, and I have carried that vision within me my whole life long, for it penetrated to the very core of my being.

For fear of inserting a trivial analogy, I failed to point out that it was during that same summer that the cactus flowered. Before finding a more passionate spectacle to observe in the mirror, I would admire the splendor of this pale pink florescence jutting up at the edge of the brick terrace. And I had resolved, despite the complexity of this blossom with its petals arranged like overlapping scales, to reproduce it in that wonderfully versatile crepe paper my sisters used to make blooms for dead people I had never met.

My mother used to tell their stories in remembrance, one after the other, but I only recall the one about my Aunt Magdalena, who died in the flower of her youth, beaten down by the ill-treatment she received from her husband, according to my father, who made a point of remarking upon his own kindness in the matter whenever he had the chance. No one took care of her tomb; the proof was a hole at ground level, and I imagined rats hiding there, watching our departure after a visit to her grave.

29

ALTHOUGH AS AN ADOLESCENT I WAS TO LIVE FOR A while in Villa del Rosario (a visit not without its consequences), the only childhood memory I have of the little town with streets of beaten earth and a colonial church of extravagant proportions is a vision of the cemetery, in the blazing sun, where people in their Sunday best ceased chattering and assumed solemn expressions as soon as they passed through the gate.

The lightness of the dresses, the wide-brimmed hats some women wore, and the gaudy colors of the artificial flowers give my recollections of the Day of the Dead a certain garden-party atmosphere. But it was in the cemetery of Villa del Rosario that I was reunited with my sorceress, a kind of mistress of ceremonies among the whirling figures on a town clock, the Scheherazade who continues, from her great beyond, to tell me of my childhood days.

La Pinotta sat enthroned in the shadow of an abandoned tomb that would have looked exactly like a sentry box if it hadn't been for the cross on top. Gripping a bucket between her knees, she laboriously turned a handle on its side, producing a crackling sound that alerted the children who began to gather around her, clutching a few small coins. Inside the bucket was another one, with a cover, and between the two was a layer of chipped ice, which I had never seen before, and so took for broken glass. La Pinotta was making sherbet. By turning, turning, she whirled away from all her lost battles, while her breath came wheezing like that of the "saint" of Luque, long ago.

There was not one feature in her face that did not speak of

sorrow and hard times. The skin of her eyelids was a dusky brown; her once-plump cheeks were now crisscrossed with wrinkles along which her sweat trickled freely, flowing down her neck into a crease so deep it looked as if someone had tried to cut her throat but had stopped halfway across.

Her majesty was profane, and now counterfeit, but wherever she might be, even there, in that macabre lair among the dead, she possessed the presence of a prima donna. And so instead of frightening me, her decrepitude became in my eyes an extra measure of splendor.

People catching sight of her turned their faces away, and a few of them crossed themselves furtively. She did not notice me among the group of urchins clustered about her, deaf to the calls of their parents, but when she decided that her sherbet had reached the desired consistency and rose to advertise its excellent quality to the general public, she stood in puzzlement for a few moments, and then cradled my face in her hands. She was leaning forward to kiss me, but drew back abruptly: my father was behind me. They did not speak a word to each other. La Pinotta nodded her head, smiling. My father stood stiffly in the haughty attitude that always gave him a double chin. She represented what he had always hated most on earth: she was disorder in person, and in the very costume of poverty, clothed in garments held together in places by pins that put off any prospect of mending until some highly unlikely tomorrow.

I only loved her all the more, though I would have preferred to see her triumphant in her reunion with my father. She held out her hand to him; he hesitated, then gestured vaguely in her direction, simply because he was concerned about what people might say, I suppose. When La Pinotta sat down again, I quickly settled myself astride her knees and looked my father right in the eye. And so I joined her side once and for all, and I evoke her memory today in that same spirit. My father acquiesced, placing on his aged aunt's shoulder a hand that was full of authority but intended to convey welcome.

La Pinotta got up again; I remember the sudden sparkle in

her eyes, like the glint of the winter sun when it sinks below the horizon. She offered me a sherbet in a paper cone and gave another one to my father, who invited a few penniless children to enjoy this manna before it melted away.

Does memory strain anxiously to capture – and recapture – the sensation? I find it again, that moment when coldness became greediness in my mouth, coldness that until then had been only the wintry wind of July buffeting me on my horse, and hands cracked with chilblains.

What then passed between my father and La Pinotta? From the cadence of her words, I detected rejoicing and a kind of indulgence that might have concealed some ruse. My mother embraced her by the side of a grave, and then I remember her humming in the car with us as we drove home. She no longer owned her lovely cariole; she had only her ice-cream churn. I suspect that it was this device – which he had carefully tied to the back of the car – rather than a feeling of solidarity or the awakening of a long-suppressed natural affection, that had gotten the better of my father's animosity toward his aunt. From then on, with the arrival of winter, the only season when we could indulge in such a treat, my father would go into the village occasionally for slabs of ice, which he broke up with a hammer. He brought to his cranking of the ice-cream freezer the violent enthusiasm of a blacksmith eagerly working white-hot iron at his forge. Nevertheless, sherbet was the result: in the bitter chill of winter, chilled sweetness. My mother would serve us some in coffee cups, and we would reverently taste this fantastic food, thinking of La Pinotta, who was no longer of this world.

Home from the cemetery, during the dinner at which she sat facing my father at one end of the table (in my mother's place, sometimes occupied by don Benito or the worker honored with the title of farm boss during the harvest), La Pinotta seemed quite at ease, while the rest of us sat in a silence somewhat alleviated by the noisy and more or less rhythmical slurping of soup.

What had happened to her boldness, her readiness to lavish praise or blame?

This woman who had once been stubbornness itself now seemed shrunken, stripped forever of her truculent manner and incantatory powers, reduced in her melancholy exhaustion to the animal existence of a broken-down old nag, a creature with cloudy eyes and a distressingly rank odor. Her cheeks were flabby, her chest sunken, and she hunched over her plate at times with a weariness we had never seen in her before. Life had drained the life from her.

In my eyes, however, she presided over our table, and when we rose at the end of the meal, she managed to hold up her head and carry herself with a dignity that was still impressive in that world where it was so important to put up a good front. And when my mother broke the silence by gently urging her to recall some past event for us, I thought the storyteller was awakening, drumming up her ghosts: they flocked to her from the supposed far corners of the limitless plain, and a few were summoned from the land of her childhood. But her words seemed to come to her slowly, almost with reluctance, and if her voice rose, it was only to fall back, stricken, to a murmur.

It must have humiliated her to be relegated to helping with the housework, but she resigned herself to peeling vegetables and sweeping out the rooms, which was all she was allowed to do.

She wandered around the poultry yard, collecting eggs from the nesting boxes in the henhouse or from the nests hidden in the bushes by the more independent chickens. I showed her where some of them were, and she found others on her own.

She wandered about the stables, sometimes going inside; I saw her stroking the sleeping animals, and I remember that night when, just at cockcrow, a small cow dropped a calf almost bigger than she was, in a sea of dung: my father busily wielded huge forceps while La Pinotta held up the kerosene lamp, adjusting the wick with its flickering flame. When I look back on it today, I see that other Nativity; even the stench now seems like a kind of perfume.

She wandered, she wandered, farther and farther away, following – and in vain – the trail of a skunk, she said, beyond the walled farmyards, over to where the cultivated fields began. Was she seeking a way out, a path that would have led her to the high road of adventure once again? She had come to the end of her road, and no one on earth would ever follow the labyrinth of her steps as she wandered, nursing her dreams.

At dawn and at dusk, she forecast the weather. This provided daily grounds for dispute, but also for reconciliation (if not agreement) with my father, who had claimed once and for all the right to out-argue anyone and was not about to give it up, even when the old witch would tire of the argument and come over to his opinion.

She would study the trees, looking them over, here and there plucking a leaf, crushing it between her thumb and index finger to release its scent – a sleepwalker gliding by, submerged in the limpid summer air.

Then the days grew shorter, and plowing began again. La Pinotta slept in the sewing room, and under her bed she kept a tightly knotted bundle that she never opened, which naturally intrigued us no end. Since her Christian name was Giuseppa (which is where her nickname came from), for the feast of Saint Joseph, my sisters made her a new outfit and my mother gave her stockings she had knitted herself, along with a pair of woolen slippers. La Pinotta agreed to put off her rags, but she did not throw them away, and the next day her bundle had grown bigger.

After that, whenever she went near a mirror, we could hear her laughing just as in the old days, but under her breath.

The swallows vanished earlier than usual, and a mild, rainy autumn suddenly drew in the horizon. That suited our fields, but when my father showed his satisfaction, La Pinotta reminded him that predicting the weather was her department, and her chuckling stung him to the quick.

The garden looked exceptionally beautiful, although the cactus had rotted away. Moss covered the bricks edging the beds and grew over cracks in the bark of trees. And one day La Pinotta – her eyesight failing, but her sense of smell intact – nosed out from a fork in our oldest locust tree what looked to me

like a moldy cauliflower, an enormous brownish growth surrounded by bulbous little satellites, a kind of bouquet that she
detached with deft, smooth movements that suddenly recalled
the unctuous manner that had so impressed me in the hovel of
the "saint" in Luque. She inhaled the odor of the large fragile
lump with delight, and smiling, elevated it above her head with
a priestly gesture. In what dim corner of memory had her joy
awakened? She twirled around, her mouth watering, and trotted off to the kitchen.

My mother and sisters were now as bewildered as I was, and
suspicious as well. They made faces of disgust, while my father
forbade any of us to touch this freak of nature that he called a
"mushroom," because he had heard from his parents that back
in Cumiana, their valley in the old country, whole families had
gone to sleep forever after a meal, for the mushroom-gathering
of one day could decimate a village.

But no warning could dispel La Pinotta's happiness: for
once, she was the one in charge of the kitchen, plucking from
the braid of peppers and garlic bulbs plaited together, bending
over the cast-iron pot, calling for the poker, quickly now, and a
nice big shovelful of charcoal for the fire.

We stood open-mouthed before her, filled with the same
excitement and uneasiness caused by those successive periods
of silence and crashing thunder that precede a storm. Was she
talking to my father? As her words swept over him, he screwed
up his face and stiffened in an attitude of noble indignation.
Still, he was curious, and along with the rest of us he watched
La Pinotta as though she were a druidess performing a ritual.
She separated the mushrooms from their cluster, gently
brushed them, dipped them carefully in two changes of water;
we began to help her, handing her the utensils, but without
showing too much eagerness for fear of sparking an outburst
from our father. He said nothing, however, and when she asked
him for a shiny piece of iron, much to our surprise he hastened
to get her a big nail from the wall, polishing it up himself.

In response to our inquiring looks, the sorceress added mystery to her own, assuming in her expression and movements a gravity that discouraged all questions, so intent did she seem upon taming unknown forces.

There was a sudden crackling sound: thinly sliced, the mushrooms sizzled in hot oil redolent with garlic. Holding the lid in one hand and the shiny bit of iron in the other, La Pinotta waved the nail in a circle and dropped it into the pot.

Only then did she deign to reveal her secret: if by some misfortune the nail should rust, we would be deprived of the most delectable treat imaginable. Was this some archaic wisdom sprung from the junction between magic and experience? Whatever the case might be, we would not taste this dish, decreed my father, pointing at each of his children in turn. We stepped back, and he ordered us to follow him. We heard the rattle of the lid as La Pinotta lifted it from the pot, and I glimpsed her wreathed in steam; the most unappetizing smell imaginable, billowing in great waves from the kitchen, followed us all the way out to the patio. It was on that occasion that I learned the word *miasma*.

My brothers and the peons were coming home from the fields. Appealing to my mother, who gave her assent (but not without a little shrug of her shoulders), my father decided that since everything in the kitchen was quite possibly contaminated, we would dine on stores from the pantry and the usual grilled meat, which was barbecued on a weeding harrow. My father presided at the grill, since he alone, in his opinion, knew how to select the wood, add the correct amount of charcoal, prepare a properly even bed of coals, and arrange the various cuts of meat upon the harrow according to size and tenderness so that all would reach the same degree of doneness at the same time, spurting juicily when sliced open – which seems strange to me, now that I think about it, because over there, at least in those days, meat was always cooked until it was quite dried out.

Smoke curls up into the trees; the embers glow like the setting sun; from the house comes the rattle of dishes, and now La Pinotta as well, who crosses the patio holding out her arms like a tragic heroine, as though she were pushing the dying day before her, and as an exordium to her confession of failure, she utters a cry that turns to laughter as she shows us the rusty nail.

Is my mother smiling at her? My father makes fun of her unkindly, then shifts from sarcasm to the usual moralizing.

La Pinotta keeps quiet, almost as though her mind were far away, and when my father finally falls silent and leans back in his chair, with one hand she slips off the faded rag she wears wrapped tightly around her head, hiding her ears. And I see for the first time, along with everyone else, perhaps, the cottony gray wad of her hair, which no comb could ever have untangled, but as she wags her head from side to side, wavy locks fall free to hang down about her shoulders. In a sleepy voice, she begins to remember the Piedmont and its autumns, the fine drizzling rain, the hills, the gathering of mushrooms in the woods. Her pride and mischievous spite will turn this retrospective inventory to account, thanks to her skillful evocation of an episode in which she once figured, according to her, as the heroine of events that were eventually distilled, in the retelling, into a proverb.

Although I do not understand her story, I think I sense how the sly old thing's very words restore her soul, the soul of an enchantress who moves easily between the harshness of her daily life and her dreams, which she introduces into everyday reality in such a way that dream and reality become, in all innocence, the reverse sides of each other.

Now, by wandering back in time, will she be able to recover her old oracular powers?

Along the way, she begins to croon a cantilena, and when she lets it fall, someone picks it up again down at the other end of the table. Humming absentmindedly, my father suddenly realizes what he is doing and breaks off. Too late: an acceptance, an acquiescence quite beyond their control has come over them both, a kind of self-renunciation. Everything that has ever led to clashes between them – on the one side, life seized in a full embrace, over and over again; on the other, an obsession with order that stifles every impulse; the one living without a care for respectable appearances, swapping and cheating along her merry way; the other exercising a ceaseless vigilance that condemns immediately the slightest stirrings of adventure – everything that has separated them their whole lives long, now seems to be melting away, second by second. Will they finally be reconciled?

A faint tremor passes through us, like a breeze in a suffocating heat wave, and reunites us. The joy that shines in my mother's face is still before my eyes.

The next morning, before the sun had peeked over the horizon, my mother awakened me while she herself was still getting dressed. I was to carry breakfast to my brothers and the peons, who had been working at the other end of the property since before dawn, and I was just about to fall asleep again when my mother's cries for help roused me from my bed. She had found La Pinotta sitting in the kitchen, dead. I saw her, in the low chair she was so fond of, her head resting on her breast, tufts of hair hanging down in her face, a scrap of bread clutched in her fingers, her hand dangling in the mushroom pot that sat on the floor at her feet. It was empty.

Bowing to the entreaties of my mother, who was moved by piety, and for the sake of appearances (the death had, after all, occurred in his house), my father decided to rehabilitate his paternal aunt. Thus, to begin with, she was entitled to one of those caskets that have oval windows in the lids to frame the face of the deceased.

After the formalities had been taken care of and the body placed in the coffin, we filed past that black box in which La Pinotta must have felt fairly cramped, and after us came the neighbors, who had begun to arrive for the wake. I took it into my head to reproach my brothers and sisters for their impassiveness, and the anguish I felt when I imagined myself lying in La Pinotta's place produced an effective catch in my voice.

There was a religious service, and the notary from Las Junturas came to the cemetery to deliver the funeral oration in praise of the wanderer, using the rhetoric of political speechifying to weave her exploits into an epic tale. My father quickly adopted this official version and in the future never lost an occasion to extol the courage of this aunt who, driven by death, had finally returned, in great pomp, to the bosom of the family.

Thirty years later, when his own days were drawing to a close, I would even hear my father holding her up as an example to us all, and in this he was consistent with the time-honored habit of families who expect their dead – particularly those who were never understood while they were alive – to furnish them with precepts for living.

30

ALTHOUGH I COULD NOT PUT IT INTO WORDS, I KNEW, obscurely, that there was something in the world that belonged to me and to no other. But this conviction, which stirred up so many dreams, was frustrated by its symmetrical counterpart: a sense of the impossibility of vanquishing the plain that stretched out all around me, of ever escaping it for good.

My brothers – not my sisters – had been boarders in Villa del Rosario at the Salesian School, which was run by members of the Society of Saint François de Sales. As for me, it was through the marriage of Cecilia, who went to live in Córdoba, that I was able to go away to school when I was eleven years old.

The provincial capital was taking on the air of a metropolis, and I was reassured by the way its streets were laid out in straight lines intersecting at right angles with the same military precision I was to notice many years later in Turin. My sister had only two rooms on the ground floor, opening onto the street, and a small patio half covered with awnings made of split canes. A passageway separated her bedroom from her sewing

workshop, where she set up a bed for me behind the pink gingham screen from the farm.

Cecilia took good care of me, the way our mother would have
done; my sister had inherited her serene vitality and even temper. And of course there were special, innocent bonds between
my sister and me.

In honor of I don't remember what person who had distin-
guished himself during our wars of independence, the street we
lived on was named Rondeau – my first exposure to the French
language and its perplexing propensity for not pronouncing all
the letters in a word.

I was enrolled in a nearby school adjoining the Franciscan
monastery and run by the friars, who taught only religion to the
mixed classes of seminarists and day pupils, while other sub-
jects were handled by different teachers. One of them was a
young and pretty woman, and I was very proud of her, more on
account of her Anglo-Spanish surname, a double-barreled
patronym that had figured in the short history of our country,
than for her teaching, which in fact reflected her deep concern
for her students.

Like the immigrant who tries to compete with his new coun-
trymen to become just like them, I was soon on the honor roll,
and the Franciscans were not long in sending me a lay brother
as ambassador. Brother Salvador was a big mulatto, not particularly bright, who trotted about with a funny walk and seemed
somewhat absentminded whenever he asked you questions. He
did not participate in the life of the monastery as far as communal prayers or ceremonies were concerned, but he always
appeared promptly if someone or something required his attention. And no one in the monastery would have dared criticize
him for his independence, because he possessed the gift of
awakening a "vocation" in a boy and persuading him to take
holy orders. That is how it happened with me one October afternoon in 1941.

Sometimes a veil of sadness would cover his face, a sadness
made more poignant by the look in his eyes, and sometimes this

sorrow would vanish in a smile of sparkling white, framed by fleshy lips of a purplish brown rather darker than the rosy tint of his skin. I remember how he would genuflect hurriedly in front of each altar without interrupting his little trot, and when he crossed himself, you would have said he was simply brushing away a fly.

Sometimes we saw him in the courtyard during recess, his hands folded idly across his belly. He kept a blissfully abstracted eye on us and always seemed about to break into a smile. He was in charge of the weekly handicrafts class, where he was so good at discovering and nurturing each person's individual skills that at the end of the year – while most of my fellow students were working with saws, doing fretwork on plywood panels – I had covered two square meters of coarse linen cloth with cross-stitched floral designs.

Had he thought he was alone on the day when I was still dawdling in the study hall and saw him in front of the student honor roll, with my name heading the list? Eager for compliments, I banged the top of the desk to get his attention. He started, turning slowly around, and peered through the windows at the darkened classrooms. I felt embarrassed, and stepped back against the wall. There was a long silence, then the clinking of a bunch of keys: Brother Salvador unlocked the forbidden door, studded with iron fittings, that opened onto the cloister. As he stood on the threshold, still looking fearfully around, I caught a glimpse of the garden in the evening light: all the serenity in the world was gathered there, around the mossy stones of a well.

In the courtyard the next day, he beckoned me discreetly with one hand while rooting around with the other – his arm buried up to the elbow – in the pocket concealed by the folds of his robe. He finally pulled out a rosary of small beads, which he offered me without a word, gesturing with a jerk of his chin at the monthly honor roll.

I sometimes ran into Brother Salvador on his way back from the market, trudging along with big baskets topped with bundles of leeks. On idle Saturday afternoons, not daring to venture any farther into the city, I walked back and forth in front of the monastery, where I sometimes saw him in the doorway of the visiting room, waiting for expected guests or welcoming them as they arrived.

One time, he was not at his post, and nothing moved in the shadow of the alcove breaching the high facade with its blind windows. I boldly went inside, and rising suddenly from the seat where he had been dozing, he invited me to sit down even before recognizing me. And as though he had been waiting for me, he began an impromptu recital of the events in the life of a young man, the son of a wealthy cloth merchant, who had sought only sensual pleasure and military glory until the moment when, touched by divine grace, he became the most perfect Christian who ever walked upon this earth – in a word, a second Jesus, because, like Our Lord Jesus Christ, Francesco Bernardone knew that happiness can only belong to those who possess nothing.

Of this story told in the semidarkness of the visiting room, I would remember only a few things, but I will remember them forever. I was first of all surprised to learn that Saint Francis of Assisi had a family name (which brought him back down to earth for me), and a very modest one – Bernardone – an impression heightened by the contempt displayed by the Argentine upper classes for all Italians. Next I was struck by the metaphor presenting the young man's conversion as a marriage with "Lady Poverty," and above all I was amazed that Signora Bernardone was able to attend the canonization of her son on the day following his death. On the third of October, 1226, lying naked on the naked earth, Francis of Assisi had sung his "Canticle of the Creatures," adding a verse in honor of the imminent arrival of his "Sister Death."

In Brother Salvador's mouth, historical facts were transmuted, in a fitting reflection of human longing, to the stuff of legend.

But what would steal into the soul – reaching the fertile soil where those images that are slowest to flower take root, one day revealing our thoughts to us with a rare clarity – were the words the friar attributed, in his monotonous voice suddenly quivering with enthusiasm, to Francesco Bernardone trumpeting his enlightenment through the streets of his native city: "Love is not beloved.... Love is not beloved...."

Delighted and a bit bewildered, I walked around the city for a long time before going home. Had my greedy heart just understood that one may possess the universe by possessing nothing? I took up mysticism the way one takes center stage, and my only concern in the future would be to catch up with the image of myself that, projected into the impossible, came back so crisply at me from the future – that image one hopes in vain to embrace some day, holding it tightly enough to become one with it at last. As in dreams or mirages, this image vanishes at our approach, reappearing only in the distance, exactly the same, but as though embellished by our expectations.

I did not know what only time would tell – but I did know, with increasing certainty or madness, that I would not remain where I was born. I encouraged myself by despising my surroundings, convinced that my only chance lay in escaping them, in fleeing my family and the encircling phantoms of the plain. Without knowing it, we make ourselves into what we are; then we are what we have made of ourselves. I felt that fate and I would meet face to face, and that I was just as free as fate was.

When my first year at school drew to a close, Brother Salvador and I agreed that I would return to the farm to inform my parents of my vocation and wrest their consent from them.

Was I taking my mother's support for granted? For reasons that are beyond me, she took my father's side. No other episode of my childhood has left me with such a concrete impression, even though in this memory the words – or the invectives, I should say – have been reduced to the inflection of the voices, the strident tone, the fits and starts of this torrent of abuse.

My father, my mother, and I are standing near a half-open door, the one leading to the gallery. The sun is sinking in the sky; a tapering triangle of light lies on the floor between us like a blade. With all the dignity of my eleven years, I have just informed them of my decision, and my father's blue eyes blaze with a ferocious hatred. He explodes. Suddenly, every vein in his face stands out, and his anger, always quick to flare up, surges through his voice. My mother's joins in, charged with both authority and alarm, but also with an irritation that drives her voice into a shrill register where it frays and breaks, no longer her own. She falls silent, fearing to lose her child; my father, however, will not tolerate the loss of the farm worker he expects me to become. He threatens me, shaking his finger in my face, sputtering and hammering out his words.

I do not move; I sense that my whole life depends on my behavior at this moment: I must remain impassive and not let myself be out-stared; I must listen without flinching, without allowing anything to shake my determination, not even if my father slaps me hard across the face. Above all, I must stand my ground, right there.

What happens all of a sudden? My father is silent; my mother looks up at him, and then both gaze at me as though from another shore. What are they waiting for? For me to have second thoughts, to give in? If I were to beg them on my knees not to love me, they would not understand, when at this instant that is all I need: not to be loved, desired, wanted. I have not a single tear, not one flicker of feeling to spare for their distress.

The sun sets; the pool of light between us evaporates. And I see that they are all there, my brothers and sisters, surrounding me, looking at me inquiringly, but I find I am no longer within their reach. And time, I will discover, can do nothing to change this. My father tells them the news, and there are chuckles, perhaps a tear, quickly wiped away, before the jokes start coming. Can one ever do something for oneself without hurting anyone else in the meantime? I have just left childhood behind: left, right, and center, for as far as my eye can see, I am free. The heavens can fall, but something greater is calling me. I do not belong anymore.

Between that triumphant late afternoon and the moment when I crossed the threshold of the monastery, more than two months must have passed, but there is no trace of them left. On the day of my departure, my mother doles out tidbits of advice as she neatly packs my clothes into a suitcase purchased for the occasion; on the station platform, in a gesture as solemn as it is unexpected, my father holds out his hand, and I am unable to disguise my confusion and embarrassment. He speaks of ingratitude, reproaching me bitterly. I feel strangely relieved, never suspecting that my father's hand will still be there, held out to me, when death has swept away almost everything else of him.

Today I no longer share the eagerness of someone who, leaving forever, believes himself now free of his past or his origins. Before the train leaves, I would like the net of words to gather up a few solitary scenes that stand out in my memory, as fixed and immutable as photographs, where they may well last as long as I will myself, coloring my ways of thinking and feeling, or simply adding to my sorrows.

Cecilia, who has learned how to drive, stops the car before the thatched cottage where the Peralta sisters now live after renting and finally selling their former property to immigrants. Chairs are set out beneath the only tree, a weeping willow. A door creaks at the third blast from the car horn. The Peralta sisters will appear one after another, at rather long intervals, their thin, spectral forms clothed in black, their faces white with talcum powder, their lips garnet-red, their speech and gestures so slow as to appear affected. Cecilia has brought some flaky pastries with quince jelly and she offers them to Nigelia, the eldest sister. Then I catch that unforgettable detail: the smile that lifts only a corner of the mouth, leaving the rest of the impassive face untouched. Now, that is the Argentine smile, in which skepticism and irony seem to share, just as a precaution. I shall always dream of a museum of expressions, of gestures, manners, and intonations peculiar to a certain time and place, often ephemeral, inspired and disseminated by custom.

My father has painted the gallery a washed-out red, and now, perched on top of a ladder, he draws his brush over a strip of cardboard with a cut-out design; when he removes the stencil, a frieze of yellow roses blooms all around the room.

I am carrying my little sister, who has not yet learned to walk, and as I dandle her in my arms, caressing her, with one hand underneath the flounces of the dress, I pinch that plump flesh of hers. No one can understand why she bursts into tears.

Out in the main shed where the rafters are hung with strings of sausages, I climb on top of a pile of crates, bowl in hand, and lift up the cloth covering the vat where the grapes have been fermenting for several days. Although they crushed the fruit with the help of hand-cranked wine presses, I had heard them speaking, my father and La Pinotta, of the olden days, when they had to trample the mounds of grapes by dancing on them barefoot. I plunge my bowl into the amber liquid and gulp it down with delight. In his *Confessions,* Saint Augustine relates that when his mother was a child, she almost became a drunkard by doing this same thing.

I am on horseback, ambling along beneath a colorless sky; the great seas of wheat have turned to pale gold. There is not a breath of air to bring relief to the countryside in this blazing November sun, but suddenly, out in the middle of a field, heads of grain begin to shiver as a wide-brimmed straw hat slowly emerges; a man stands up, whom I recognize from his drooping blond mustache as our neighbor, while the woman who then gets to her feet, straightening her clothes, is his eldest daughter.

My father is driving the car, and we are far from the house – from any house, in fact. There are not even any animals to be seen out on the plain. Lying by my side on the back seat is the stray dog that turned up one morning at the farm and liked it there: short-haired, white with gray spots, she somewhat resembled a pig, and so seemed even uglier than she already was. I had named her Pearl. The car slows, stops. My father gets out and carries the panting bitch, who is about to have puppies, to the side of the road, where he leaves her. We drive off; through the rear window I see Pearl's sharp little muzzle poking out from the couch grass at the edge of the ditch, and then the dust from the car billows up, and she is gone.

There is also, way back in the past, the thunderstorm that surprises my eldest brother and me as we ride in a sulky late one night; the lightning bolts seem to chop through the darkness. And another time, my mother sets a piping hot dish down on the table and says, with a candid smile, that thanks to a touch of oregano, she has recaptured the flavor of the risotto her grandmother used to make.

What is it that drives me, a half century later, on this wretched August afternoon in Paris, to gather up these crumbs?

31

WHEN I FOLLOWED BROTHER SALVADOR ACROSS THE threshold separating the world from the cloister, I thought that Heaven was bidding me welcome from on high: at the instant the heavy doors closed behind me, and the vaults of the colonnade surrounding the garden began to echo with the sound of my new shoes, I heard piano music coming from one of the monks' cells – the music I had once tried so hard to remember and had always regretted having forgotten. I was to learn, that day, that it was the andante from the "Moonlight" Sonata.

I questioned Brother Salvador in great agitation, fearing that the melody would vanish forever, and he, rather taken aback, interrupted the performer, who was soon to become my first music teacher.

Father Rodríguez was a very big man, but trim, without a paunch or double chin at that time, and he looked more burly than fat. The ends of his short fingers were as broad as the white piano keys, and I had never seen anything like them in the countryside, where hands – those ancestral tools – hardly ever develop in proportion with the body and are often too long or too wide. Father Rodríguez pounded away conscientiously at the keyboard, and since his fingers were not very nimble, his playing lacked subtlety, and even at the harmonium, his hands tackled the keys with superfluous strength, because the force with which the notes were struck could never affect the modest capabilities of that instrument, with its gummy sound more suggestive of an accordion than an organ.

Well, that day, thanks to my ignorance and excitement, Father Rodríguez was the divine messenger – in an opulently corpulent disguise – who unsuspectingly returned to me one of my very first treasures. He greeted me with a kindly smile, but his glasses frightened me: like his fingers, they were startlingly thick, reflecting Brother Salvador and myself in their curves, where his eyes would occasionally surface like fish rising to gobble tossed crumbs. He told me the name of the Beethoven piece, and also that the composer had begun to grow deaf in his thirties.

Fearing that I had not grasped the importance of this fact, Brother Salvador – that teller of educational tales – asked me in amazement just to imagine: a deaf composer! Judging from his own astonishment, it was the first time either of us had ever heard of such a thing. And the more he harped on this, the less perplexed I must have seemed, for he ceased exclaiming over this marvel in mid-phrase. I could not put into words for him what I half understood. Hadn't I listened to that melody in my head for an entire afternoon? It seemed natural to me that the musician would benefit from his deafness, be able to grasp more surely the untouched substance of the music, which comes from elsewhere to course through him alone.

As an *au revoir*, Father Rodríguez returned to the sonata, and when Brother Salvador and I went on our way, the silver-fringed tonsure of a friar just disappearing around the end of the colonnade seemed to me, in the dim light, like a full moon slipping behind the corner pillar, for the bald spot on his large head was a perfect circle.

It was the father superior. We turned around and went to meet him via the opposite side of the cloister. I tried out my first hand-kissing. His fingers seemed flabby. Still preoccupied with his reading, he welcomed me at first simply by looking up inquiringly and asking the brother to repeat my last name, which he murmured to himself while spacing out the syllables, with his eyes half closed, as though he were committing my name firmly to memory. His eyes brightened as he warned me that it was not enough to choose saintliness as the purpose of monastic life, that one must do what is necessary to achieve this end with patience, day after day, and he was immersing himself in his book once again when he realized that there yet remained one required admonition to deliver, so he added, in his hollow but impressively grave voice, that God sees all things at all times, even into the very depths of our souls. And with his hand he seemed, for a moment, to be protecting himself from the scrutiny he was evoking, thus emphasizing its penetrating nature.

With this, he returned to his meditation, and Brother Salvador picked up my suitcase. I held the package of sausages wrapped in newspaper that my mother had asked me to give to the fathers. I was ashamed of the packet and would have liked to be rid of it. I looked around the cloister, with its funereal serenity, and was filled with the quiet peace of this old garden surrounded by its arcades. From the world of plains and sky and endless horizons, I passed to this enclosure where the geometry of the stones took on the weight of all pain and uncertainty, letting the soul stretch its wings. They would have had to drag me out to make me leave that place.

I believed that living there would make my life innocent, and I was making that vow when the sight of a well covered with ivy so dark it was almost black brought one of my oldest memories back to me: La Pinotta seating me on the edge of a different well, to the rhythm of a different music. That La Pinotta should return at the very moment when I was longing to break completely with my past struck me as a betrayal by forgetfulness.

Brother Salvador set down the suitcase and told me that the well had been closed since the death twenty years earlier of its purifying tortoise. He had not found one to replace it at the time, and now, years later, no one dared drink the water anymore. I remember thinking, as though to raise myself anew to that level of nebulous beatitude where I found my contentment – without being able, for all that, to remain long at those lofty heights – that the small stone circle in the heart of the garden represented death, which surrounds and closes in on us as the years go by. And as I was evoking the words of praise added *in extremis* by Saint Francis to his "Canticle of the Creatures" in honor of Sister Death, Brother Salvador began on the spot to recount an episode from the life of Il Poverello. Having finished reading his breviary, the father superior now joined us, and he let Brother Salvador finish before chiding him on a point of historical accuracy, reminding him good-naturedly, as if he did not expect his words to be heeded, that the capitulary assembly of 1266 (knowing only Argentine history, I was surprised by the remoteness of the date) had ordered the burning of all legends concerning the life and deeds of their patron saint which had been written before the authorized biography by Saint Bonaventure.

With a promptness and a familiarity that disturbed me, Brother Salvador retorted that Bonaventure himself had presided over the assembly in question, which undermined his authority to issue such an interdict. The father superior shook his head from side to side, while his contradictor nodded up and down. I was to see those two going over the same tired arguments on many occasions, each stubbornly defending his position, but having once gotten into a serious disagreement, they were now careful not to let the dispute grow heated. Somewhat reassured, and worried that this discussion would continue, I picked up my suitcase, and, to my great relief, Brother Salvador sheepishly took charge of my package of pork sausages.

We took the stairs leading to the pleasant galleries of the first floor, and I was already imagining myself stepping from my cell to contemplate the garden below when we arrived on the landing, where my guide shook out his bunch of keys and opened a small door that blended perfectly with the rest of the wall, being of the same color and lying flush with it. And suddenly I felt as though I had stepped inside a prison, like the one I had seen in an American film the previous year: before me was a large rectangular courtyard surrounded by buildings with several floors, each one equipped with a gallery with a balustrade and slender iron colonnettes. Just as the convicts in prisons are separated according to the seriousness of their crimes, the seminarists were housed according to their levels of study.

The peeling walls still retained, here and there, a hint of ocher. Cracks zigzagged across the cement floor of the courtyard; big garbage cans without covers were crowded off to one side. I was warned never to amuse myself by tossing things down into the cans, not even if I had good aim, and I was never to lead my comrades into temptation, or do anything I felt a desire to do without thinking it over twice.

It had not yet occurred to me that even the shortest step toward perfection requires some sacrifice of well-being, and that such steps will never mark the end of the journey, until the very last one necessarily brings us the joy mixed with terror of tumbling headlong into death.

Ever since my religious vocation had triumphed over the wishes of my parents, filling me with the bliss and peace I felt in conforming to the divine will, I had lived turned toward the Light, with the stubborn rectitude of seedlings striving to reach the sun, and I drew nearer to that summit where one confides one's troubles no longer to the stars but to the splendor above them that alone veils the countenance of the Lord.

There was no one around. Brother Salvador invited me to tour the premises, explaining that my fellow students, as well as the rector, were on vacation in the sierra and would not return until the following day. In the dormitory, he assigned a bed to me, as well as some shelves set into the wall where I might keep my things. Then he showed me the study hall, where about forty desks were lined up in front of the blackboard, and finally, what he called the library: a hundred or so different volumes, some of them without covers, arranged on a few narrow planks tied together by a cord and hung from a single large nail in such a way that they moved at the slightest touch. At first glance I could pick out a few textbooks, a dictionary, and a Lives of the Saints.

Brother Salvador promised to return at noon to fetch me for the midday meal, and in response to some little movement I made, he clasped the package of sausages to his breast and assured me, before disappearing through the little door he closed and locked behind him, that the brethren would not forget my family in their prayers.

I was afraid of my own footsteps, of the many rooms we had not visited; aching to examine the books on the "library" shelves, I remained leaning on the fragile balustrade, looking down into the courtyard at the invading sunlight and the retreating shadow of the building across the way.

Not a sound reached me from the city; the rectangle of blue sky seemed to defy me. What space would these prisonlike surroundings take up in my life? Only after eating lunch in the cellar kitchen did I return to my mystical musings, when Brother Salvador took me into the huge church, where daylight entered the nave with its three bays only through fixed windows high above the side chapels. Hanging in the transept, where the darkness gathered, was the tiny, flickering flame of the oil lamp that watches, day and night, over Jesus sleeping in the eucharistic hosts of the tabernacle.

Nowadays I sometimes visit the empty churches of Paris and experience a kind of rush of happiness because the little flame still watches from its cup of oil, the mute signing of wandering shadows to a shadow without a name.

While Brother Salvador was tending to the altars – throwing out the faded flowers, rearranging the votive candles that had burned unevenly, lining them up by height – I strolled around the nooks and crannies where light and gloom set fleeting stages for my awe at meeting the eyes of saints gazing down at me from their niches, and once I thought, upon discovering two symmetrical angels atop an altarpiece, that the rustle of their wings was stilled at my approach. I was preparing the setting of my devotion.

Free to choose a confessor, but not knowing any of the reverend fathers even by sight, I began by learning their names, revealed by small copper plaques on the confessionals. At the first communal service, I would study the monks' faces, observe their bearing, and choose my guide. Was I intoxicating myself in a dream of holiness? I wanted my confessor to have the look of a saint.

32

ON THE STROKE OF THREE, BROTHER SALVADOR appeared at the prison, and while the abruptness with which he locked the door might have wounded my sense of self-respect, the uneasiness I felt in that deserted place gave way to a kind of pride: God was putting me to my first test. I would overcome my deep distress all by myself.

I went to the "library." At first I was discouraged by the disorder there – some of the books stood upright, some lay on their sides, while others leaned crookedly – but suddenly I sprang into action and began to sort them by subject, dusting them off with a handkerchief.

My jailer appeared several times in the course of the afternoon, allowing me to remark the speed with which he could appear and disappear. Whenever he sat down, it was on the edge of his seat, as though he were eager to go tearing off again at any moment. Since no call could reach him up where we were, he seemed slightly embarrassed every time he found some excuse to leave me once more – you would have thought he plucked them from the corners of the room, or the floor, or the ceiling. He got on my nerves, and I tried to suppress my irritation as an offering to Heaven.

As I was finishing my rearrangement of the books, which I had divided in a way intended to bring some small measure of stability to the shelves, I came across some volumes of poetry. I took this as a good omen and a reward for my work. I was not familiar with any of the poets, so I selected one whose name impressed me with its majesty: Rubén Darío. I passed over his *Prosas profanas*, for fear they would distract me from my devotion, in favor of his *Cantos de vida y esperanza* (Songs of Love and Hope). Taking up a little volume with a kind of anticipatory fervor, I sat down at a table made of two planks laid across some trestles and so badly planed that my clothes kept catching on them.

In imitation of Saint Francis, who opened the Gospels at random one day, according to Brother Salvador, in hopes that his eyes would alight on a specific command from Christ, I opened the *Cantos* with trembling hands. Despite the book's title, the poem was called "Lo fatal." The poet's theme is one of man's oldest longings, a desire we have all felt at some time or another, one expressed in so many different ways ever since writing began: the wish not to be, or to be without being conscious of one's own existence. Many years later, I would find the South American's poem again in a line by Michelangelo: *"Caro m'è il sonno, e più l'esser di sasso."*

I read and reread Darío's verses in silence. My inner ear told me they were bound by a flow of rhythm and laced with repetitions of specific sounds, and I had the same impression I had had in don Varela's classroom, a feeling of great upheaval inside me, provoked by a magic whose source lay beyond the poet, in the very highest realms of language, on the borderline between language and music. I wondered if the pleasure the poet was allowing me to share might coincide with faith, since to my ears the meter of the poem charged its meaning with a certainty that bore me along to that place of understanding that passion craves and the heart desires.

I reread the poem once more, listening to the images rather than imagining them, and the fear that "Lo fatal" was the only poem intended for me kept me from turning the page. I had conferred the value of an absolute upon it then and there, having discovered in it a rule, a law that I aspired to obey with my entire being, wishing most of all to go farther and ever farther from myself, within myself.

The confusion of my own emotions, the torment I felt at the memory of my precocious misbehavior, my regrets, the hope of a life elsewhere – an unstable and rather disjointed mixture – now flowed into the world of verse. No more hesitation, anxiety, misgivings: disciplined by form, all would be good and true, whereas the refusal to bow to such discipline would be the mark of error and of evil itself. The soul had to foresee, to predict, to renounce those wanderings I so delighted in; all these paths had to merge into the straight and narrow, and from now on, as though they were words, the actions of everyday life had to rise above existence like a great vault of language.

At some point I began striding up and down the room reciting this poetry, without needing to look at the book anymore. The prison became an empire; had these grimy walls ever heard a poem before? I was exultant. From the innate abjection that had been my lot, I had risen toward the cold and crystalline realm of chastity. Thus Lady Poverty offered me one of her treasures as a reward: I conceived of poetry as a kind of prayer. I did not know that it is not in exultation, but on one's belly in the dust, that one climbs up to God.

The seminarists returned from the sierra, where they had spent their vacation together; I remember their boisterousness in the recreation yard and their loud shouting, like the cries of some pathetic, crazed animals, but despite having lived with them for an entire year, I cannot remember a single face. As for the rector, I recall an old man sitting on a rickety chair in his cell (which doubled as his office) with an unlit cigarette dangling from the corner of his mouth. However, my memories from the other side of the prison – the cloister and the church – have remained extraordinarily vivid.

After a few days and a few services attended by both monks and seminarists, I picked out one of the brothers as my official spiritual director: he seemed to stand out by virtue of his aura of timeless asceticism, as though he had stopped life at the point when it unfolds into needs and desires, and as though in taking the habit he had chosen conclusively the behavior and bearing to go with it. He resembled those Gothic sculptures that present only the diagram of a face, a death's-head with its holes, its sutures, its protuberances showing through the gleaming marble. I do not think I have ever seen such transparent skin in my entire life, or such prominent bones. The ivory forehead jutted over his eyes, and the flesh that hung from his cheekbones was gathered in at the small but square chin. I no longer have any idea what his lips looked like. Still, a smile occasionally flitted about his face without disturbing his features and vanished back into his dark eyes, which were those of an attentive and sagacious child.

He was only twenty-four years old but was already spoken of as a great theologian. A professor at the university in the city (Córdoba, of which it was then said that every one of its natives was a "doctor" of something), he heard penitents in confession so as not to lose touch with their reality, like those bigwig physicians who teach in medical schools without neglecting their patients or leaving them in someone else's hands. In any event, this mania for confession that afflicts the believer (and – who knows? – perhaps each one of us) is something that a dedicated doctor can often soothe even better than a priest, acting for a while as the repository for secrets that will, in time, find their way to the confessional.

At the very moment when I knelt in the blind side of the little booth to make my first confession to Father Salgado (that was his name), all mystical fever left me. Plunged back into those depths seething with inchoate mysteries, guilty of evil thoughts I had sought to escape by driving them away (but how could they ever have appeared unless they announced sins *in posse*?), I felt at one with everything that is vile.

Instead of launching into a general confession, which is customary when one asks a priest to become one's spiritual director, so that he may know with whom he is dealing, I began by describing to him the distress that had just come over me. Doubtless encouraged by the monotonous calmness of his voice, I listed instances of my dissolute behavior, most of them lustful; some examples, which seemed harmless to me, concerned my disobedience toward my parents, which had culminated in my forcing them to accept my decision to enter the monastery, and of course I confessed this out of pure pride, feeling deep inside myself that such disobedience drew me closer to Saint Francis.

Father Salgado asked me my age, and I was a bit disappointed when he skipped over my depravities to focus instead on inculcating in me certain thoughts, rather than principles, that would ward off temptation. He told me – and I am amazed now at his confidence, which was of an intellectual nature, although I was not at all surprised at the time – that my pleasure implied pain for someone else, a stranger or someone close to me, and that any joy, however innocent, should seem less precious to me than the necessity of not delighting in it.

So, another's pleasure would flow from my suffering, and impiety from my piety?

I was told that my suffering consisted in not giving in to temptation and that my piety might decide the outcome of a battle waged at the far ends of the earth, or ensure the eternal salvation of some unknown soul *in extremis*. Father Salgado added that everything is interconnected and that the most idle thought affects the future; I remember how he hesitated at this word, substituting it for *fate*, which was already on the tip of his tongue.

I was to accept the idea of a law of compensation, the counterbalancing of good and evil; I was about to admit to him that I did not understand these words when something occurred to me that revived my doubts: if the sinner stopped sinning, would a saint somewhere else cease being a saint?

I took advantage of his patience and asked him to forgive me. I had the impression he smiled when he advised me to answer the question myself, not by thinking about it, but by devoting myself to the accomplishment of each day's tasks and by asking God to strengthen my faith, because were I to question Him, He would simply withdraw into His shadow.

Father Salgado must have handled the situation quite well, because I felt reinvigorated the moment he gave me absolution – even delighted at having to consider all sorts of delights suspect, beginning with the one I felt on leaving the confessional: like hands full of flowers, mysterious passions were blossoming on my body when I aspired only to subdue my flesh, put it to the test, force it to submit to the arid authority of the soul. The height of saintliness was to be measured by the depth of one's disgust.

That evening, in the sleeping dormitory, sexuality flared up again as though my enjoyment of the state of grace meant to cleanse my past had instead set my body on fire: I who knew so well how to bring sensual pleasure to its highest pitch was no more than an irrepressible hand gripping my sex, and before I knew it I had reached an almost unbearable climax.

Something my mother once said came back to me, something she had blurted out the only time I ever saw her lose that smiling composure everyone who ever knew her still remembers. She was peeling potatoes on the terrace; from over by the sheds came the sound of my father's voice, berating my brothers. After a long and difficult silence, she dropped the knife, and with a sob, murmured, "I wish I were dead and buried."

The night of my great sin, I wished, as she had, that I were lying in my grave. And in that state of mind, I fell asleep, to find Death waiting to conduct me to Hell.

When I awoke, even though I was terrified by the gravity of my offense, my first thought was to hide my face at the basins where we all washed in the morning, when my fellow students always checked to see who had those telltale circles under the eyes, the signs of satisfied lust. One week of communal life had taught me what lay behind the insinuations regularly proffered by a malignant fellow whom I remember only as a head hunched between dwarfish shoulders. And while I never participated in this collective inquisition, I had myself noticed shadows of a rosy mauve smearing the sallow skin of some cheeks.

So, in the seminary, we used to scrutinize one another's faces every morning, the way we had studied the hands of girls back home in the countryside, laughing at those who wore the nail on their middle finger cut short.

The fact that I did not take communion that morning confirmed the suspicions of my comrades, for whom I became the object of relentless surveillance, but fearing their mockery even more than I feared God, I resisted temptation, so that they were soon disappointed, and more than one would not forgive me for deceiving his hopes on this score.

Since Father Salgado only heard confessions late in the afternoon, and since death, according to a figure of speech I had just learned, could fall upon us like a thief in the night, I decided to seek out another priest to release me from my state of sin. Not without a bad conscience, I passed from repentance to attrition.

I turned to Father Anselmo, who had been the senior confessor for an eternity – an old man whose constant murmuring was like the buzzing of bees inside his cowl, which was always pulled up over his head, even in church, where he continued his conversation with the angels while waiting for penitents. He felt the cold in winter and summer both, and because of his great age was granted a dispensation from the regulation wearing of sandals. If you passed him anywhere near a door, he would warn you religiously about the treacherous nature of drafts, with his transparent blue eyes bulging in horror, and he would cross the threshold only walking backward, holding one hand up to protect his neck. They said that when he celebrated mass, he sometimes sneezed when he opened the tabernacle. I never saw such a thing, because he said mass at hours when there was not likely to be much of a congregation and when there were hardly any seminarists among the faithful. That was a prudent precaution, on the whole, taken by the father superior after the nonagenarian had apparently celebrated a funeral mass for the repose of his own soul.

The cowl cast frightening shadows upon the old man's face, and his great beak of a nose stuck out over sunken lips like the grimace of a Harlequin mask, but in his expression one sometimes caught a glimpse of the shimmer of prophecy.

I slipped into the church at the hour it was most deserted. I found him in his confessional, cased in darkness, leaning his cheek on his clasped hands. He was sleeping, and sighing, almost squeaking as he breathed. I knelt before him, so close I was almost touching his knees. And he awoke with a start, on the Mount of Olives.

The confession was brief; the absolution, absentminded. I arose in a state of grace, according to the catechism, but felt no inner peace. Restored to freedom by my judge, I yet remained a prisoner. I had cleverly kept Father Salgado from learning of the sin committed on the very day of my general confession, so that he would not reflect back to me a demoralizing image of myself. I was thus able to preserve between us the idea of contrition, which would help me feel the emotion.

As I perfected my system of precautions, trying to justify my trickery to myself, I was overwhelmed by a sense of unworthiness that kept me from taking communion for three whole days. Something had come apart within me: I was becoming my own adversary. Finally, like one who has crossed deserts and suddenly catches sight of the glittering promise of a sheet of water, I overcame my shame and confessed my sin and betrayal to Father Salgado. I no longer remember his reaction and advice; I recall only the sensation of overpowering and mastering myself, of making myself whole again, as happens each time we wrestle with ourselves to throw off falsehood.

I discovered the one thing worth more than all the rest: the annihilation of thought in the patient execution of one's duty, in perfect obedience. It was my duty to think against thought –

thought, what the soul loves the least, since it seeks only to justify what one is, and consequently, to vindicate the demands of the flesh.

Had I dreamed of religion as a liturgy perfumed with incense, a procession of days leading to beds where death agonies came to an end in a rustling of prayers and extreme unction? I emerged from Father Salgado's confessional a completely different person, I thought, capable of believing without seeing myself as saved at the journey's end. I renounced my claim to Paradise for the benefit of some other soul who had neglected to praise God. And by this imaginary sacrifice, I imagined that I had left pride far behind me. My prayers would no longer be for my own salvation. I found myself praying for my mother, and then, not without effort, for my father. I was reassured and resolute. This lasted for a few days, without any other sustaining fervor beyond respect for discipline, lessons well learned, and dictations written out with great care. I forbade myself all satisfaction, and in the refectory I ate with slow application, as if savoring each bite, but in reality as a form of mortification, since the food (the ingredients of which we could sometimes identify) was on a par with the tin plates, which were coated with the film of dull grease that clings to dishes rinsed in cold water.

And when the customary apple arrived, as we gave thanks to God, the triumphant serpent reared its head behind my back.

I was becoming used to the privations of asceticism. And did faith occasionally waver, as faith will? It was important to believe not in victory, but in the mission itself.

And then one evening the rector, our mystery smoker with his ever-present unlit cigarette, gathered us all together after dinner to listen to music. He wiped off the records with the sleeve of his habit. It was piano music, the liquid and yet mathematical voice of the piano. I did not simply yield to it – it filled me and seemed to carry me away somewhere inside myself, beyond pleasure, beyond the happiness granted by grace. And I understood, in this rapturous flight toward a Heaven without God, that just when you feel the safest, something stronger than any temptation may arise: beauty – a sunset, a particularly happy rhyme, the opening of a Chopin nocturne – and once again you are lost, fallen among the damned.

33

DESPITE FATHER SALGADO'S WARNINGS NOT TO exaggerate my conduct into an obsession, I persevered in the discipline of abasement. And so as the school year wore on and I continued to win praise, both at the school run by the Marist fathers where we attended classes and at the seminary, where the rector often held me up as an example, I decided to slip a bit – in my behavior, at least, although not in my studies, since my vanity would not accept banishment from the honor roll.

The Marist school catered to the well-to-do, and most of the day-students there belonged to the upper middle class. I had only one rival, and for a whole year my main concern was to best him at everything, every day. He was quite intelligent and enjoyed the marked preference constantly shown for him by the Marist father. And theirs are the only two faces from that time that have stayed in my memory.

The Marist's features were delicate but still rather common; I remember his expression as imperturbable, except when his favorite was reciting the lesson: then the teacher's eyes would widen behind his little round wire-rimmed glasses until they seemed even bigger than the lenses, and his lips would stretch into a smile. As for the boy – frail, but with the poise and assurance of the *grande bourgeoisie,* a class not given to matching wits for sport – his face was so small and thin that his cheeks almost seemed to touch each other. His lips were thick and fleshy, however, and their bright orangey-red color reminded me of my sisters' nail polish, which had a medicinal smell I found intoxicating.

This other boy was almost ugly, but – I realize this only now – he had the advantage of resembling those models who, so plain in real life, appear transfigured in paintings.

I resolved not to hate him, but my rebellious heart went its own way, especially since the dear fellow – full of confidence and well aware that he was the teacher's pet – would watch me so attentively during my regular visits to the blackboard or whenever I was quizzed orally that my wish to astound him was even greater than my ardent desire to demonstrate somehow, thanks to a scrap of knowledge gleaned outside of our lessons and textbooks, the incompetence of the teacher.

I should say that there was never the slightest suggestion of connivance in the attention paid to me by this rival (who was one for me without my being one for him) until the day the teacher asked each pupil to learn by heart a poem of his choice in honor of the Virgin Mary, for the end of the school year was approaching, and the Feast of the Immaculate Conception would mark the last day. When it was my turn, I recited a set of sonnets of my own invention. The first developed the hackneyed metaphor of the virginal lily; the last, a hypothesis furnished me by the theological permutations of Brother Salvador: the Immaculate Conception, envisioned *ab aeterno* as the crowning work of the Creation, above even the Incarnation of the Son.

The consonance of the rhymes, the correctness of the meter, and my inclination to pathos won over my audience. Grudgingly, the teacher congratulated me; as a member of the Society of Mary, he could not very well take offense at my praise. And for the first time, I saw tremors of dismay disturb my rival. He probably understood nothing of my precocious theological quibbles, but perhaps he detected in me – the way animals can hear a distant footfall – a sense of rhythm he himself did not possess. I knew this: his recitation of a canticle that day confirmed it for me. The quaver in his voice and the gestures he affected fooled no one. On the other hand, I fooled myself into believing that the lead in the end-of-the-year play would be mine, when in fact I was allowed to play only minor parts.

While my jealousy grew constantly stronger, I still occasionally felt the desire to appear at fault in the eyes of my superiors, to mortify my reputation as a good student, for despite the pleasure it gave me (that gentle swelling in the breast), such a reputation kept me enslaved to vanity. I had had early experience of that singular dismay you feel when, having in a kind of ferocious innocence presented a certain image of yourself to others, they then send it back at you, demanding that you top it.

Rehearsals began. The play was written in verse and set in the land of the infidel. The author? The Marist. The meters he observed (after a fashion) were rather ill-assorted. My first role, if I may call it that, was a wall: two fingers of each hand spread to represent a chink through which (as in Shakespeare's *A Midsummer Night's Dream,* where the characters engage in some risqué wordplay) a priest and a princess conversed. Then I played a messenger who shouted out his entire part: one hemistich. I cannot recall the other bit parts I played – and they were many, for I remember changing all those costumes in the wings – except for the small role of the converted infidel who expired, after a few lines, in the arms of the protagonist, who was played by my rival.

After a few rehearsals, I knew the play and stage business by heart, and although I sometimes tried to stifle my growing eagerness, I was beginning to hope that one of the actors would come down with whooping cough at the last minute. There was someone inside me ready to pounce at the first opportunity – like that aging chorus singer I would see one evening in 1964, wearing a long, red velvet scarf over her attendant's costume, watching from offstage for any signs of weakness in Maria Callas, who was singing *La Norma.*

I hid my ambitions under a modest demeanor, however, and strictly followed the Marist's stage directions, which were austere and devoid of interest. Then came the dress rehearsal. The scenery was set up (exotic vegetation with the sea in the background); the footlights and stage lights (a humble garland of rainbow-colored bulbs) were turned on. Despite the spareness of the room thus roughly transformed into a theater, I imagined overhead the vigilance of the wide-open sky, the circle of the Pleiades up in the flies, and wondrous mysteries radiating throughout boundless space like the music of the spheres.

Then there was the donning of wigs and costumes, and the sensual caress of makeup. I would wear tights and an undershirt to play the wall, a costume all of gold and ribbons to portray a courtier, and an outfit of skins for my role as a savage during the finale. My adversary, who was quite short, got to wear a bishop's robe; the miter gave him added height, and a silvery, fan-shaped beard symbolized his great age.

Finally, our first and last performance: the play was in full swing, with the audience observing a respectful silence that magnified the rustle of cellophane candy wrappers. After each tableau, the closing of the curtains would set off a storm of coughing, just as in real theaters.

It was only at the very end that an incident occurred to disrupt the performance, passing unnoticed by the audience, as these things often do: I do not know what came over me when I fell, pierced by a lance, into the arms of the bishop, who was about to give his big speech. Taking advantage of the fact that my skins had gotten tangled up in his cape, I behaved like some marionette controlled by evil spirits. Pushing my rival toward the wings as I flailed about in my death agony, I clamped my hands on his beard, which of course came off. The helpful arms of our director whisked the now bald-faced bishop off between two flats, so it was I who delivered the last tirade (an impersonal speech, in any case) before crumpling to the stage between the multicolored footlights and the curtains closing behind my back.

The play was over, but what had just happened in the heat of action had quite an effect on reality. Like one possessed, beside myself and yet still myself, I suddenly understood why the Church had once refused to bury actors in consecrated ground.

The audience burst into applause, the curtains parted again, my comrades helped me up, and I took my proper place among the rest of the cast.

People were chatting and still applauding as they collected their things; elderly gentlemen wagged their canes in the air, while ladies in hats fluttered their gloves. And suddenly, a delighted voice was heard calling for an encore: it was the inspector of circles under our eyes, the wet-dream accountant, who waved his little fists at me and shouted at the top of his lungs. Everyone around him laughed, even our teachers; instead of scolding him and telling him to behave, the fathers seemed to egg him on. And on stage, while we kept stepping up to the footlights and then back again, over and over, I saw the dwarf's jubilant expression, as though his head had opened up like a window, revealing to the light of day the very face of idiocy: a huge, triumphant, blissfully stupid grin.

The curtain closed for the last time. Our revels were ended. I was not too worried about the consequences of my sabotage, because elementary school was over, too, and I would be going off to a seminary in the outskirts of Buenos Aires. The Marist might report me to the rector, however, and – who knows? – to the father superior himself. And so, growing more and more uneasy, I was just about to rush off and apologize to my teacher when he stopped me abruptly in the corridor. His impassive features were not used to expressing emotion, so his anger showed only in the slow, sad way he shook his head at me. Not for an instant did I think that either he or my rival would ever forget.

34

WAS IT A GOOD OR A BAD OMEN THAT THE DAY CHOSEN
for my arrival at the seminary coincided with the solar eclipse
astronomers had been predicting for some time? The fathers
had never spoken of the event without making numerous bibli-
cal allusions.

During the holidays, which we spent in the Sierra de Córdoba,
we had been obliged to search the Gospels for passages in which
Jesus threatens mankind with disorder in the heavens, and texts
describing how the stars act in concert to fulfill this prophecy.
Free access to the Old Testament remained the privilege of the
senior students.

Each of us collected his little harvest – the variants of two or
three passages that might be described as atmospheric theater –
and tried to write a paper.

I do believe our teachers, and even the taciturn rector with
his unlit cigarette butt, succeeded in filling our slow and muddled minds with a dread of divine punishment, a dread that
turned to fear in the more passive spirits among us, while those
of active imagination fell prey to outright horror. And our literary babblings, however inept, can only have contributed to this
vague but pervasive distress.

The harsh countryside was graced only by some bushy shrubs
and a river with such a rocky bed that from a distance, its gargling
sounded like the rushing of a mighty torrent. As for the house, it
might at first glance have blended entirely into the landscape of
grayish stone had its doors not been painted green. Together, the
house and its site prefigured a world deserted by life.

As the only confessor we had during our vacation, the rector must have grown tired of being so much in demand – and to make matters worse, at the very time when all his charges were supposed to be finally in bed, leaving him to sit with his ear glued to the wireless, free at last to take deep drags on a cigarette that would by no means be the last of the evening. After having sown a terror of the Apocalypse among us to ensure good behavior, he had to suffer the consequences and understand that souls made deeply aware of the unforeseeable aspects of death would naturally entertain suspicions that each visit to the river, each sunset, might be their last, and that every bedtime might last, this time, forever.

As for my composition, which was doubtless superbly gloomy, I remember the phrase taken from the Acts of the Apostles, from Luke: "The sun shall be turned into darkness, and the moon into blood." For a long time, my favorite of the Evangelists was the exquisite writer who retold the Gospel according to Saint Mark, filling in the blanks or inventing scenes that reach the sublime, such as the Visitation of Mary, pregnant with Jesus, to Elizabeth, who carries the Baptist, and who feels her child leap with joy in her womb as the voice of the Salutation reaches her ears.

Today, perhaps because life seems to me like a fable that words go on weaving as they please – and were I to unravel them, I would disappear – I prefer the unembellished words of Mark: honest, austere, consistent with what he saw and heard, and all the more persuasive in that they do not seek to persuade.

Was it a good or a bad omen that I arrived at the new seminary, accompanied by the worthy Father Rodríguez, on the very day of the eclipse?

With its whitewashed walls and roof of red tiles, the big building looked for all the world like a huge chalet. On the park side were the chapel, the music room, and the long central section housing the dormitory; the refectory and classrooms were on the other side, by the kitchen garden. Only the gallery, with its semicircular windows, had the look of a cloister; this gallery gave onto the park, where the few priests who lived at the seminary would take their walks, breviary in hand. After life in the "prison," however, I was quick and happy to see a resemblance to the summer homes of the wealthy people I had once admired in the pages of *Rosalinda*. And for a moment I quite forgot about the eclipse, while we walked among the tall eucalyptuses at three o'clock that afternoon, in a dull light that drained all color from the scene, and then gave way to a fluid darkness that absorbed the shade beneath the trees and our shadows as well.

Startled birds filled the air, darting in every direction, but their twittering sounded different from the cheerful tumult of their late-afternoon homecomings. The sound of their scattering was damped, and there was a sudden quiet throughout the motionless foliage, as if they were already asleep. The sky seemed charged with power; the earth, with submission.

The rector, my new rector, came to meet us, and this small man with a gleaming bald pate embraced Father Rodríguez, who was a giant. As in the encounters of saints in Gothic paintings, they clasped each other's forearms while they talked over a few matters concerning me.

Father González invited us to set down our things, and as we walked out onto the patio, the sun was dying overhead, a dark disc haloed by a milky splendor. Dressed in the regulation drill smocks, about forty boys between the ages of thirteen and twenty barely greeted us, so intently were they gazing up at the black sky. I recall the scene in that corner of memory where dreams are born – it is as though it were happening in a space without gravity, like those constellations that sometimes dance beneath our eyelids, change color, and drift away to return in a completely different guise. The boys' gestures seem apathetic, without purpose, and in that constantly dissolving and re-forming circle, each spectator, as if intoxicated, releases a kind of gentle madness. Does anyone laugh or utter an exclamation? The noise explodes in the waiting silence.

Does anyone move? All are still; suddenly, the ossature of the earth is gone, and time no longer beats its measure. Abandoned, exiled forever from its stately rotations, its atmosphere growing unbreathable, with this dead sun in a vanishing sky and absence crowding in everywhere like an onrushing void, the world has lost its way, and so have we.

Then, gradually, with a slowness of centuries, the darkness pales; a breach is opened to the daylight now scintillating all around us: will the moon's silver coin be rolled from the face of the sun?

We are all struck dumb. Then, in the growing brightness, we hear talk and laughter, and soon everyone is chattering away. I am trying to join in, to strike up a conversation with my future fellow students, when I feel someone's gaze alight on me. One of the older boys is standing off on one side. I begin to tingle all over. I manage to look up; our eyes meet and we stare at each other for a few seconds: I as if in fear, he as if in recollection, and suddenly he is already inviting me into our secret.

35

I AM NOT EXAGGERATING WHEN I SAY THAT YESTERDAY, when I was trying to recapture that first look in words, I felt a surge of emotion beyond all reason. Something happened that I had never imagined experiencing. While memory was carrying me away from the present, as it so often has, to take me back over there, into a past that begins to live again, so that I feel the splendor of those moments preserved without my knowledge, without me, in my absence – I became convinced of the impossible: he was still looking at me, just as he had on the day of the eclipse. And I knew he had been dead for more than twenty years.

Just as on that day when we first saw each other, I feel my

whole being caught up by his, my body trembling with anxiety, my heart pounding. And that long-ago hope is reborn, welling up within me, immortal and undeniable, simply so that I might find him again.

I cannot remember his name; I spent part of the night and the morning trying to recall it. It was a waste of time. I went through every Spanish given and family name I could think of without finding the right one; it is as though he had acquired his name in some other world.

Am I raving? But there is nothing of delirium in this renewed faith, the completeness I feel at this reviviscence, which is from now on bound up in what remains of my fate. How is it possible that such a memory can have slumbered for so long?

I know that all kinds of memories are available to us, usually those connected with our sight and hearing, and I am also only too aware that the labyrinth of remembrance grows daily in complexity, while whole sections of its maze can collapse without reason. And yet, many things perceived but immediately sent into storage at the moment of sensation may suddenly blossom without explanation, simply on their own.

A gesture, an intonation, a way of walking or laughing, the texture of a certain fabric – once I have noticed such things, I never forget them. And then there was Latin, a language I studied every day for five years without ever managing to figure out its syntax; at the perilous moment of my oral exams, the words would spring to my lips in just the right order, so that the examining teacher thought I was a brilliant Latinist.

My memory persists, however, in refusing to provide me with proper names. As a child I grew ashamed of my family name, doubtless because of the contempt displayed in my native land toward the Italian, that despised immigrant. I felt tainted by having to bear such a name. And I still feel that way: when I hear people going into ecstasies about the musical qualities of the Italian tongue (all languages are musical, as any well-turned phrase will prove), I cannot help wondering what they are talking about, as though – in spite of Dante, Leopardi, and

certain pages of *The Fiancés* – I were condemned to hear a vulgar babbling drowning out any literary beauty in the language,
and most Italian patronyms annoy me exactly the way my own
does.

But it is time to return to the seminary, where for an entire
year I moved like a sleepwalker among the tutelary shades of
the eclipse, with a light burning in my heart.

36

LOVE ALWAYS COINCIDES WITH THE CENTER OF THE
world. There is a restriction concealed within "always": this
center is never a place where one may rest, only a place to
travel through – deserted, uninhabitable, belonging to no one.

I was fourteen; he was twenty-two. The difference in our ages
suited my nature. Many days went by without our exchanging
the slightest word, and even during our recreation periods,
which were spent gardening, or when we were assembled after
dinner by the rector to listen to music, when we might easily
have drawn closer to each other, we kept apart. I never looked
at him unless I felt his eyes on me – erasing all distance
between us, a look that had taken possession of me straight-
away, penetrating the darkness where my childish passions
were huddled.

We had to be careful, and so could do nothing, for few things
excite more suspicion and watchfulness in boarding school than
a budding friendship. Mysterious dangers haunt the approach of
happiness, and the fear of losing what we do not yet possess
makes us timid, so I devoted myself to the constant observance
of the strictest discipline in order to appear above reproach.

Did the bell ring, calling us to fall silently in line? I was among the first to obey, standing where the rector would see me, and I would hiss at any students who continued to whisper. And I was even more of a prig if the noise in the dining hall at the beginning of our meal, when someone always read aloud to us, made it difficult to hear the harmlessly boring story of some saint's life.

I had understood, if I had not known it instinctively, that everything linking someone in love to the world where he lives becomes a source of suspicion and mistrust. All the orderliness he has brought to his life, to his various daily chores, now seems insipid to him, and although he may well perform these tasks diligently, he will not be wholly *present* wherever he is. Those who live and work with him will notice this and begin to spy on him, for even if they cannot guess the cause of his distraction, they will be convinced that he is hiding a precious, shameful secret, something from somewhere else that now fills him with happiness. He feels he is being watched, and he tries every trick, stoops – politely – to anything in an effort to convince them that he is truly present among them, that his vocation is unshaken. But no one is fooled.

Distracted, my mind would wander during prayer, and I tried in vain at the time (as I would in the future) to fathom the double action of the brain: providing the lips with words learned by heart while allowing thought to go off on a tangent or simply up in smoke, in the same way that an image sometimes takes us away from a text our eyes continue to peruse, and when we return to it, we feel as though someone else has read those paragraphs.

What happened when I returned to my prayers? I would slip away again, far away, especially in the evening in the darkened dormitory, along the open roads of the night, borne as far along by the thought of him as an impulsive heart could carry me: to the edge of suffocation. And since our hearts are always ready to believe we have been forsaken by someone who may well not even have thought about loving us, I suffered to think that only a few beds away, he had abandoned me by falling asleep, while I struggled to stay awake as long as I could to increase my suffering, so that I could reproach him all the more, when the time came.

When the windows grew pale in the morning light, and the rector clapped his hands until every sleeper was sitting on the edge of his bed, I would try to steal a glance at him just as he was waking up. Since he stood right behind me when we lined up according to height, I knew that he was looking at me, that I was bound to him by the illusion of feeling his breath upon my neck, as I had felt the cowherd's sour breath so many years before, and the world would then begin to breathe again as well.

Yes: many days went by without our exchanging the slightest word. Were we afraid of damaging what was happening between us? We stayed away from each other, and often had no idea what the other was doing. I knew that his life would be a part of mine forever, and I cherished the hope that the same was true for him. In reality, I was certain of this – but the prudent expression "I cherished the hope" was dictated to me just now by experience, that great teacher, to correct the past by toning down its madness.

Thanks to the relaxation of discipline caused by the visit of our benefactress – whose generosity had built the seminary, provided for its maintenance, and given us the park – the day finally came when I felt an increased intensity in his gaze, and soon he gave me a sign, inviting me to follow him. I did not hang back. A blinding certainty led me toward him.

We went into the visiting room, where a painted plaster statue of the Assumption portrayed the Blessed Virgin crushing the Serpent underfoot as she began her ascent into Heaven.

Hand in hand, we gazed at each other, as at the end of every road. His gentleness was firm; his first caress, as light as the touch of fingertips smoothing a length of silk. A dark, eager light came into his eyes. Attraction did the rest, and I could see his face no longer.

37

ALTHOUGH I WAS BORN GUILTY AND INCLINED BY
nature to invent qualms of conscience, I did not feel at fault,
that day or afterward, even though the disturbance of love per-
sisted, increasing with each encounter. The world? Finally a
safe place. Our caresses? The first ever exchanged. Our lips?
The first ever to kiss. That fulfillment in which two become one
was bathed in innocence. Our hands had never strayed below
the waistline into sin, nor would they in the future. Our bodies
were simply cut in half.

I was experienced in pleasure, and even more so in vice, but
the feverish thirst that had raged during my childhood – and
been curbed for more than a year – did not flare up again. And
if I am to believe his actions and his words, which now rustle
unintelligibly in the depths of memory, it was the same with
him. We lived in such an excitement of our entire being, in
such bodily enthrallment to our souls, that it was perfect bliss
to hold each other's hands and take pleasure in a thousand
ways from their touch, so that our joy possessed our hearts and
faces and was expressed with every look and breath, filling that
part of our bodies so enraptured by music when it sweeps us
from the grasp of time that when we return to the present once
again, tears come to our eyes.

I know that we are rarely conscious of that moment outside of
time when one heart pledges itself to another, but I know that I
was aware of this moment, and that our love and faith somehow
touched the earth, and the universe itself. No illusion could
have come so alive for me again today, decades after our secret

encounters in the visiting room, if he and I had not kept our passion pure, and unsatisfied.

And that is how we lived for an entire year, unable to be either together or apart.

38

THE VISIT FROM OUR BENEFACTRESS – WHOM SOME OF the older students ridiculed as "Lady Charity" and whom the rector had urged us to remember in our prayers – gave us an opportunity to see each other when refreshments were served.

Our guest was a woman in her sixties, attired with an understated elegance; the print material of her dress (little gray flowers on a black background), which might have seemed austere, gave her appearance just a hint of stylishness when worn with a hat and gloves. She had an air of calm authority about her, particularly in her bearing, that discouraged both familiarity and obsequiousness.

Had she suffered, experienced great passions? Her features seemed asleep, already carved in marble for her effigy. Could anyone doubt her proverbial munificence? Yet it was as though she kept everything for herself – her generosity, her goodness, her sweetness – and might stifle from not knowing how to laugh, and die from not daring to cry. She must have loved duty for the satisfaction derived from its fulfillment, and always preferred this satisfaction to the truth, thanks to a faith unshaken by doubt. Aside from the hat and gloves, there was no notable difference between herself and the lady's companion who followed her, a few steps back and to her left, except that this shadow hung on her every word.

Our benefactress asked questions – not really of anybody in

particular – about daily life and the program of studies in the seminary. Were we taking good care of her garden? Then, after soliciting the rector's approval with a knowing look, she observed that there was no task, no matter how modest it seemed, that could not aspire to greatness. She herself, early every day, even before her breakfast was served, would change the water in her flower vases, trimming the stems of the bouquets, removing any dead leaves, offering in this way a morning prayer.

She wished to visit the oak split by lightning when she was a child, with its low fork where two people might sit face to face; there she had played, learned her catechism, done her homework. It had truly been her own little house, and if her governess had let her, she would have slept out there under the stars.

She toured the property, with us in attentive if somewhat unorderly attendance, and when she visited the orchard, where we rarely ventured, I shivered to see, beyond the orchard wall, the sky of the open plain, anchored to a horizon of clouds.

After our guest's departure, we were allowed to receive her little gifts of sweaters, socks, and shoes, used but clean: washed, mended, resoled. I remember cardboard boxes covered with glossy paper; one of them, a long, dark, narrow shape, reminded me of La Pinotta's coffin. It must have been – what I could never have suspected at the time – a dress carton for an evening gown.

In the pile of shoes, one pair stood out from all the others, and I coveted them. They were two-toned: the pointed toes and the counters were an orangey brown, while the rest was a yellowed white. When my turn came, I snatched them up. Unwilling to imply that anything provided by our benefactress might be inappropriate, the rector did make some remark about the size of the shoes, which were obviously too big for me. I had never seen any shoes as beautiful as those, even in the pages of *Rosalinda.* I stuffed newspaper in the toes, and wore them the next day.

They provoked murmurs, laughter, scoffing, humiliation. I did not give in, and offered my mortification to the Madonna in the visiting room, even when the toes of these shoes that were way too big for me began to curl upward, giving them the look of medieval poulaines.

So all day long, everyone had fits whenever I went by. I would have liked to back down, but pride became mixed in with my imaginary offering to the Virgin, and as for *him*, well, he still looked at me in the same way – although I was feeling quite low that evening, when he signaled me with his eyes to meet him in the visiting room.

Not one word was spoken. He knelt on one knee and with the skill of a conjuror, unlaced my shoes, removed them, offered me his own, put on mine – and served at mass in them the next morning.

He wore them all that day, and that day only. They did not curl up as much on his feet. During mass, looks were exchanged as heads turned with a slowness that spoke volumes. Afterward, if any of my former tormentors began whispering at the sight of me, he would quickly appear, silencing them by his mere presence, watchful, with the hint of a smile in his eyes for me. They respected him because of his seniority, which automatically gave him a supervisory authority, and because, on the eve of his novitiate, it was said that as a theologian he would prove well-suited to triumphing in any argument with those Thomists, those Aristotelians, those *Dominicans*. And so he had the right, as did certain of the resident priests, to display a marked partiality for someone, his favorite.

In fact, of the three monks who lived with us (except the rector, a saintly man who preferred caution to scandal, and Father Dutto, who played the harmonium – rather clumsily – all day long), two seemed for all the world like dramatic characters who had wandered into the wrong play.

Hard as it was to imagine, our Father Salgado was the brother of my confessor in Córdoba, the Gothic ascetic; I shall always remember him racing off in the seminary car to do some errand in town, and upon his return, dashing back to his room as if a horde of bandits were at his heels, with his habit of light woolen serge (which he wore very short) flapping around his skinny legs. He said mass as though something urgently awaited his attention elsewhere. I suspected that his favorite, a blond imp of Polish extraction, suffered more disappointments than he enjoyed advantages. Whenever the curly-haired boy was about to enter his protector's cell, or when leaving it, he would hesitate like a doe sniffing the air for danger.

Father Rincón, on the other hand, was quite sickly, and spent most of his time lolling about on the cushions of all sizes piled upon his bed. He lived in semidarkness, and when he left his door ajar, the lighting in his den seemed murkily obscene to me. Medicinal odors and the scent of eau de cologne would drift out into the corridor.

When he spoke to you, an expression of unctuous malice came over his face, and with the look of someone who has peered deep into your heart, he tried to ferret out your secret. I overheard him and his protégé, a sneering rascal whose last name, appropriately enough, was Siciliano, discussing the exchange of shoes between myself and my friend. I had just finished my music lesson, which never lasted long enough to suit me; a piano falling silent makes me feel as though life has come to a halt, that nothing else exists, and at that time, since I took particular pleasure in musing upon the impermanence of things, I would be overwhelmed by a vague sadness. On the day in question, however, I was still moved by my friend's gesture and was feeling happy in spite of the backbiting all around me.

Without noticing it, I had stopped near Father Rincón's room. A yellowish light filtered through the shutters, along with whisperings, giggles, and the scowling boy's voice; I heard him say the word "shoes," and then add, "This morning, at mass, was their betrothal."

From the depths of his nest of cushions, Father Rincón answered eagerly in a hoarse voice, "Their wedding, my dearest, their mystical wedding!"

At first I thought I would repeat these words to him, because they made me feel so proud. But I did not, for I understood almost immediately what he knew only too well – which explained his silences, all those glances seemingly charged with things unspoken. I had understood that reality is too fluid to resist the assault of words, which caress it only to erode it all the more, to transfigure reality and make it into an image. Things take on proportion and their true power only after they have been said.

Those who by revealing their feelings turn them into obligations are unfortunate indeed, but more unfortunate still are those stories left untold, because they will never have existed.

39

THE SCHOOL YEAR WAS DRAWING TO A CLOSE. THE DAYS went by, highlighted by our rendezvous in the visiting room, and also by the examinations we had to take every month. Actually, I never studied until the week before the exams, which was enough to satisfy and even impress those good old Franciscans, who only half-understood what they taught us – or in matters of religion, drummed into us.

Did they keep an eye on the two of us? We were like each other's conscience; we hallucinated ourselves. Surrounded by suspicion, our encounters in public were the subject of conventicles held by those of our fellow students who had been alerted by the affair of the shoes. Luckily, my friend was respected by the student body, and my cleverness at showing up our teachers was another point in my favor.

Summer arrived, and the entire seminary went off to the

Sierra de Córdoba, to that clump of inhospitable little cottages in their grim setting, where the heat was stifling even in the shade of the few scattered trees. Drought had reduced the river to a rushing stream in its rocky bed. But at least *he* was there that year, and I was with him – and that painted the landscape in the brightest of colors.

I remember the heat, and the shouts of bathers echoing off the stony walls, and mass celebrated – since we did not have a chapel – beneath the only tree with spreading, leafy branches, on an altar like something out of an opera about druids. But the heat, the cries of the bathers, prayers out in the open air are only the prelude to the most important moment of that summer, when the future, our future, simply stopped, without my realizing it. This hiatus has lasted until today, when the pitiless coherence of words has led me back to the beginning of that end, awakening in this worn-out frame the body of my youthful days – and when I think what it cost me to leave everything behind, and more than once, the way one leaves oneself!

On the pretext that I wanted to correct a translation from the Greek, I received permission from the rector one day for us to skip both the swim period and the daily walk. We were alone. We sat facing each other astride a low dry stone wall, and for the first time, our knees touched. He had set a big book down between us, and I had opened my notebook. As a precaution, I held a pencil in my hand. We did not read or write a single thing.

He took hold of my wrist, and something in his voice told me that I should not interrupt him. He said that he would not be returning to the seminary in Moreno, that he would be going directly, and soon, to the monastery in Buenos Aires. It had become urgent for him to leave for the novitiate before the end of our vacation, so that he might have a few days of solitude before the other novices arrived from seminaries in other parts of the country.

Did I protest? He tried to persuade me: we would see each other again by Easter at the latest, when the students and faculty of the seminary at Moreno made their customary visit to the capital. After the sung mass and breakfast with the provincial, there would be a program of entertainment in which I would surely participate, given my amazing progress on the piano.

We would never again return to the visiting room – that last time, had he already known this?

He continued his monologue hurriedly, gently, firmly: he would not forget me, and the wait would be part of the novitiate that I would begin myself in three years' time. A year after that, we would live in the same wing of the monastery, the philosophers' wing, where everyone has his own cell. His smile was faintly sly, like the smile of someone trying to deceive a child.

But love, love, that word never mentioned between us – how could he believe it compatible with monastic life? In despair, in anguish, and with a kind of brutal determination as well, I suggested that we go off and live together according to our nature.

He replied that there was no other way of saving what bound us together than to persevere in this vocation that isolated us from the world. He said that he had truly set out upon the path leading to God, and that he alone risked losing me; with an enthusiasm and, now that I think about it, a grandiloquence of feeling that were not at all like him, still keeping his voice at a murmur, he encouraged me to walk along with him, although at a distance, toward the road to perfection, and when we were both the same age.... He had taken hold of my wrist again, gripping it hard.

When we would both be dead and it would be too late? He smiled: Heaven had blessed us by allowing Heaven to begin for us here below, and we were already there; a difficult journey through the shadows lay ahead, and the first one to cross over would await the other.

Did he paraphrase a line from Virgil? *"Ibant obscuri sola sub nocte per umbras...."* We laughed. To keep from crying? We were laughing – then his face crumpled and he looked away. I felt his hands trembling on my cheeks, on my eyelids, and the slender tip of his index finger glided across my forehead like the tip of a knife.

Time-honored wisdom would have it that ignorance of the date of our own death is indispensable to the fulfillment of our destiny. And so life is full of last farewells that we had thought were merely good-byes.

He left a few days later, well before the summer was over, without telling me. When the rest of us woke up that morning, he was already gone. I found out when I saw he was not in the line for washing basins; each boy would empty the one he had used, fill it with clean water, and give it to the student behind him. I handed the basin to someone else that day.

As the sky grew lighter and more spacious, the landscape seemed to turn hostile once again. The sierra looked to me like piles of rocks thrown up in haste, or something dropped from the clouds to crash into the ground. Dormant from time immemorial, as it had been before I met him, and strewn with stony rubble, without that animating energy my happiness had brought to it, the gray scenery hemmed me in, imprisoning me in the heart of an unfinished and abandoned creation.

After the morning service, I asked to see the rector. In the monastery I saw faces that reflected great thoughtfulness and serenity, but his was the only one that shone with the light of simple faith alone.

To my surprise, while showing me out after a lengthy conversation, the rector suddenly advised me not to think about what was troubling me for three months and not to ask for another appointment unless I felt a serious need to speak with him. As usual, his flat, thin little voice gave no further hint about what he might be thinking.

40

It would not be long before I had convinced
myself that love would never withstand the divisive forces of
time and distance.

For a few weeks after our return to Moreno, I found the childhood haunt of "Lady Charity," that oak sculpted into a love seat
by lightning, to be the ideal spot for reverie and reliving old
memories. But what was the first sign that my adoration was
fading, that a desolation like the dusty plain around the farm
was closing in on me again?

I tried in vain to maintain the power of his gaze over me, over
my body, which had been chaste for a time out of an illusory love
of God and then out of love for him, and which was still filled with
the memory of his presence and with my devotion or inclination
to study, so that my slightest actions still drew on this hidden
strength. But soon my efforts faltered, as old desires swarmed
back to life; the moment came when I felt the object of my constant longing and dreams pull free of me like the pulpy flesh of a
fruit coming away from its pit. That wave we call our one true love
receded; ties that had bound us together as one came undone. He
drifted away, ever farther and farther away, carrying something of
myself along with him forever into oblivion.

What seems like only a short while to me today was in reality
a long period of despair. At the end of three months, I asked to
speak with the rector again and was promptly ushered in to see
him. Although my first words were the same ones I had carefully thought over not so very long before, I now had a completely different purpose in mind. Had I thought to admit to
him frankly that I had no vocation, so that he would allow me to

leave the seminary, thus letting me punish the one who – without having any more of a vocation than I did – had urged me to join him years later in the monastery instead of going off to live with me? Ever since his departure, I would have liked nothing better than for him to know that I was in a state of sin.

When I pronounced the words that should have made my case seem beyond remedy, I ran the risk, of course, that I would gain my freedom and then be obliged to return to my family and the desolate countryside. I hoped, however, that the rector would try to persuade me to stay by offering me certain privileges. He saw through my little ruse quite easily, and observed that there was still time for my vocation to announce itself, or to return.

Did he realize that we were forbidden to read anything besides a few expurgated anthologies of secular literature and the Latin and Greek classics – all handpicked so that we would encounter in them only those heroes who in some way prefigured the saints of the Church? What would someone whose waning sense of vocation precluded his admission to the novitiate be able to do, if he found himself back in the outside world equipped with a religious education that would only rarely prove useful to him?

Neither Father González's genial manner nor his voice betrayed any change when he told me that from then on I would be allowed to go into town once a month, and that a small sum would be given me to purchase books. I was to buy whatever I liked, on condition that I neither gave nor lent any to my comrades.

This was even more than I had hoped for, and instead of feeling guilty, I felt voluptuously self-satisfied: impossible barriers had sprung open, allowing me to pursue my destiny. Did I think I was above average? No: far superior to everyone around me.

With the rector's tacit permission, I looked at the Index, because I was certain that the works listed there reflected the very pinnacle of human thought. Aware as I was of the Serpent's high reputation, I had no doubt that every book had been carefully selected.

When I try to recreate with words the intoxication of my first trip to Buenos Aires all by myself, I can hardly picture the city. In fact, all I recall is my anxious attempt to investigate everything on the bookstore shelves, and my distress at finding *The Critique of Pure Reason* unreadable. From my meager harvest, I gleaned a few impressions in Kierkegaard's *The Concept of Dread,* and a few more lively ones in Unamuno's *The Tragic Sense of Life,* and, finally, I read Ibsen's plays with the utmost excitement: I fell in love with Hedda Gabler, who kills herself to make up for a lack of courage in the man she loves; her gesture seemed to conform to the dogma of the communion of saints, and to that law of compensation taught me by my first confessor, Father Salgado. And I loved Nora Helmer, the one who goes away, the one capable of leaving because she knows, in her childish cruelty, that to sacrifice oneself for another is to rush headlong into ruin, and sometimes to bring ruin on the other person as well.

When I took part, as my friend had predicted, in the entertainment in honor of the feast of Saint Francis in the monastery in Buenos Aires, I presented a short play I had written, chock-full of words lifted from Ibsen's heroines. I seem to remember that it revolved around the blameworthy action of a monk who, at the crucial moment of his ordination, accepts for all eternity the dignity of priesthood, knowing that his nature will soon compel him to break his vow. It was easy to smuggle in ideas censured by the Franciscans. Only one of the spectators that day was able to recognize Nora Helmer under the frock of the intransigent monk whose part I played; he was some sort of society man of letters who had taken holy orders late in life and who wrote me, although we had never spoken to each other, upon learning that I had left the seminary, urging me to reconsider, suggesting that I had chosen the wrong monastic order and that the Society of Jesus would suit me better. I was proud to hear this but did nothing about it, much to my occasional regret.

After the evening's entertainment, students and seminarists scattered through the classrooms, the cloister, the library, and the orchard, where we finally found each other, he and I, amid some trees whose name I could not have told you, their branches laden with a gleaming orange fruit: kakis. This intimacy was short-lived, lasting barely long enough for me to look into his eyes once more, which did not seem so much to see me as to speak to me, as they had on the day of the eclipse.

He selected a ripe fruit, offered it to me, and even though the message in his look was clear, he sought to intensify its meaning with every possible nuance. Then the kaki slipped from my hands to splatter softly on the grass.

We were never to see each other again.

As in the naive illuminations of old missals, the sky is cut off, the young monks stiffen into stillness, and each fruit, each leaf on every tree settles into its own distinct outline: nothing has any volume. Feeling fades away. The heartbeat that made the moment quiver with life is silent.

41

AFTERWARD, I WAS TO HAVE VERY LITTLE NEWS OF HIM. I learned of his ordination from one of his fellow students, who had himself decided at the last minute against entering the priesthood and who came to see me years later at the real estate agency where I was pretending to be a secretary. Then, silence again; his image faded, disappearing peacefully inside me, the way ripples from a tossed pebble flow out to the edges of a pond.

Had I more or less forgotten him – perhaps even completely – that summer day in 1967, more than twenty years later, when I opened the door of the apartment where I was staying with some friends in Paris, and found myself nose to nose with a hulking giant, who was wearing the frightening smile, moreover, of someone who has finally ferreted you out? He had thick lips and eyes that swam at the bottom of his glasses, where they seemed to expand and fill the rimless lenses like spreading drops of ink whenever he screwed his chubby cheeks up in a smile.

When I recognized his voice, his features fell into place for me: the Franciscan who had been playing the andante from the "Moonlight" Sonata the day I first came to the monastery. His fringe of hair and tonsure were gone; now he wore his hair combed straight back, and like most priests at the time, he wore as a kind of lay dress a shapeless suit of a nondescript gray and a turtleneck instead of a shirt, probably to dispense with the frivolity of a tie. And so you always knew they were priests when you saw them in the street, without even having to think about it.

Father Rodríguez, who had been quite husky even as a boy, had put on a lot of weight, and his step on the parquet reminded me of the way he used to bang on the piano keys, but despite the impressive sway of his belly, his gaze had remained clear, unsullied by the slightest tinge of greed.

Seated at a table in the living room, we had tea with short-bread cookies; his stumpy fingers handled the china with timid care. He reminisced about the seminary, the fathers, our music lessons, and so on, up to the time of my departure. Had I kept my faith? To please him, I said yes, while adding that I still prayed, which implied some mental reservation on my part. How far away it was, that day when I served at the mass he celebrated in our chapel during one of his visits to Moreno; at the moment of the elevation, the little vault sheltering the altar had seemed to grow larger as I watched.

I tried to keep from staring curiously at his shabby outfit. As for him, he never once looked at either the pictures or the unusual objects that filled the room. Suddenly, he seemed to become somewhat uneasy. There was a silence; then he spoke, and his voice had changed its tone. I remembered the distinction he established, in the realm of emotion, between the keys of C major and C minor, when he had me play the first measures of the "Moonlight" Sonata.

He asked me (his question was in C-sharp) whether I remembered – and then he said, very distinctly, the name I have since forgotten, and I cannot recall either the number of syllables, or the initial, or even the rhythm of this name, as has often happened to me with other names as well. He told me that after my friend's ordination, in view of his gift for subtle theological argument – mentioned with a very Franciscan tinge of condescension – he had been sent to Rome to complete his studies. Father Rodríguez paused for a moment, gathering up crumbs from the tablecloth; his eyes sought the brightness of the windows behind me, where the daylight peeped through a tangle of leafy plants.

Had I heard? My friend had left the priesthood. With some effort, my visitor added one word: "defrocked." And then, with a sigh, said that he had died two years later, in Switzerland, but not without confessing his sins on his deathbed, my informant hastened to remark with satisfaction.

Even though Father Rodríguez had never hinted at his motive in telling me all this, he seemed to feel intensely relieved, as if he had just accomplished some mission, in accordance with wishes that were beyond him. And now a vision opened up before me of a part of life that had been hidden by the innumerable adventures that had taken me so far from the plains and the world of La Pinotta. I was convinced that the good father had tracked me down with the sole purpose of bringing me news of my friend.

I felt no particular emotion upon hearing of his death. That he had given up the priesthood, on the other hand, bore out the predictions of the boy who had once asked him if they might leave the seminary together. But I felt suddenly stabbed to the heart by one question: for whom had he returned to the outside world? For there was no doubt that there had been someone else involved, whose existence I deduced not from the fact that my friend had thrown his frock away, but because instead of going home to his own country, he had gone to live in Switzerland, a fortress without any attraction for a penniless South American.

We poured ourselves another cup of tea; it was lukewarm, bitter, and the shortbread was all gone. Father Rodríguez had nothing more to say.

I reread the preceding pages and am surprised by the gap between the emotional upheaval provoked by the words that brought my friend back to me and the impotence to which they abandon me by retiring into the shadows, bearing only a little votive lamp, leaving me alone and stunned by an onslaught of jealousy.

Sometimes we can feel hailed on all sides by the dead without understanding what it is we can do for them. Surrounded by nothingness, they watch us: waiting, hoping. But how very *present* this one is, how tenaciously he hangs on, and after having drawn me back into the past through the awakening of all my senses, how he has become a part of my days!

Will I try to trace his wanderings toward the end of his life? Will I ever see that gravestone lying somewhere on Swiss soil, a stone cut to precise measurements, on which the fragile light of October is falling at this very moment?

42

As we all know, time quickly teaches us not to be surprised at the inconstancy of our feelings, which move from one sole object to another at the heart's command. One fine day, our thoughts about the other person become a simple habit of memory, and then they fade, scattering into the shadows. The light is snuffed out.

Had I dreamed of submitting my nature to the laws of

Heaven? My faith withered away. Had I believed my friend and I were united by a sacred bond? The stirrings of sensuality gradually subsided, and forgetting did the rest.

I took pleasure in arguing with the fathers about matters of doctrine. I was not lacking in insolence. Overindulgence in such behavior, of course, makes one ridiculous. I often was. Whenever I badgered one of the fathers with questions, it meant I could never be budged from my own position. In fact, I would come up with almost the same objections today: the transmission of original sin; suffering used as a kind of currency; the role of pain (whether man's or a beetle's) in the economy of the world; ransom by prayer; and, most of all, the free will that enables us to choose our actions and their consequences – Heaven, the reward that does not help us to live, and Hell, which works to prevent us from living.

As for Heaven, I maintained that whatever we do with our liberty, we are never either better or worse than the next man. Concerning Hell, I claimed that it would be impossible to be happy in Paradise while knowing that more unfortunate sinners were suffering eternal punishment.

I remember Father Dutto's answer on this point; he was the youngest of our teachers, the most pious, and a very ingenuous, simple soul, whose countenance shone with a gentle, defenseless innocence that was quite affecting. I can still see the strain and concentration in his face, as though he were striving with his whole being to recall things he had learned by heart, but many years before, and I remember the relief that swept over him when he found the right words: it was not God who condemned man, but man who condemned God to punish him. Moreover, in Heaven our benighted intelligence would be enlightened, allowing us to *intelligere* – he was translating his proof from the Latin – and thus to accept the indispensable justice of Hell.

And if he himself, in Paradise, were to know that his mother was burning in infernal fire?

The tears sprang to his eyes. I was proud of myself. Today,

when such things just seem like sad little games, I feel ashamed. If Hell were real, that moment would be part of it. Another feeling of remorse binds me to Father Dutto. I was the director of the school choir, and on one Easter Sunday we were performing a mass in three voices by Perosi. I had been given a baton. Father Dutto was providing accompaniment on the harmonium. At one point, between two choral sections of the mass, he played a melody, for which he changed the stops and shifted the keyboard, forgetting afterwards to return to the proper settings for the choral part, so that the baritones found themselves in the tenor range, the tenors had to attack their parts in falsetto voice, and the sopranos were screeching off key as if they were being throttled.

I gave the signal for them to stop and whispered to the accompanist to change registers. In a panic, Father Dutto kept on playing, and although I begged him to break off and begin again, his hands continued to move over the keys as though he had no control over them. Then my blood began to boil, and I do not think I have ever been so mad in all my life. Beside myself, certain that I was in the right (the poor chorus, reduced to helplessness, was proof of that), I raised the pointed ivory baton high above my head and brought it down upon his own, and even though the baton only ruffled the circular fringe of hair that made him look like Saint Anthony, what I had done was still a sacrilege. Hunched over the instrument, he finally brought himself to change over to the correct key, and we began again. There had been murmuring from our audience, made up of people from the neighborhood, and slight scraping noises as the pews shifted on the stone floor. Looking down from the choir stalls for a moment, I noticed the face of a young man who reminded me of Tomasito Carrara. Almost at the same time, two long-lost images from my childhood returned to me: the second was the tennis player, whose racket left its mark forever on my forehead; but the first memory, which had resurfaced a few seconds earlier when Father Dutto was being so stubborn, was of a broken-winded horse with a bumpy gallop, whose head I had once walloped so hard with my whip handle that the animal had stopped short and collapsed, as though dying. His coat had been highlighted with fleeting greenish reflections, like the glints on the wings of flies.

After the mass was over, while the harmonium player bent laboriously over the keyboard, striving to coax triumphant sounds from the modest instrument, and the celebrant was returning to the sacristy, followed by the deacons and the altar boys, I wished – more than I ever have since then – that I were dead.

I took no part in the rejoicing that followed. I felt paralyzed. It was the same on the following day, and the day after that. Was I afraid of being punished? I would have welcomed punishment. But it was as if nothing had happened. My fellow students said not a word to me, nor did the rector. Three days passed without anyone taking any notice of me. Banished into nonexistence, unable to endure any longer the unreality in which I had been imprisoned, I went to Father Dutto to ask his forgiveness.

He looked up from his breviary with a beatific light in his eyes: he was happy, not for himself, but for me. And his smile of compassion – in the etymological sense of the word – has never ceased to make my offense worse as the years go by.

When remorse lasts forever, it becomes difficult to forgive a pardon so freely given.

43

I WAS TO SEE THE YOUNG MAN WHO HAD SO STRONGLY reminded me of Tomasito Carrara that Easter Sunday and on every Sunday thereafter. He sat in the fifth row on the right, in the company of two elderly women, one of whom displayed a superb simplicity of manner, while the nervous impatience of the other was advertised by the clinking of her charm bracelets. When she crossed herself, their jangling competed with the four rings of the altar boy's little bell, leading the faithful into the error of falling to their knees at the wrong moment. From my post at the harmonium, where I played very simplified transcriptions of piano or vocal music, I saw the three of them from the back during the service, and afterward, from the front, for as long as it took them – given the ladies' age and the young man's respectful pace – to walk the few steps separating them from the mezzanine where I sat and beneath which they would disappear until the following Sunday. They resembled those people whose poses and gestures had fascinated me in the photographs in *Rosalinda*. They were neighbors, living on a large property opposite the seminary, and from the train that carried me off once a month to the bookstores of Buenos Aires, I had occasionally glimpsed some young ladies in short skirts playing tennis there. The family's name was Penaranda, and as friends of Lady Charity, they were also patrons of our institution.

I would wait for the moment when the young man would rise and step aside to let the two ladies pass. His face was pale and smooth; his cheeks, heavily shadowed; his hair and eyebrows, black and bushy; his lips were red. His eyes, which were quite far apart, turned to look at me one time when I had just begun to play an arrangement of a song by Schumann, "Lotus Blumen." As I read the music, I could see him from the corner of my eye, in silhouette; his movements were only those prescribed by the liturgy, but he looked abruptly over his shoulder at me, with an expression of both astonishment and malice, and, as he turned away, I saw that he was smiling.

What hopes did I not found on that stealthy glance, that hint of a smile? The young man quickly took the place that, in spite of (or thanks to) absence, belonged only to *him*. As though my heart had been nothing more to me than an empty mold, I welcomed the newcomer, enveloping him in the endlessly spinning web of my daydreams. Might we perhaps have a better idea of what we can become than of what we are? Do we really know the little we do know? When we feel the need to love, we already hear our blood pounding at the thought that our bodies may touch, melt into each other, join as one in boundless surrender.

Sunday after Sunday, the three Penarandas entered the chapel at half past ten on the dot, always in the same order, to take their places in the fifth row. I would not begin to play until after their arrival; I liked to hear the gravel crunching (*morendo*) under the wheels of their car, which I recognized among all others – unless this is something I have dreamed up only now, in thinking back on it.

Whatever their positions in the pew, they sat, not stiffly, but with a kind of hieratic attitude relieved from time to time by the clinking of the bracelets worn by the younger lady, who held her head in precisely the same way as did the woman I took to be the youth's grandmother. I thought about how easy it would have been to elicit from the young man some small sign of complicity with the harmonium player, if only the budding musician had dared to replay the "Lotus Blumen" that had already earned him a glance, and perhaps even a smile. But the young musician restrained himself, hemmed in as he was in any case by all sorts of scruples of a religious nature – or perhaps for fear that the other man would simply remain impassive.

Each Sunday the same ritual was repeated, although it was

in fact a ritual only to me; how long this went on, I could not say. I remember that the clothes of the Penarandas reflected the passage from autumn to winter (I can still see the red fox collar of the "grandmother" and the youth's overcoat with the half-belt in the back), and then, gradually, the change from winter to spring. At the approach of summer, the lady with the bracelets wore dresses sprigged with flowers, in fabric of an almost ethereal lightness.

One day, toward the end of the afternoon, Father González ordered me to put on my habit and collect the implements necessary for aspersion. I filled a brass bottle with holy water; I did not have to go over the text of the *De profundis*, for I knew it by heart. There had been a death in the neighborhood, and I was to accompany the priest. He put on the appropriate vestments – the surplice, the black stole edged with gold – and we set out in the car, driven (cautiously, on this occasion) by Father Salgado.

The avenue through the park on the Penarandas' estate led straight to the house, and it was bordered by the tallest poplars I had ever seen. The noise of the gravel was different from the sound of the more sandy variety in the seminary courtyard. Someone on the first floor of the house was walking from window to window with a lamp; then many of the rooms in the vast mansion began to blaze with light, and the facade grew darker.

At first I did not recognize the woman in the severe black dress, standing at the foot of the wide staircase with steps paved in checkered tiles of ocher and rust-brown; she had taken off her bracelets. We followed her up the stairs. I was thinking of the grandmother's hair pinned up in a bouffant twist, now flattened by the little cushion of her coffin, when I glimpsed that lady standing on the threshold of the mortuary chapel. This small *chapelle ardente* resembled a fabulous grotto: all that could be seen in the light of two fat wax candles was a mass of flowers, or more precisely, the same flower endlessly multiplied, covering the walls and the catafalque: a mauve orchid, with purple velvet at its frilly heart – the only orchid known in those parts at the time, before the horticulturists introduced new varieties and the cattleya became a rarity. I knew what it was because I had seen a silk orchid pinned to the lapel of Cecilia's suit jacket on the day of her civil marriage. And I remembered not having believed that this artificial flower, which seemed quite like a butterfly or the scalloped hem of fine lingerie, could really be part of nature.

I fervently recited the *De profundis* along with Father González. Standing at the foot of the coffin, I looked and looked at the dead youth, without looking my fill. I can keep my eyes open for a long time without blinking. His lips, once a startling red in his pale face, were drained of color and ever so slightly parted, right in the center, to let through one last syllable from the other side.

Family and friends filed past; for each one, I dipped the aspergillum into the onyx cup I had filled with holy water. Next came the servants, and last of all, a red-faced old man, the only person in tears. It was the gardener, who had been initiated in the cultivation of orchids by the young man.

I would have liked to see, beneath those closed lids, the eyes that had once thrown me a furtive glance, a look – who knows? – of understanding. His beard was still growing, giving his hollow cheeks a dark green cast. For days afterward I would think of this dead youth turning green in his grave. Although I knew the color of his eyes, I had never heard his voice.

Some months went by before I learned the reason why he had turned toward the person playing that Schumann lied. One day when I was looking for the approved station on the rector's radio, I discovered the truth. Did I think I had happened upon "Lotus Blumen"? It was Cole Porter's "Night and Day." That grouping of four or five notes musicians call a *cell,* and which determines the development of the melody, turned out to be identical in the two pieces, whether through plagiarism or by coincidence. So the young man's gesture had been sparked by his surprise at the seemingly sacrilegious playing of a popular song during mass.

I felt ridiculous, and my fantasy of a secret passion was pathetic. My overexcited imagination had once again left me high and dry on a strange shore: a confused and dismayed cast-away, condemned to go on living.

Young Penaranda might have been lost, the way the shape of a striking cloud dissolves in time, or a phrase that flashes through our minds darts suddenly beyond recall, the precise arrangement of the words seeming a sufficient assurance of their survival, so that we neglect to make a note of them.

I learned recently that Leonard Bernstein went to Fontainebleau to see Nadia Boulanger when she was dying. According to those close to her, she was already in a deep coma, from which she emerged when her former pupil asked her if she was listening to music, and if so – listing some of her favorite composers – to what kind. In that indefectible voice of hers, she replied, "A music without beginning or end." Those were her only words; she lapsed back into unconsciousness.

I no longer recall when the episode of young Penaranda occurred during my stay at Moreno, which lasted almost five years. Was it the luxuriance of the cattleyas in the mortuary chapel that engraved his image so deeply? Among the things that insist for no good reason on being remembered in the course of a lifetime, it is a rare one that does not require some editing by the mind, which is subject to the changes in distance and lighting forgetfulness may bring.

Penaranda reappears promptly and discreetly, disappears, returns, and has done so regularly through the years. "Lotus Blumen," "Night and Day," the word *orchid*, freshly shaved cheeks still shadowed by a trace of beard – these are enough to recall him to mind. And I, believing that the web of the universe quivers when the spider touches her own silken strands – I tell myself, in moments of reverie, that with his death, fate allowed me to mourn, once and for all, my first, clandestine love, and those brief caresses in the visiting room that have lived so long in my memory.

44

I HAD JUST TURNED SEVENTEEN WHEN I LEFT THE
seminary, at the moment when I would have had to take the
plunge and shut myself up in the novitiate to meditate, reflect,
and decide at the end of a year if I indeed possessed the qualities and abilities that make up a vocation for the priesthood.
Meditation is not one of my strengths, and neither is reflection,
slightly lower on the scale of spiritual activities. I did not
choose a path; I followed my footsteps.

For one whole day, I tried to find the words to tell Father
González, who must surely have known what was coming, that I
was definitely leaving the religious life. I remember walking to
the orchard wall, beyond which stretched the plain that quickly
shed its fields dotted with trees and houses, passing from
greenery to dust as it rolled toward that hateful spot on earth
where I had left my childhood.

Once again, I had no real misgivings about my decision, and
although I was aware of the dangers ahead, I felt unconcerned,
buoyed by new energy and enthusiasm. The illusion of God,
with all its promises, was fading; the intimidation was left
behind, intact. The raptures of religion had allowed me to
glimpse only inaccessible possibilities and inimitable marvels.
Through my reading, I had slipped down from the infinite to the
finite; from the universe to myself. Sometimes, through music, I
floated between the two.

Actually, the change was gradual, and in a way, it was
accomplished through substitution. One Sunday in August,
1945, Monsieur Teste took God's place.

Paul Valéry had died on the twentieth of July. I could draw

from memory the first page of the supplement devoted by *La Nación* to the poet whose name I did not even know: in the center, surrounded by articles that were doubtless hagiographic, two poems were printed with a border around them: "Air de Sémiramis" and beneath it, "Les Grenades." Although it is true that every translated poem requires an act of faith, it is still possible for intellectual poetry to cross this barrier – not without suffering in translation, of course, but preserving the ghost of the idea and something like the echo of music fading into the distance.

I can still see that newspaper, which I was not allowed to show my comrades, and the midday sun shining across my desk. And I remember the amazement, the admiration that took me completely outside myself. From one thrilling discovery to another, I would go from "Cimetière marin" to the first volume of *Variété*, which ends with *"La Méthode de Léonard de Vinci."* I compared Valéry's desire to isolate poetry from everything but itself to the ideal of chastity, as fundamental to my nature as it was inaccessible. One kind of theology was being replaced by another. And soon, prayers yielded to stanzas, to single lines of poetry, or the elegant despair of this paragraph, which is always with me: "We pass through the idea of perfection as the hand passes safely through a flame, but a flame is uninhabitable and the dwellings of the greatest serenity are necessarily deserted."

Purity, and at the same time, a wise understanding of one's inability to reach perfection; life lived without fear of subsequent punishment, or hope of reward; a striving for a body of work gathered in upon its own mystery, obeying its own laws – I saw in all this the program for a religion that was not burdensome but toward which I felt the same obligations of behavior as I had with the preceding one.

In this new clarity, I was losing my shadow. Was God avoiding me? He was abandoning me to a feeling of transgression.

I quickly obtained the original French versions of the Spanish translations of those Valéry poems, and a bilingual dictionary. That was how I entered the delicate labyrinth of the French language. One day, I sank my modest savings into the purchase of

La Soirée avec Monsieur Teste. I am not a bibliophile, but I like to reread this work in that 1931 edition, published by Sagittaire, which I deciphered with such difficulty at the time.

"Stupidity is not my forte." Valéry, who did not care for fiction, had taken it up so that he might write that first sentence without any appearance of vanity. I would have been so pleased to be worthy of the phrase; as I was not, I admired it. On the other hand, I took my secret motto from these four words found on the second page: "I have preferred myself." And with time, without noticing it, I added a fifth, the adverb *always*, between the verb and its auxiliary.

I had read a great deal when I left the seminary, had read everything I could get my hands on, feverishly, with a fervor not untinged by snobbery. One after the other, I had been Ivan Karamazov and Lafcadio, that precursor to Meursault, the "Stranger"; I had shared the courage of Ibsen's heroines; I longed to play Hamlet. But I listened to Monsieur Teste, and each sentence he let fall from his lips – hidden by Valéry's mustache, itself surmounted by his clear gaze – was suddenly worth the whole of literature. In much the same way, I was trying to discover music from the inside, by playing the piano. Certain pieces were beyond my ability, but sent a crystalline pleasure coursing all through me. When did I understand that music imposes its life upon our bodies, the same life that literature asks to borrow from us?

I visited many islands and was charmed by songs of endless variety, but of them all, there was one I felt could have been meant for me: the pensive, wintry song of Chopin, the very sound of remembrance. In a voice like no other, this messenger of the night speaks to us of our soul and its burden of confusion, fear, and regret; his music is not a sweeping flood of orchestral tone but a melody he has awakened in a past of which we know nothing, a slender, subtle melody that comes to us in our gloom and somehow touches our hearts.

When I left the seminary, I knew that I would have to live for a few weeks, if not a few months, with my parents. They had moved from the farm to Villa del Rosario, that little town halfway between the emptiness of the plain and the bustle of Córdoba.

Were my parents happy to welcome me home? I felt they expressed joy only to humiliate further and spoil the return of the child who had once demanded to have his own way. Even though he had acquired a certain stock of cultural knowledge, he would still have to begin all over again, since the studies he had completed at the seminary had been in a lateral direction, so to speak, and had led to neither a title nor a diploma. And no one was waiting to give him a helping hand.

But I had not wanted to hear about it, like someone who already knows and prefers not to reply, filled with the certainty that whatever move he makes brings him closer to his destiny. As I had done before, I did what I could, which is to say that I jumped ahead of myself and followed on my own heels.

Did I find the words I needed to tell Father González I did not feel called to the priesthood, and did I speak firmly enough to ensure my departure? I cannot recall talking to him or packing my belongings; in a way, I never left. There is a gap, a blank, a kind of nothingness through which threads the fragrance of the peach trees, their boughs laden with fruit, and the distant chiming of the rector's clock as it continues to strike the passing hours.

45

I WENT FROM THE KEYS OF A PIANO TO THOSE OF a typewriter, a portable model borrowed by my parents from some neighbors who had welcomed them warmly to their new home. I mistrusted these neighbors the most because they might be useful to my parents' project of keeping me nearby, in

Villa del Rosario. I was told that learning how to type was indispensable for someone like myself, unable to boast of even a single diploma. My father decided it would be a good idea if I became a clerk in a notary's office, working on deeds, contracts, and real estate sales.

As a child, I had visited Villa del Rosario on All Saints' Day, the year that La Pinotta had taken up sherbet making. The town had been laid out in a grid, like all Argentine cities intended to serve as military outposts for the Spanish Conquest. The church, which had been constructed at the same time, bore comparison with that of the Franciscans in Córdoba, for despite its smaller dimensions, there was a definite family resemblance between them. And I remember that visitors instinctively lowered their voices and walked on tiptoe inside the dimly lighted church, doubtless because it was almost always deserted.

The town had slumbered through three centuries, and there was no reason to hope that it would one day begin to grow and develop; it stopped right at the original limits, although only ruined houses and clay huts filled the last blocks.

The streets looked like strips of earth plowed into furrows in all directions, because farm carts heavily laden with sacks of grain and trucks bringing merchandise from Córdoba for the town stores would dig deep ruts in them when it rained; when the mud hardened, vehicles would drive around the ruts. Municipal neglect did the rest.

Four streets crossed at right angles to mark out the town square, a rather large space planted with eucalyptus and plane trees in alternate rows; a decrepit cedar near the church provided a surprising exception to this rule of symmetry. Not a single blossom graced the flower beds invaded by couch grass and thus turned into a kind of lawn by default. Although the place was charmless, one could still find shade there.

Bordered by four blocks of single-story row houses, whose entryways allowed glimpses of a series of patios paved in a checkerboard pattern, the square provided an open-air refuge; I was at first surprised, then delighted to discover that people never gathered there except on Sunday, after mass. To feel safe, I needed only to avoid sitting down facing one of the streets that led to the square, or, rather, that were born there, only to die a few hundred meters away, swallowed up by the plain. Still, one of those streets showed a view obstructed by trees that looked small in the distance, but if you knew that they were growing along the banks of what the local people thought of as a big river (which did manage to make its gurgling heard after nightfall), then your imagination could restore them to their full height as poplars.

Three months after taking up typing, I was trying my hand at being a public letter-writer, with a slight twist: like all the others, I strove to set down my clients' thoughts, but in a form that would seem incontestable to them (and even more so to the recipients of these letters) thanks to the crisply typed format. I hammered out love letters, for the most part, and I learned that one customer who took advantage of my services won the heart of his beloved within a few days, after two years of determined resistance on her part, and that when they subsequently began seeing each other every Saturday, the obstinate girl demanded to receive a letter before each rendezvous.

I led the reclusive life of someone earning a pittance, exercising my fingers assiduously all day long in the hope of reaching the speed of forty words a minute that would allow me to apply for a job with the notary, with whom my father thought he had some influence because he had once signed a bill of sale for a small farm in the man's office. We lived in a house with four rooms separated by the entrance hall, which opened onto a patio paved (a bit like the gallery of my childhood home) with odds and ends of tile, most of them gray, and so less conducive to the play of fantasy. These tiles did not cover the entire surface, and my father was so delighted with this space of beaten earth that, even before my parents were settled into their new home, he rushed to build a brick henhouse with a high, complicated roost constructed of poles on the sides to make up for the narrowness of the site. He planned to raise only purebred poultry.

For as long as I stayed in Villa del Rosario, I watched my father go busily about his constant repairs, preferably perched on top of a ladder, where, judging from the beatific look on his face, you would have thought he enjoyed a divine vision of the world from a golden balcony. He had a particular fondness for whatever was happening on the ceiling: an imperceptible crack, the slightest sign of flaking; day after day, the hook for the hanging lamp gave him a reason to climb his ladder, which he learned to use with the skill of an acrobat. He got on my nerves just as much as he always had, and even more when he lectured me on how not to be wasteful with food (each mouthful had to be accompanied by bread) or razor blades. He sharpened those large Gillette blades of blued steel by passing their edges one over the other, back and forth, the way butchers sharpen their knives, and when they had become useless for shaving, they were still not to be thrown away, because they could be used to sharpen pencils.

Electric light amazed him, and he reserved the right to switch it on in the evening. Even though he had never used electricity before, he had come up with a theory about how to save energy: according to him, turning on the light represented a good quarter of the cost, so it was better not to switch off a lamp when one would be using it again shortly.

He never tired of teaching me ways to be thrifty, and I was careful not to contradict him, listening attentively until he ran out of words. He was never really satisfied, however; proud of having preached economy, he would leave you, muttering softly in his frustration, then more loudly, as he headed for the hen-house, and soon he would be surrounded by a confused swarm of words.

He was full of images he could not master; they seized control of his arms, his hands, driving him to make the gestures that once accompanied his soliloquies and were too vigorous, too sweeping for his new surroundings. If someone came upon him unawares, he did not even try to fool this involuntary witness, although in a pinch he might invent a quarrel with the neighbor, whom he treated with haughty disdain, on the pretext that since she was a Creole and surrounded by a pack of famished-looking brats, she would soon be making off with the rare eggs, if not with the hens themselves.

He missed the plain, the great spaces where he could freely stage this theater of old grudges he carried about inside him. I had suffered too much from them to feel sorry for him. Still, on the day of the red rooster, I saw how homesick he was, and how distressed by his confinement.

In the evening, he would shut up the hens, each in her niche, and padlock the door. The setting sun bronzed the plumage of the rooster who perched fearlessly at the top of the henhouse like a splendid weathervane, chasing off any chicken bold enough to try and settle on any of his poles; he was the conqueror of the sun, whose rebirth he would summon the town, emerging from the night, to celebrate on the morrow even before the awakening of the bells.

Awaiting the darkness, the rooster stood like a statue, indifferent to the commands of my father, who crowed a few *cock-a-doodle-doo*s before condescending to cluck invitingly at the stubborn bird, as though he were calling the docile hens. And the two of them, standing stock-still, face to face, resembled each other.

In a burst of temper, did my father try to catch him? The rooster pecked at his hands with that quick unerring aim of farmyard birds who spot a grain of sand lying in the dust. And when the rooster suddenly spread his wings, my father panicked, flailing his arms and pouncing on the lord of the chicken coop, who wriggled free and took to the air, heavy and uncertain at first, then surprised at his own lightness, after landing for only a second on the low wall, where he touched down with just one foot – like a dancer entrusting the prowess of a great leap to a single leg – before hurtling away in a coppery whirlwind of feathers.

My father, his arms outstretched, slammed into the wall (yes, he sadly missed the vast, open plain...) and then struggled over the obstacle only to discover, to cap the humiliation, that his rooster was perched on the neighbor's roof.

The Creole woman's dexterity with a lasso retrieved the fugitive and placed my father in her debt. As for the rooster, my father attached a weight to its foot, and although the bird could no longer flutter up to his perch, he dragged his ball and chain about with a lordly air.

For as long as I knew him, even when he grew older, my father always wore shirts made by my mother (cotton with narrow stripes, cotton flannel in the winter) and trousers with tapering legs and ample room at the waist, held up high over his middle by suspenders. He wore a felt hat straight across his forehead, even inside the house. Actually, he never really changed much until the very end of his life. He was eighty-six the last time I was over there. Old age had only slowed him down a bit. Although a few inches shorter, he still displayed the haughty bearing that had always exceeded his humble circumstances: back straight as a ramrod, military step, head drawn stiffly back as though in indignation – an attitude I recognize each morning when I shave, as though that reflection were not me but my father, passing through who knows how many mirrors to lecture me on the proper care and maintenance of razor blades.

46

I WENT TO MASS ON SUNDAYS WITH MY MOTHER, and while she agreed that the altar boy was clumsy and made a great show of being inattentive, she did not suggest that I speak to the priest, her confessor, for fear that somehow the religious life might get a hold on me again. My mother never paraded her piety and went to mass the way she tended to all her daily chores, with the reserved serenity of someone who considers every misfortune as a thing already past, and every happiness as a blessing it would be unwise to celebrate too much.

It is no exaggeration to say that my mother had an aura of wisdom sensed by everyone. Her grandchildren, who knew her only when she was quite elderly, were ignorant of the harshness of her life and the obstacles she had had to overcome, because she never boasted of her accomplishments, but when they speak of their grandmother, a look of amazement comes over their faces, and you can hear the wonderment in their voices.

When she attended mass, it was only at the moment of the elevation that she became even more present and at the same time unattainable in her supreme contemplation: she would watch the priest bending first over the paten, then over the chalice, as if she were observing the millennial formation of a diamond and a ruby. It always struck me that she never lowered her eyes.

And she would still have that competent air of a clever housewife who would return to her kitchen and prepare, from minced chicken giblets, herbs, parmesan, and bouillon (made of all the bouillons saved up throughout the week), a risotto, the favorite dish of my father, who would advise me to spread the rice out upon the plate and begin eating it at the edges, so that I might savor every mouthful at the proper temperature, even to the last bite.

During this stay in Villa del Rosario, I rediscovered for the first time the simmered flavors of childhood, which depended on the exact amount of that pinch of nutmeg or oregano, and the point in cooking at which the proper seasoning was added.

I can never understand why people pretend to despise the pleasures of the palate, when they live for those that may be obtained from music, the cut of a garment, cosmetics, jewelry, perfumes, a room where the chandeliers are lit in preparation for a party. Do they not know that the delights of taste return as caresses, melodies, smiles – that they are at the origin of the spot of rosy pink that brings together and sets off all the elements in a beloved painting, that they preside at the birth of harmony in this or that arrangement of words or notes? And that it is in the perception of a flavor that all the senses unite, from sight to touch, body and soul melding in a happy tingling of tastebuds, of distinct and fraternal cells animated as one by contentment, or distaste: all that is invisible in the body comes to the rendezvous, to whirl in a circle of elation or dignified retreat. Habit leads us to overlook the complicity that springs up among the eye that perceives the yellow color of the fruit, the nose entranced by its perfume, and the tongue that savors its ripe flesh, but a feverish germination is at work, and slender streams join into a single torrent. Commotion, muffled agitation, fusion: thought goes to sleep at the feet of the animal self (busy savoring its happiness), where it dreams of huge flowers and birds that swoop and blossom only in the dark night of the body.

My mother had nothing to fear: I had no wish to make the acquaintance of the priest, still less to place my long experience with the liturgy at his service. But when I abandoned my typewriter for an hour or so toward the end of the afternoon, I would stroll to the town square and sit on a bench opposite the church, later, I began going inside the church, where I would remain for quite a while, but off to one side, near the main door. I loved the grandeur of the vaults, which contrasted so strikingly with the flatness of the town. If I had walked up the nave, which was deserted during the week, I would have approached the harmonium, which had no one to play it and so sat over by the pulpit with its cover down, near a pile of prayer stools probably once used by the choristers. I dreamed of raising the cover to glimpse the yellowed smile of the keyboard, and my fingertips itched with longing. Were they – was I – remembering those little pieces I used to play at the seminary, that day in the town church when I heard (too late to slip away) the sound of echoing footsteps and, in counterpoint, the clinking of a bunch of keys that reminded me of Brother Salvador? It was the priest. He almost froze when he spotted me, and the glance he shot

over my shoulder alerted me to the slender silhouette of a girl
moving stealthily toward the door. I was to recognize her several weeks later because of her bleached hair, which hung
down her back all the way to her waist and seemed to float
behind her as she moved.

As for the priest, I cannot forget the impression he made on
me that day, and at our subsequent meetings as well: from a
distance he seemed to possess an uncanny power of attraction,
but if you dared look deep into his eyes, the black irises
reflected only the sadness of the damned.

Most people thought he was around forty years old, but how
could anyone know for certain? Sometimes his complexion was
pasty, his face puffy, and he seemed as beaten down as any
peasant of his generation; later during the same day, an other-
worldly serenity would shine from his pale countenance,
almost lighting up the darkness. When he spoke to you, however, you could sense the strain behind both this heaviness and
this calm. He would come so close that his breath was almost
unbearable; his voice, although powerful, lacked timbre, and
seemed strangely flat. You felt he was about to confide some
terrible secret to you – which he eventually did try to do – and
it was hard to imagine what violence could be lying in ambush
behind his impassive expression, apparently ready to burst out
at any moment, although his gaze might suddenly withdraw into
the depths of the pupil, hesitating between this world and the
other – unless he was retreating so far inside himself that he
could no longer see the person who stood before him.

He held out his hand in what was already an antiquated gesture at the time, and I kissed it, following the rules of etiquette.
He knew who I was, and mentioned the seminary, but some
reflex of common sense kept him from dwelling on the subject.
Knowing of my interest in music, he told me that the instruments of his church would be at my disposition; no one else had
used them for quite a long time. Then we went up to the organ
loft, and there I felt somewhat at a loss: I had only the barest
knowledge of how to work the levers that linked the manual

keyboards, but as for the pedal board, which the organist plays with the tip and heel of the foot – well, my feet just stood there. Besides, I did not care for the organ. With its turgid sound, its muddy groaning and swelling sonorities, it seemed to me like some dying monster that swallows up the music, letting the melody come through only in the lulls.

Telling me that he knew nothing about music, the priest dusted off a few scores that had become stuck together over the years, opened one of them, and placed it on the music rack. Then, as if he had suddenly noticed someone down in the nave, he left me hastily, asking me please to carry on, and would I be good enough to play during Sunday mass; I could still hear his voice when his tubby figure reappeared in the transept, where he stopped and stood motionless, on the alert, looking to the right, to the left...before proceeding slowly, reassured, to the sacristy. I would never have suspected he could scramble down the spiral staircase and scurry the entire length of the nave as quickly as he did.

I returned to practice on the organ every day. Even though I hated that instrument, I was happy to run my fingers over ivory keys again and discover the complex magic of sounds, of voices that I played separately or together, without really knowing what I was doing. I experienced the luxurious self-satisfaction of being an entire orchestra, and countless choirs, and the awesome cataclysms of nature, whirlwinds and tempests that shook the vaults – which did not, in any case, do much for the quiet concentration of the faithful.

One Sunday after mass, when the priest asked me to play more softly, I felt as though I were being forced to renounce the outpourings of my soul, to give up the mountains, the oceans, almost the entire universe.

47

IN THE PAST I HAVE DESIRED THE DEATH OF CERTAIN
people who had in some way wronged me or those I love, and
twice, by chance, I enjoyed the agreeable illusion that I had
some control over reality in that respect. But the man I have
hated more than any other, the notary in Villa del Rosario,
escaped the combined efforts of my will and hatred unharmed.

The petrified young man who stepped straight from the sidewalk into that room with the dirty walls, punctual to the minute
for the appointment obtained for him by the parish priest, had
no way of knowing, of course, that the individual enthroned
(and with what corpulence) in an upholstered armchair –
tufted, here and there, by strands of escaping horsehair – would
prove in the future to be the cause of the most painful episode
of the young man's life.

His hands, clasped upon the pommel of a cane planted
upright between his legs, imparted to it a slight but constant
circular motion. He was impassive, like the models for those
portraits in museums who seem to have waited too long for you
to come see them. Without making the slightest gesture of welcome, he observed me from beneath eyelids at half-mast. He
had the large, violet-edged mouth of a carp sleeping at the bottom of a muddy pond.

He slowly passed his hand over his yellowish-gray hair to
tidy the deeply crimped waves, adjusted his lavallière tie, and
finally spoke, in a voice that was both hollow and falsetto.

Nodding toward someone typing in a corner of the room – on
an ancient Underwood with a rackety sound that would
brighten my days – he told me, in accents of feigned bitterness,

that his clerk was abandoning him for a miserable teller's position in a bank that was about to go under, since its customers were all insolvent debtors, as he knew from experience. The clerk turned toward him, laughing, and held out his hand to me; I shook it feebly, not wanting to displease the boss.

Although certain faces may not actually resemble one another, they have something intangible in common that transcends their real features, awakening the feelings and even that jolt of sensuality inspired in us by the first one in the series, which was perhaps only the sign of a face that will remain forever unknown.

Did Luis's smile, his confidence, risk winning me over? A tic, a twitch in his right eyelid that shot through his smile in a flash, was enough to save me. I did not wish to become friends with anyone in this town, since I felt I was only passing through, and I understood right away that his friendliness would give him a hold over me.

I would inherit his position if I could prove myself worthy of it. Since the notary trusted Luis completely, despite his supposed ingratitude, I was handed over to the clerk for approval. At the time, good calligraphy was more important than skill at typing, because every deed was written in the registers by hand.

I passed the test, thanks to the immediate complicity that had sprung up between Luis and me. On high, or somewhere in the future, the spider of fate had just spun the first long thread of the web that would ensnare me five years later: accused of forgery, I would return to Villa del Rosario in the custody of the police, for a confrontation with an elderly lady who had been the victim of a swindle. With the help of the notary, her heirs had tricked her into selling them her only property, her little house, for a paltry sum.

Aside from the fact that the handwriting of the deed was well and truly mine – hardly sufficient proof since I was the notary's clerk and the register was full of documents in my handwriting – had I not personally taken the register to the lady's home, and had she not signed the bill of sale at my request?

It seemed absolutely vital that I deny this last allegation, as I risked spending at least one year in prison. I remembered the small house at the end of a street on the outskirts of town, where the grassland began; the woman, all in black, sitting in her garden with a rust-colored dog at her feet; I remembered reading the document, trying to pronounce each syllable clearly, and having to shout each word practically at the top of my lungs; I remembered holding the register out to her, and giving her the pen; I remembered how quiet it was. But my lawyer had advised me to forget everything.

All this trouble must have happened during the winter of 1953; I had been living in Buenos Aires for two years, ever since I had turned twenty-one years old.

One morning, in the real estate office where I was still earning my living at the typewriter – while also trying my hand (without success) at selling apartments, or as they said over there, "horizontal property" – I received a call from someone at police headquarters who asked me, quite affably, if I would please come in and see him at my convenience that afternoon.

At the time (which I would so much like to forget), if you wore a raincoat or a tie of an unusual color, or if a lock of hair hung down over your forehead in a flagrant display of eccentricity, you were at the mercy of a corrupt police force that was paid a commission based on the number of people brought in for a simple identity check, which meant you had to spend the night in a jail cell that was often packed solid. So I was not really worried about this phone call, because there was clearly nothing to prevent the police from arresting me where I worked, had it been a serious matter. That is why I did not take the precaution that had become commonplace in those days – warning one's friends and employer – before going off to see the official who had practically apologized for asking me if I would be so good as to stop by his office.

The humble insignificance of this amiable man was written all over his face; his voice was of such a higher rank that it seemed unconnected to his body. If his lips were moving, then his eyes went blank. If he was looking at you, his mouth became a straight line. His affability had been a mere ruse. And I still sometimes believe that if you trust someone, you will persuade him to be trustworthy!

48

WAITING FOR ME WAS A WARRANT FOR MY ARREST, ISSUED by the police in Villa del Rosario through police headquarters in Córdoba, where I was to be transferred shortly. The charge? I would be informed at the proper time. Was I a homosexual? I denied this. When the insignificant man rang a bell, a guard appeared, clicking his heels at attention behind me; he was ordered to take me to number 3. First I was carefully searched: they confiscated what little money I had on me, my tie, belt, and shoelaces.

The courtyard, with its handsome ocher walls, reminded me of the cloister in the Franciscan monastery, and the staircase made me think of the one I had climbed with Brother Salvador. Prodded along by my jailer, I went through a small, hidden door into what looked at first like the set for a prison movie. But this was the real thing. Instead of the deep silence that had greeted my arrival at the monastery, I heard lively shouting and hand-clapping down at the end of the long room, bursts of laughter and mockery, foul language, insults tossed off as if they were compliments. Two guards, slouching against the bars, were taking quite an interest in what was going on in the chalky light of number 3 – a long narrow patio with a ridge roof of frosted glass, lined on one side by cells without doors or bars, and on the other, by a dormitory with arcades that looked like a ruined shopping gallery. There were iron bunk beds, most of them furnished with rusty wire springs that creaked at the slightest movement, when they weren't coming apart; some of them were reinforced by planks. You had to watch out for the dilapidated straw mattresses because they were crawling with vermin: if you shook one out, a reddish shower of bedbugs rained upon the tile floor.

Standing with my back against the bars, not daring to take a step, I was slowly and silently surrounded. They fell upon me abruptly, one pulling me by the collar of my jacket, another dealing me a backhanded blow to the chin in slow motion, a third sniffing and nuzzling at me while a fourth, like a vision of imbecility incarnate, pretended to kiss me with greedy lips and then cackled maniacally.

When they tired of harassing me, they bombarded me with questions: What had I done to earn a place in their company? Since I had no idea myself and could not manage to say a single word, I gave a little shrug, or shook my head to mean no when they ran through the list of possible offenses.

What a treat it was for these seasoned crooks, the arrival in their midst of this bewildered blond fellow, pale with fear, incapable of even a little snatch-and-grab job!

They finally backed off and treated me with mocking hostility. Then I saw a man sitting on a small bench. Everything about him was tidy: he was close-shaven, with neat, smooth hair and a clean shirt, as though dirt could never touch him, no matter where he might be. He was looking at me. Suddenly he put his hand down flat beside him on the bench, signaling me to come sit down. After a moment of hesitation, fearing that his gesture would set off a new round of bullying and uproar, I did go over to sit down, but only on the edge of that bench improvised from two planks and a couple of broken-down braziers. The man remained silent, and he never spoke a word to me during the entire week I spent in number 3.

Now I took a good look at the other prisoners. They were young, for the most part; street riff-raff, probably petty thieves, and not one of them seemed upset at being there. It was as if having a roof over their heads, even a prison roof, were a stroke of luck that sheltered them from even greater misery.

Smiles were exchanged; someone ventured a knowing remark and was quickly hushed, but then I heard a laugh, like a voice cascading down the musical scale. It came from the cell into which I had seen a long train of pink silk disappear when I arrived. Disguising his voice, the occupant asked to meet "the new boy." While the others roared with laughter, the man next to me touched my elbow, and with a vague wink, indicated that I should obey.

Crossing the threshold of the cavern inhabited by the pick-pocket who called himself "La Madelon," one passed from the stagnant air of the patio, thickened by musty smells from the dormitory mixed with the odor of soup, into a spicy atmosphere.

In the seedy half-light, I first made out a baby-face almost as shiny as the ample satin dressing gown draped over an equally ample paunch. Then I noticed two boys sitting on the lower bunk bed next to the wall, playing cards. And raising a dimpled arm with a silken rustle, her dear little hand drooping beneath a weighty cargo of rings, *she* welcomed me with all her fleshy majesty, ordering one of the card players to switch on the bare bulb hanging from the ceiling. Rummaging through an enormous handbag of peccary skin lying on her lap, she pulled out a pair of Harlequin glasses with white frames that she perched, with a sweeping gesture, on her turned-up nose.

Pursing her already tiny mouth, she studied me, leaning her head back against a pillow decorated along the edge with a panel of satin-stitch embroidery of the kind my sisters used to sew; talking to herself, the creature searched her memory for just the right image for the occasion. Was I aware that she was an internationally famous pickpocket? She was respected in prisons all over the continent, to which she assigned stars, continuing to practice her profession only for the pleasure of revisiting choice establishments. And if her stay would be a long one? She would shower gifts on a youngster, who, if he accepted them, would gradually become her servant. And if she tired of his good offices, she was not the slightest bit ungrateful – she would seduce a second one to serve the both of them, and so on. In Cuba, one time, a poor handsome devil had had to take care of…she couldn't remember how many, now. "Cuba," she sighed pensively, snapping open a lacy fan all gleaming with mother-of-pearl; a Caribbean languor had come over her. She could just see the palms, the guava trees…. She fanned herself lazily. Prison was of no interest to her as such. It was a theater in which she recounted her exploits before a willing and definitely captive audience.

When she stirred up the phantoms of her imagination, her voice took on a dreamy tone, but also, at times, a terrible hoarseness, as though she were picking up an old, unfinished argument with some ghost from her past. When she began punctuating her tirade with clacking sound effects from her fan, the laughter of her entourage brought her back to reality, and an expression of extreme gratification spread over her flabby moon-face. Shooting up one eyebrow as sharply peaked as a chalet roof, she sang – or rather, oozed – one of Marlene's favorites: "Falling in Love Again."

How did I react to all her gracious words, to her promised gift of a chocolate bar every day to help make up for the inadequacy of the prison food? I felt even more afraid. No one could ever have guessed how much I felt at the mercy of invisible tormentors. Then she dismissed me with a benevolent gesture that relieved me of the personal obligations normally entailed by the acceptance of her gifts. I was not her type.

As I left La Madelon's lair, I discovered a trait in my nature that occasionally gets the better of me: I find myself turning obsequious through cowardice, without being able to tell if it is my lack of nerve or my contempt for the other person that sends me down to defeat. I was a good audience, and was treated to my daily chocolate bar.

My silent protector strode up and down the patio, either to get some exercise or to work the stiffness out of his limbs. When he passed me, he boldly gave me a long, penetrating look. I sat down on the bench, slumping back against the wall this time, trying hard not to let the tears come to my eyes. The other man soon joined me, and made some small show of doing so, just to make the claim he had on me clear enough to everyone.

At supper time, guards set down in the middle of the patio a dented bucket from which arose nauseous smells that invaded my entire body. I have encountered the same lukewarm stink given off by that greenish-brown stew in the third-class sections of ocean liners, in the sleepy fug of night trains – and my stomach, shrunken and knotted by fear, would have none of it. Hunger? Only a memory.

My "pal," on the other hand, was busy with his soup plate – they were of tin, like the ones in the seminary – and had filled a second one for me, containing a thick liquid in which lurked bones that seemed to have already been gnawed. I rested the plate on my knees; a bitter taste came into my mouth, and I swallowed hard. After the other man had gulped down his portion, he took back mine, and that he ate calmly, with an aloof air.

Had he taken me under his wing to obtain the double ration? He made me eat some bread, without bothering to look at me.

At lights out, I took an upper bunk at the far end of the dormitory. The beds nearby seemed empty. A dim light seeped in from the patio. There were jokes, obscenities, laughter, farts, the groaning of rusty iron, then snores that were quickly joined by others, a tidal wave of slumber crashing through my insomnia. I was living a waking nightmare. Then someone climbed onto my bed, with professional stealth, and began by stretching out on top of me to pin me down. Just when I was being turned over onto my side – to give in would have made things worse for me, and perhaps it was a trap – my unknown visitor sprang back off the bed as if he had been bitten by a viper. Someone had grabbed him by the neck, pulled him off the bed, and let him fall; then I heard muffled noises, panting, and the sound of a head being slammed against the wall.

Some sleepers turned over, exchanging dreams, perhaps, or maybe each man's dream began to go astray. Against the pale light from the patio, I saw a hunched shadow scuttle off, holding its jaw in one hand. There was the abrupt squeaking of a bed; another shadow stood up and came to sit on the bunk beneath mine. I knew that someone was there, that all I had to do to touch him was let my arm hang down; I would have so loved to do it, but I did not dare, and I could not even hear his breathing. After a while, I don't know how long, the shadow stood up, and I thought I recognized the firm step of my taciturn protector as he stole quietly away.

The next day, when they doled out some chicory-flavored dishwater, I had no trouble identifying my visitor of the previous night from his swollen lip and cheek. He was handsome. When my mysterious friend offered him a cigarette, the injured man glared at him bitterly, but his longing won out, and after a moment's hesitation, he accepted the cigarette. Blows or gifts, one had to accept everything from him. And that is how I think of the monastery or prison when I sometimes dream of ending my days there, but alas – as far as prison is concerned, my luck would no longer be as good.

Why did the silent man behave that way toward me? What reasons could he have had?

Four days after I was locked up, I had still had no news from outside. Finally my friends discovered where I was, and for the rest of my stay in the thieves' ward, I vied with La Madelon in the eager distribution of provisions. It took three days for the lawyer who had been called to my rescue, and who found out why I had been arrested, to obtain my release, if not from the police station, at least from number 3. I was moved to an office.

At the moment of my transfer, I would have liked to shake the hand of the silent man, to thank him, but everything about him discouraged such behavior and stymied this impulse, which remained completely bottled up within me, for I had not been able to betray this feeling of gratitude – and yes, attraction – that I felt toward him, either by the slightest gesture or by anything I was conscious of expressing with my eyes.

Perhaps it was all in my head and not at all in his, and perhaps he had protected me as a kind of duty, or to make up for some former loneliness, suffered without a single word of compassion from anyone else.

I lived for four days completely alone, shut up in a huge office that rather resembled both a courtroom and the choir of a cathedral, having dark woodwork, a long bench with a high back, and a table that ran all the way around the room, leaving a gap only at the doorway. The grandeur of this piece of furniture, which sat on a low dais that seemed like a pedestal, evoked both a judge's tribunal and a preacher's pulpit.

Twice a day I was escorted to the toilet, and around noon, after the guard had inspected them, I was given the lunch box and basket of fruit my friends had brought. Later I learned that they had also sent me some books, none of which I received. One of the slogans of that time – "Shoes, yes! Books, no!" – enjoyed quite a vogue in political demonstrations, which were the only kind we had. I no longer dared budge from the corner where I was supposed to remain seated, hemmed in on both sides by the long table. At night I stretched out on the bench, which was slightly worn along the middle of the seat and had a rounded edge, pleasant to the touch.

I was taken by bus to Córdoba, flanked by two policemen who told me straight out that they were not going to make me wear handcuffs, but that if I tried to escape during one of the stops along the way, they would shoot me down like a rabbit.

We traveled across that endless plain from eight in the morning until eight at night. I was put in the infirmary at the police station; my sister Cecilia had obtained this preferential treatment for me. I remember how cool the sheets felt. In front of the staff, I had to feign illness, which I did with such imaginative skill that my arms and legs seemed to obey me only with great effort, because everything inside me was slipping toward that insensibility that attracts and lies in wait for me, the indifference that forms the bedrock of my soul and on which I would so often like to stretch out, except that something always manages to recall me to the light of day. I knew I was innocent, but I also knew that I would not have the strength to fight back if I were found guilty. Just another prisoner in the eyes of others, in my own I was a prisoner locked out of the world. And the one thing that troubled me, lost in this lethargy, was the thought of my parents and their shame.

In Villa del Rosario, before the police-court magistrate, I was placed in a lineup of six young men obviously chosen for their height and age, the only points of similarity between them and myself as the accused. And soon the elderly lady appeared, pushed along in a wheelchair by a bailiff. Had they put me in the middle of the line to draw her attention to me?

Gripping the armrests with hands that were nothing but jutting bones and bluish veins, the old lady was wheeled to a stop before the first of the youths on my left. Bent nearly double with age, she stuck a frail tortoise neck out from between her shoulders, and as she raised her little head, first one eye, all milky, was revealed beneath an almost transparent eyelid, and then the other, jet black, widening with a piercing look as it fixed on the suspect. My fear grew as she spent no more than a few seconds in front of any of the others; didn't this prove that she remembered clearly what the criminal had looked like? When it was my turn, however, she did not pay any more attention to me than she had to the rest, and I felt a huge surge of relief. Then she turned her head, slowly, to look at me over her shoulder, and wheeling her chair back, inch by inch, keeping her eyes fixed upon me, as though she were searching for a memory that would not come to her, she came toward me. I was lost. With a look of deep regret, she feebly shook her head, back and forth: I was not the guilty one.

Perhaps she had recognized me; perhaps she knew only too well who was really responsible for her misfortune and had gone along with the pretense of this confrontation for fear of incurring the wrath of her heirs – and especially of the town's leading citizens, with whom they had many old ties. Unless she had suddenly understood everything only at the instant she recognized me.

There are moments that no amount of words can fully express; afterward, a person may no longer understand how he ever lived through them, and like a memory projected into the future, a threat will hang over all the rest of his days, perhaps even bringing his life, in a way, to a halt.

49

NOW THAT I WAS WORKING IN THE NOTARY'S OFFICE and earning, not my living, but enough to set my parents' minds at ease – and give them, as well, increased prestige among our neighbors and the townspeople – I had no qualms about going out in the evening after dinner. I liked to walk through the deserted town in those hours when the only footsteps are your own, and sometimes, as you pass by, you hear the sound of dishes being washed.

Convinced that a poet can and must remain alone with his thoughts, I walked as an outsider, a citizen of a world I was anxious to discover, trying out metaphors of the moon, or sleep, convinced that I would find some that had never been used before, certain that each successful image, each duly accomplished action, was an escape from dull reality.

I never went beyond the border marked by the last streetlight: on my side, the humble geometry of straight lines, a network binding the town together; on the outside, the cessation of time, its dissolution in emptiness, its return to a kind of perceptible nothingness – the immense sweep of the plain.

I shunned the center of town to avoid the only bar that stayed open until midnight, fearing that someone might recognize and hail me; I skirted the main square, stopping at the intersections of the streets that led over to the park, along which drifted the bitter fragrance of eucalyptus. In reality, these solitary walks only made me laughably proud of being different, better than everyone else. I dreamed of other places, dreamed of being there, and walked along unfamiliar streets. And I made myself ridiculous in my own eyes by strolling at a measured pace when deep inside I was running, frantic with longing, sick of bumping into shadows in the labyrinth of my imagination, and at the end of my wild galloping, as before, I found only the mirage of a horizon I now carried inside myself, but could never quite reach.

There were so many stars in the sky over there! And no one at my side to pretend to count them. And so, one evening when I spied the gleam of a cigarette in the darkness after walking to the edge of town, I did not let myself feel afraid or turn back toward home. The dim figure was coming in my direction, and, who knows, perhaps to meet me. When he drew near the streetlight that stood between us, its feeble glow was not enough to illuminate more than his face: it was the priest, and his features reminded me of those weathered bones I used to find at the farm when I went looking in the rough grass for eggs the stubborn hens had hidden there. He stifled a cry when he saw me, but recovered his composure, and, switching his cigarette over to his left hand, he automatically held out the right one for the baisemain; realizing how strange that seemed under the circumstances, he pulled his hand back as I bent to kiss it. At that hour, in that place, we were both shady characters. He made a belated attempt at a smile, which froze on his lips for a few seconds. He, too, had been walking in a world of his own, God knows where, and although meeting me so suddenly had brought him back to earth, he had not yet fully adjusted to the change. His face, which took on a phosphorescent glow whenever he took a drag on his cigarette, was that of a dethroned king on the stage: sad eyes peering from between swollen lids, and a body past caring about danger, at ease in its defeat. He took me by the elbow and we walked a long while, chatting – rather awkwardly – about nothing in particular. Suddenly, as I halted facing the street that led straight to the presbytery, he seemed to shudder, and looked at me, as if awakening from some nightmare we had dreamed together. Lighting another cigarette, he turned on his heel, placing a hand on my shoulder to bring me along with him, and we walked back the way we had come. He asked me to listen to him, telling me that I would understand later.

The night was so quiet all around us and we walked so close together that I seemed to hear, beneath the harsh rustle of his clerical garb, the secret sounds of his body. The two tips of his hob-nailed shoes clacked along the pavement like high heels. Did I glance down at his feet? He remarked ruefully that quiet shoes would make him seem suspicious.

We walked on without another word, going deeper into the darkness until we had reached the edge of town again, where there was no difference between the sidewalk of beaten earth and the street. The metallic clicking that had relieved the silence then ceased; I felt that a host of phantoms seethed beneath his lethargy, ready to pour out in a flood of words that finally came, leaving him gasping painfully every time he began talking again after some momentary uncertainty or reticence. Even though he was speaking to me, he seemed to belong all the more to the night, the houses, the solitary street-lamp, the ember of the cigarette he waved in front of him, and his remorse.

I gathered that he had managed to attain a kind of anonymity, an intimate anonymity in the very depths of his soul, where one is no longer anyone at all, and now, after all this time, he was throwing off this forgetfulness of self and breaking his own rule: that he should lock away everything that had tormented him for as long as he could remember.

Would I believe it? Almost immediately after his ordination, he had been offered one of the most sought-after parishes in the capital, but the bishop had granted his wish to live among the poor, in those villages lost in the immensity of a country where the church was in decline. There were times when the priest curtailed his eloquence, telling something in only a few words, and these abridgements gave his story an allegorical quality; at other times his outbursts came close to despair. In his simplicity he had thought to extinguish his own private hell, to cast off all temptation by fleeing the capital – for if I did not already know it, I would soon learn that every body is a hell, a cave of feverish desires, a pit thirsting after pleasures, a darkness into which, in our sleep, the light of God's glory once shone, but without leaving a single trace behind. The flesh cried out so strongly in solitude, and with my return to Villa del Rosario, his torment had returned as well. Yes, as soon as I had arrived, he had known he was caught again: an ex-seminarist would bring about his downfall, unmasking him. And now, would there not inevitably follow catastrophes that I had not foreseen?

When I forced myself to ask him a question, in an effort to channel this disorderly harangue in some coherent direction, he refused to listen to me and fell silent. Occasionally a sentence might emerge from his muttering – "Nakedness, that is what separates us from the animals" – and then dissolve into a scattering of words: "To undress, be naked, nudity, Eden...." He urged me abruptly to leave town as quickly as possible. I had been right to quit the seminary, as I was, like him – wasn't that so? – both a religious and an impious man, an ungodly man searching for God.... It was not so much God we needed, but forgiveness.

His pathetic tone and his observations on human nature, which he qualified, with a sigh, as "sempiternal," were not going over well, and he knew it. He stopped, turning his face away to study the backdrop of the night sky, looking for something lost and secret.

In a more solemn voice, rather flat and monotonous, he wondered: Did he dare tell me about the sacrifice of a child – an innocent, simpleminded child – committed by the boys in the orphanage where he had grown up?

I remember the sinuous evolution of the tale, and that it was stuffed with realistic details designed to convince a skeptical listener. The child in question loved to listen to his comrades tell him of the life of Christ; his favorite episodes were the wedding at Cana, the miracle of the loaves and fishes, and Calvary. I no longer remember if the priest claimed the child desired, or felt called, to be crucified, or if the crucifixion was plotted and carried out entirely by others. The way he described it to me, the child was smiling, lashed to the cross. Each day, each minute, each encounter may bequeath to us an undying nightmare.

His last words? The storyteller whispered, "I was the one who brought the nails." His last gesture? He took my hand between his thumb and forefinger, and turning the palm toward himself, lifted it up before his face as he mumbled words of absolution.

Even though I could not remember when or where, I was sure I had heard some version of this story before.

I stood there with my hand in the air, watching him disappear into the night, and since I was already in position, I gave absolution to the stars.

Shortly afterward, I noticed something that changed my interpretation of what happened that night. Of course, the endless walking, the fragmented, allusive confession were signs of a disturbed mind, but the harshness of this story that provided evidence of a crime rather than of madness was a clumsy tactic: by admitting responsibility for an outrageous action, he was only trying to cover up his real concern, his interest in pubescent children, which would not escape malicious notice.

I understood this on the afternoon when Luis, the former clerk, stopped by with some friends at the notary's office to see how I was getting on. He introduced me to the young woman with whom he was holding hands, but since he was ignoring the younger girl with them, I nodded to her, just to be nice. And then I recognized her bleached hair: it was the girl I had glimpsed in the church, when the sunlight had revealed her slipping away from the priest toward the door. With the self-conscious expression of a strutting child, she glanced at me furtively, and an evil smile crept over her lips.

Since spring had come early, with exuberant splendor, we

decided to have a picnic down by the river on Sunday. And if the weather turned even warmer, we would have to remember to bring bathing suits!

We burst out laughing for no reason, and just as suddenly lapsed into an awkward silence.

50

THE MILD MORNING AIR HAD WARMED UP BY THE time Luis and I made our way through the ash-gray thorn bushes dotting the half-mile-wide stretch of land between the river and the edge of town. We were looking for the previous year's path, which was largely overgrown. We carried wicker baskets full of provisions; the sisters walked behind us, singing softly: Luis's fiancée, Isabel, sang in a high-pitched voice, and the younger girl in a lower tone. For three days I had been thinking of her in my imagination as "the Girl with the Flaxen Hair" in memory of the still-recent past when I used to play a little Debussy. The four of us plunged onward through the bushes; other people were heading for the river, too, and we could see their heads and hats bobbing along here and there over the brush.

Fate takes care not to let us know too much about what is in store for us, and at the time, I did not realize the full significance of what happened that afternoon; other memories of other Sundays have clustered around that one, so that they all fuse into a single day. We pay no attention to certain events, and as the years go by, we live our lives without understanding why we are swept by storms of hatred or compassion, shaken by sudden arousals of the flesh. We have moved so far away from any thought of what is in the past that when we remember, all at once, we sink to the bottom of our own hearts. Familiar with the absurd way memories have of flooding back to us, we ascribe to the past the momentary quality of a scene from a play, or, at the most, the fixity of a painting, unaware that it can become a force, an element provoking actions, attitudes, behaviors, undertakings that themselves become strata of memory.

The four of us leave the field of thorn bushes with their clinging, scratchy branches, and when we look up, for a few seconds there is nothing beneath the midday sun but us, stillness, and the endlessly rippling water. And on the opposite shore, a stand of poplars, like important personages observing the arrival of some people arguing over who may claim the shade of a few weeping willows. Voices reach us, brief cries, laughter – distant, and yet intimate. Irma, "the Girl with the Flaxen Hair," rushes off toward the iron bridge, and we fall in behind her. She knows of a ford beneath the bridge itself, and off she skips, happily zigzagging from stone to stone. We have barely begun to follow her across when she is already leaning against the last piling, hands behind her back, as though she has been waiting for us for a long time. She dips her toe into the water, and, as she tosses her hair, I think of horses twitching at the irritation of a wasp, and of Pouliche standing stolidly, oblivious to the swishing of her own tail.

A sound like a dense humming puzzles us, for the sky is too blue for thunder, but gradually a rhythm emerges from the approaching tumult, giving it consistency, and Irma shouts, "The train, the train, the freight train!" as she runs through an entire repertoire of histrionics denoting childish excitement. I remember thinking, beneath the bridge rumbling from the onslaught of the train, that she was hiding her breasts to try to look like a little girl, while Isabel's whole physical being was expressed in the exuberance of her ample bust.

We leave the shelter of the bridge, our bodies still shaking with the cadence of the wheels as the train heads into the distance, tossing off ragged clouds of steam and whistling repeatedly, uselessly, chugging across that great plain toward the place, so far away, where I was born.

Since all the willows have already been snapped up by families early in the day, Irma chooses a flat rock, where we sit down. We open the picnic hampers, drink some orangeade, and a kind of uneasiness overtakes us. Words are spoken; sentences drift off into silence; absently, we watch the water bumping into little boulders, churning through narrows, idling in eddies. Then Isabel solemnly spreads out a tablecloth and each of us sits down on one of its corners.

There is no awkwardness among us now, and we take inventory of the other picnickers. Tired of being scolded by the grown-ups whom they constantly menace with their clumsy ball playing, some boys lounge almost naked in the dirt, resigned to watching the game being played out overhead between the wind and the clouds, and perhaps they feel the strange impulse to stretch out their hands and stop the clouds in their course, questioning, as I do, the reality of this time and place.

Bathers crouch in the water, and, not knowing how to swim, they cling to clumps of weeds growing on the river bank. Men with rounded bellies and women with large rumps sit fully clothed on the grass, where they take off their shoes and gaze blissfully at their gently wiggling toes.

And these people advancing at a ceremonial pace in the distance, small silhouettes against the light, grouped around a figure whose gestures have the stamp of authority – who are they? Why, the priest and his flock!

As she announces the news, Irma undresses, and straightening up again in a clinging red bathing suit, she holds her head high, thrusting out her little breasts in a pose that jars with her candid expression. Fresh-faced, with such a rosy complexion, she seems the very picture of innocence, but suddenly there is so much wounded longing in her eyes, and I know how she feels.

She takes a running leap into the water, splashing us all; when she turns away from the shore and lets the current carry her along, I notice, in the middle of her back, slightly to the right, a swelling beneath the tip of the shoulder blade – a brutal discovery that immediately erases all thought of an angel taking flight: Irma has a hump. She is hunchbacked.

Venturing beyond a little archipelago of jagged rocks, she drifts along, motionless, gazing up at the sky, floating farther away, still farther, until she disappears around a bend, whereupon she immediately begins pretending, with great screams, that she is drowning. Without really believing her act, Luis and I dash into the water. He pulls ahead of me; I can see his arms, and sometimes his back; his broad shoulders and slim waist form the points of a triangle of rippling muscle. Luis has what would be called an ideal physique, while I would be ashamed to show myself out of the water, because my body is lithe, but thin, and my arms look like sticks. Without even thinking about it, I avoid the people in the passages between the rocks, keeping my body out of sight.

I can hear Irma giggling; at times she sputters into laughter, or moans, or gasps out inarticulate words and mewing sounds. And my strength is about to give out when I see Luis swimming back up the river with one arm, dragging Irma behind him by her hair. As they go by, she notices me and kicks her legs stiffly, twisting and writhing her trunk like a fish trying to cast off a hook. I grab her ankles, swimming along in their wake; as soon as he can touch bottom, Luis lets go, and in a flash she grips my face between her thighs, just for a second, and then her body slides along mine.

Beneath the fabric of the wet bathing suit, her nipples show clearly on their gently curving mounds, just at the surface of the water, like the severed breasts of a martyred saint carried on a platter of liquid silver. We look at each other, chatting foolishly, perhaps, and although we are separated by a suitable distance, our legs are touching lightly, then lingeringly, and gradually they become entwined, entangled, and I find my way to little places I have never reached before, in a fluid, ardent sweetness, a downy softness where flowers bloom and are swept away by the racing waters.

She is the one who began the game and who now ends it abruptly. Off she races to our rock; she climbs to the top where, throwing open her arms, as though she had won a great victory, she seems to provide the landscape with a focal point: everything converges on her – the curious stares of those lined up along the banks who have been eagerly watching the incident and are registering their disappointment; the willow branches trailing in the water; the meandering perspective of the river sketched by the line of poplars. And with a mixture of satisfaction, nervous confusion, and renewed respectability in his own eyes (because my being seen with Irma helps shield him from suspicion), the priest calls out in a fluting voice, like an infant awakening to the world and all its wonders, that we should thank Heaven for the splendor of this springtime, and for the river, which is a true blessing. And glancing around to catch the attention of those nearby, he reminds his audience of the distant source of these waters, high in the Sierra de Córdoba.

I feel almost dizzy, hearing those words explode in my head, and as I repeat them to myself I am no longer where I am: I am in the same river, but it is six years earlier, during my first vacation as a seminarist, when, on the bank of this very river, the youth whose name I would eventually forget refused my plea that we abandon the religious life and live together.

We never swim in the same river twice? No river ever welcomes the same swimmer again. Time is nothing like a single line along which we advance like an acrobat on a tightrope: each life has several lines, and if one of them leads to an impasse, we follow another, parallel or diverging, that we have spied in the meantime. Each second belongs in part both to the past and to the future, where perplexing crossroads await us, one after the other. We are creatures of mystery: we think we are moving forward, stepping into the future, and all the while time carries us toward the past, bequeathing us its horrors and its marvels – memory, the shifting, changeable thing that makes us what we are.

The sun draws out its arc; the tubby priest's slender shadow reaches our rock and climbs upon it. Irma makes a point of sticking out her foot to touch this dark, fluid patch – and the priest whips back his head as though he has been speared by the Devil himself. Then he forces out a laugh and waves playfully as he continues on his way, but his bewildered, even dreamy gaze gives the lie to this performance, and when he turns around to call out a last good-bye, the look he gives Irma will always remain the most despairing expression I have ever seen on a human face.

He almost bumps into an ice-cream vendor, whose cart is promptly surrounded by a throng of eager children; the juxtaposition of their clamoring for ice-cream cones and the billowing cassock that seems so out of place in these surroundings revives the memory of my first visit to the cemetery in Villa del Rosario, which lies only a few hundred meters away, beyond the viaduct, where the river narrows. Before me once again is La Pinotta, so proud and regal in defeat, and the taste of lemon sherbet is in my mouth.

We have eaten and watched as others folded up their tablecloths and blankets along the river bank; women have slipped shawls around their shoulders, and men have clapped their hats firmly on their heads. They are gone, dazed, it seems, by the end of this peaceful, sleepy, perhaps even happy day. The young people taunt and jostle one another, pretending to wrestle, but their horseplay is half-hearted.

Now the sun is sinking behind the poplars, sending its rays darting along the ground and leaving a sudden chill in the air, but we stay on our rock like castaways marooned on an island. Sparrows swoop overhead, land on a branch, fly off again at random, wheel about, and flock back to their perch. Luis strokes Isabel's hand; Irma tosses a pebble at them, which I proudly catch on the fly.

The river picks the immense rose of the sunset, and swarms of flitting shadows blur the surface of the water.

We can still hear people calling and someone shouting threats, but then the squawking dies down; after a few last sounds, a vague feeling of the end of the world settles in, the way it does after love making.

Luis rises, and before he has stood all the way up, the rest of us are on our feet. By the time we reach the edge of town, after wending our way through the thorn bushes, the darkening blue of the sky has turned to night. And everything – the streets along which we pass, the houses where so many people live, love, hope, hate, and despair – seems part of the same whole, encompassing the barking of a dog, the clatter of closing shutters, the dancing glow of a cigarette, and the four of us trudging in the middle of a dusty road – or, rather, the three of us, Isabel, Luis, and I, since Irma has gone tripping on ahead out of sight, probably so that she can jump out at us as we go by.

How about going to a movie after dinner?

51

IN THOSE DAYS, WHEN THE LIGHTS WENT DOWN IN A movie theater and the white screen lit up in a silvery rain of needles, when the buzzing of the audience gave way to the fanfare introducing the searchlights of Twentieth Century Fox or Columbia's goddess holding aloft her torch, I would feel released from everyday reality, and slumped down in my seat, with my solitude reinforced by the presence of so many others around me, I would forget even my own body, which spoke to me only in the quickening of my pulse, the beating of a heart greedy for excitement.

Being there with friends that evening had disturbed the sense of reverent expectation that always came over me on such occasions. Perplexed first of all by our taking seats in the last row (Isabel paid attention only to Luis and seemed to accept her sister's sly tactics and exaggeratedly childish behavior without question), I was equally surprised to find myself sitting between Irma and Luis, whose fiancée sat on his other side.

Absolutely the only thing I can remember about this film was being suddenly distracted from it when Irma's hair brushed against my cheek. Neither can I say if I was aware at the time of the series of casual contacts and little bumps with which she sounded me out, or if I realized only in hindsight how carefully she had made her moves. She had let her hand hang down from the armrest a few times so that her fingertips grazed my thigh, but it was not until her hand settled itself firmly there that I understood how recklessly I had behaved during our swim in the river. Soon I was quivering at the warmth of her palm; her fingers squeezed me for a moment before her hand began gliding slowly, softly, rhythmically, up and down my thigh, and then she gripped me hard.

I have never met anyone more skilled in the art of undoing buttons using – and with what perseverance – the little finger, which sported a long nail like the ones seamstresses grow to lift out basting stitches. She could clearly sense where pleasure might eagerly be awakened, and how boldly she aroused and toyed with this sensual delight without ever – how did she manage? – allowing it to climax!

There was one moment, shortly before the film ended, when Luis's leg touched mine, probably by accident, and then pushed strongly against it; the four of us sat there as though welded into one formless entity by a unique current, on the verge of crossing a last frontier, when we were startled to see the words THE END on the screen. The house lights went up, returning us to ourselves, the reality of our surroundings, the routine of idle conversation, the pretense of respectability, and our own self-conscious reserve.

The house where Isabel and Irma lived was in the southern section of town, on the last street with public lighting – a few bulbs scattered along a cable stretching between two poles. I remember the house as a kind of theatrical backdrop about to be whisked up into the flies, leaving an empty stage to the night, an impression reinforced by the two empty lots on either side of it. I never went inside their house, either through the main door, which probably opened onto the usual front hall, or through either of the two doors that flanked it, creating a modest effect of symmetry. The thickness of the walls and the width of the doorways allowed two people to shelter there quite cozily.

As soon as we turned into the street where they lived, Isabel told us to talk only in whispers, and we tried to stifle our laughter. Did I ever really believe that these parents existed, or that they were such light sleepers?

That evening after the movie, we separated into couples without hesitation, as if by long habit, to stand in separate doorways; once we were ensconced there, like statues in their niches, Irma pulled a slingshot from her shoulder-purse and snapped a pebble at the bulb whitening the facade with its pale light. A faint crunch plunged us into darkness. And now this gawky adolescent boy who had once been so precociously devoted to sensual pleasure felt he had to take on Irma: I wrapped one arm around her waist, the other about her shoulders, and in my excitement, beneath the flowing mass of her hair, my hand closed over her hump. She wriggled free like a viper, pushed me away with a punch in the chest, yanked me back by my tie and drew me close again, but without letting me kiss her on the mouth. That was for lovers, she warned me scornfully, sneaking a glance at the other door, where a compact, two-headed shadow reeled in the darkness the way dancers twirl to the music of a waltz. I had no claim on Irma who broke the rules at her own risk. Actually, during the course of those few nights when Irma drew me into that doorway after her, I decided that her happiness consisted, for the most part, in bringing happiness to the body of her partner, and that she satisfied this unusually solitary hunger with such tenacity so that nothing would linger between them afterward. Where her own pleasure was concerned, no matter how licentious she was by nature, she rebuffed and ignored all my initiatives, so that I finally had to admit that I was wasting my efforts, while she herself preferred to remain unsatisfied.

Yet if she had ever shown the slightest inclination, during her devoted and expert attentions, I would have – in spite of my inexperience – brought to a climax the shuddering longings so keenly evident when she sat astride my raised knee with her hands on my shoulders, squeezing my leg between her thighs. She was always quick to reject my advances, however, and so I can recall no image of Irma satisfied in turn, her face no longer disfigured by desire but calm once more, with that candid expression she always wore in public.

One may take countless steps in raising oneself or another to the heights of bliss, and, with caress after caress, Irma knew how to take me higher and farther, but it was useless to seek in her eyes the look that adolescence has always hoped to find ever since the world began. Did I feel any remorse at how I treated her?

Soon I broke off our relationship, for fear of becoming too involved; something inside me kept my eyes trained on a future in which I saw myself reaching the most inaccessible shores.

Remorse would break through this icy crust only a good twenty years later, during my only trip home; I had gone back for a family reunion, and we had reached that moment when the evocation of times shared begins to falter, and each person tries to conjure up an extra memory or anecdote connected to this common past, in the hope of somehow keeping the parade of phantoms marching along.

I remember my mother leaving the room on the pretext of some household matter when my father, a man quite proud of his deeply ingrained atheism, launched into a sardonic evocation of the priest in Villa del Rosario, who had been denounced to his bishop – too late, in my father's opinion – by the women of the parish themselves, the sanctimonious souls behind whom he had hidden his taste for girls. And my little girlfriend – did I remember her? Could I imagine her serving at mass? He had never seen her at church, of course, but others had told him about this. He had passed her occasionally in the street; she had begun by cutting her hair, and overnight – would you believe it? – she had looked older. Having thus unveiled her deformity, she turned it to her advantage through a simple scheme: Sunday, after mass, those ignorant Creoles would troop through the sacristy and pay to touch her hump, giving a dozen eggs, for example, or a chicken for a whole family, and some people paid her money.

As we sat down at the table, my father questioned me about the origin of such a superstition, but I could think of nothing to say. And as usual, I saw my mother smiling – in this case, at my embarrassment – with her hands clasped in her lap, as though she knew.... In that silent smile I see the mark of a mind enlightened by wisdom, sustained by deep conviction in the face of the unknowable. Whenever I manage to calm down after losing my temper, I tell myself that she is the one influencing me, holding me back. Without realizing it, a man often speaks his mother's language.

Although dreams are not important to me, I suspect that when I fell asleep that night, it was a desire to keep from feeling guilty about Irma that made me dream of her, dressed all in ivory, while I lavished attention on her, and silence, and dazzling whiteness.

In any case, after she had been released by my father from wherever forgotten memories are kept, Irma would reappear now and then, like a tutelary demon, embodying the primitive innocence that animates insects. I will always remember the desperation in her eyes whenever she tried to subdue me simply with a look. And the moist sweetness that followed.

52

SEVEN MONTHS AFTER I MOVED IN WITH MY PARENTS, I left Villa del Rosario with the heartfelt but foolish conviction that I would never set foot there again. I would never see its streets of beaten earth anymore, or the peeling walls of the notary's office, or the notary himself (and when I was brought back to the town under armed guard, I would feel all the repulsiveness of his sickeningly effusive farewell to me), or the priest, that tormented soul, or Irma, who was already lost, and I would never again listen to my own footsteps as I wandered there at night.

Aside from the short jaunt from Moreno to Buenos Aires, this was the first time I had traveled on a train since my departure from the farm when I was still a child, and it was a rather long trip. I seem to remember the way I gradually relaxed, leaning against the back of the banquette, which was made of thin wooden slats, like the benches one used to see in public parks. I had found it hard to believe that a simple country train could hurtle so swiftly along the rails. As the landscape streamed by, I turned my back on everything I was leaving behind. My nightmare was over; the November air sparkled, the wind whistled against the window, and I felt safe. Whenever the train stopped, there were voices, shouted orders, laughter, and the grinding screech of cars being shifted to other tracks; then bells would clang, the rhythmic chug of the wheels would begin again, and soon we were speeding along so fast that the sunshine invested things with a lightness that made every contour diaphanous, and dissolved colors into a mist that vanished in a twinkle.

In Córdoba, I would not have my own room in Cecilia's apartment, which had only two, but a corner behind the same screen of pink gingham, now faded, that had once stood next to my camp bed. Since I had never had the pleasure of living in a room of my own, I felt happy; they say that were the slave not to know he had a master, he would enjoy complete freedom. Happiness kept me awake late into the night, so the morning was well advanced before I awoke to women's laughter and the clatter of a sewing machine. My sister's dressmaking shop was also located within the twenty square meters that served as a dining room in the evening and a bedroom at night, once the table had been cleared away.

Of the three women who worked there, I remember only Maria the Turk; she fluttered her eyelashes like a starlet, manipulated her boyfriends as though they were chessmen, and brought me toasty little balls of cracked wheat stuffed with forcemeat and onion prepared by her mother, a woman I remember as a kind of Arab reincarnation of La Pinotta, swathed in black clothes gone green with wear, sitting on a very low chair in the middle of her patio, poking at the fire with one hand and holding the huge black cast-iron frying pan with the other. She knew the names of things only in her native language from across the seas (Syria or Lebanon?), from the land she had left to follow – like so many others – a man who was off to conquer America, no less, armed only with the desperation and audacity bred by poverty, weapons that sometimes prove to be powerful indeed. He had wound up as the "Turk" on the corner, whose grocery store also stocked merchandise for housewives and schoolchildren, mechanics and seamstresses. A man of the bazaar, the souk, a forerunner of the department store in the towns and villages of the plain – and his wife had been swallowed up by the hush of the little room behind the shop and the tiny courtyard, where she spent her days alone with her memories, unconsciously passing on to us, along with her knowledge of cooking, just a taste, but a vital one, of their culture. That was Maria the Turk's mother (or some other woman – there were so many others): without a life of her own, her sole horizon the facade of the house across the street, behind which death was waiting, and when death finally came for her, it would speak in a foreign tongue.

The "workshop," which was below street level, seemed to me like a basement on that first morning. When I had stayed there before, I had been the perfect height to peek out the low window set at the level of the sidewalk, and I had loved to watch the legs of passersby and try to imagine what the rest of the person would be like, judging by what I could see from the knees down: shoes, socks or stockings, pant legs with or without cuffs, a narrow or full, swirling skirt. Now, I had to kneel down to get a look at the sidewalk across the street.

The passing years would not erase that detail, doubtless because I was conscious not only of my greater height but also of something that concerned the country, the nation, and, in the minds of some people, the fatherland – a situation that would grow increasingly serious, until it reached a state of meticulous and thorough horror, like a spreading, thickening fog, or an epidemic that, without being fatal, would prove to be highly contagious and impossible to eradicate: suddenly there was the sound of marching in the street, and goose-stepping boots, stamping ferociously, appeared framed in the sunny window.

Then everyone in the workshop paused, but without making a show of it: the sewing machine stopped, needles hung poised in the air as ears pricked up, and you would have thought my sister and the other women were steeled to face some grave event. Not one voice, not even a command or any cheers rang out as the parade went by, and the silence that greeted all this tramping crept into the room while we looked at one another and stared up at the shadows moving jerkily across the ceiling. We felt threatened, and even more so when we realized what Maria the Turk, wide-eyed with apprehension, had already noticed: one of the seamstresses was still bent over her embroidery hoop, and she was even humming. We could hear the pounding noise fading into the distance when Cecilia, with a half-smile that was meant to be reassuring, informed me in a tired voice, "Peronistas."

I come, I know this only too well, from a class lower than the masses, and I knew that the people of the country where I was born resented me, as though I had been above them. I do not know how and when I learned this, but I had been convinced of it for a long time. From then on I would feel as though I were in danger, and my joy at finding myself in a real city at last had vanished. But the laughter of Maria the Turk bubbled up like a fountain, and I took heart once more. Washed, shaved, dressed with as much care as I could manage, I smiled at myself in the mirror to banish all traces of the night and brighten up my day.

I stepped out the front door: the city belonged to me.

On all sides, things called out to me, demanding my attention: a face, a walk, a yellow streetcar bouncing happily along, shop windows, and whenever a little park provided a respite from this industrious tumult, the city's bustle made a solemn oasis of these squares planted with trees and blooming rosebushes. Amid all this coming and going, turning right and left, I lost my way, drawn on by whatever caught my eye. A giant kaleidoscope showered me with images while keeping many others hidden away: the semidarkness glittering with coppery highlights in a hotel vestibule, a woman's gloved hand holding out a tip, a drunk's big puffy strawberry of a face with its two black pinholes for eyes, the bouquets of flowers in a florist's window – I found these sights fascinating. I possessed nothing, but my longing for these things was eased by the knowledge that the world was spread out before my eyes, so close that I could touch it. Clods of earth no longer crumbled beneath my footsteps. I walked by the wall of the monastery, wondering if I should go see Brother Salvador, but I quickly shrugged off the idea – or perhaps it was the idea that shrugged me off. I had had enough of the past.

Then the sun began to sink in the sky; the din of traffic seemed to die down, and the idea that quite early the next day I was to take an examination in the offices of an aircraft manufacturer filled me with trepidation. All my joyful reveries came crashing down about my ears, leaving me plunged in anxiety. I needed my sister and the gay laughter of Maria the Turk. There is always something silly about feeling happy.

53

WHAT KEPT ME GOING WAS THE HOPE OF GETTING somewhere in the end, and I sustained that hope by looking at my life so far as a series of stages. After childhood, the seminary, and Villa del Rosario, Córdoba represented a new step. But to what could all these steps be leading?

I was already telling myself that as I was determined to create something, this creation could only flower into the light if the seed had been sown in the farthest, darkest recesses of a past where poverty would prove a more fertile soil than affluence, because the mind creates only to compensate for the deficiencies of life. Desire and suffering serve only to be turned to account.

The streets where I had so happily wandered on that first eager morning now formed a rather precise map, and each one was potentially a way to reach a hypothetical future, while the world slipped away before me – and what else was I but a kind of plan, a project? I was like someone who, upon hearing exhortations in an unknown language, would rush on ahead, convinced that he had merely to hurl himself at obstacles in order to overcome them.

Before doing my military service and then moving on to Buenos Aires, I would have to spend two endless years getting up well before dawn (except on Sunday) to catch a bus to the factory. The buses were always packed; the trip took an hour, and there was so little space between the rows of facing seats that people's legs fit together in an alternating pattern like a herringbone stitch, with each person's knee wedged between those of the passenger sitting across the way. The central aisle was so narrow that the drowsy standees remained on their feet only because they were jammed tightly together. We clocked in at 7 A.M. and did not leave until nine hours later, so that my life – the one I had to save from the daily grind, constructing it minute by minute as though I were building a tower to rise above disappointment – did not begin until late in the afternoon.

Should I mention that as I recall my stay in Córdoba, I feel the very same longing to leave that city as I did when I was there? And yet, it took almost nothing to fill with excitement those few hours that followed the relentless monotony of the factory. I made a few friends; our group of young people was like a gang of aimless conspirators. Four of the men were named Ricardo, and the women, who were of German, French, and Scandinavian extraction, were named Ingeborg, Bella, and Selma.

In honor of Hermann Hesse, whom I was the only one not to revere, we called our review *Abraxas;* I recall that most of the articles concerned architecture and that there were scads of typos. We learned Valéry's dialogue *Eupalinos l'architecte* by heart, along with Rilke's *Letters to a Young Poet,* which at the time were the breviary of every Argentine who had anything to do with literature. Since we all loved the theater, we set ourselves up as actors, directors, set designers; we championed Meyerhold against Stanislavsky, and Gordon Craig against all his peers. Not all our productions were flops – except when Ingeborg, with her face like a terra-cotta moon, insisted on playing *La Dame de la mer.*

We went to lectures, and to all the art galleries; once we had lunch with Borges, who could still see our faces, and another time we brought Brazilian butterflies of a dazzling blue to Walter Gieseking, who placed the box on the piano before his concert. We dreamed of being what we were: Europeans in exile. And I remember Carlos Tecco praising *Tonio Kröger,* and Lucho Farina offering us a copy of his translation of "Un coup de dés." And I particularly recall one of our four Ricardos, a man who worked in the same office with me at the factory, and who still retained, along with his petit-bourgeois taste in clothes, a sense of indignation and disgust: when he discovered that I had a bent toward more than literature and Le Corbusier he was appalled, and admitted that he could not understand why I did not commit suicide. We made a cult of frankness, which can be so wounding, and advocated free love whenever we were not in love ourselves. I remember how impatient we all were to share this or that discovery with one another, and one day I got to tell them of a grand event at the factory: her yellow hair gathered at the back of her neck, her figure trim in a checked gray suit, Eva Perón stood on a tractor haranguing three thousand or so workers and office personnel assembled inside a hangar, where the corrugated iron walls echoed with the violence of her shouted commands and slogans.

I was able to avoid military service through a ruse. I could not say either when or how I discovered my ability to speed up my heartbeat – probably when I was trying to slow it down in order to conceal my distress over something – and that was the trick I used to fool the doctors in the barracks, who were interested only in cardiac irregularities and hemorrhoids. I can still see them, taking notes in the dim light, making the recruits bend over and spread their cheeks for a brief inspection; then the cardiologist went down the line, clamping his stethoscope to each chest for a moment. As naked as worms, we formed a kind of gigantic worm that stretched the entire length of the room. I had been ceaselessly exercising my emotions by imagining myself in a car (in the death seat, of course) with the speedometer needle about to fly right off the dashboard, and then the sudden curve, the skidding wheels, the car turning over and bursting into flames.... My imagination was working on the steep slope of a ravine and the squeal – too late – of brakes when the stethoscope landed on me, staying long enough so that the little cup of glass and metal lost its chill on my skin before I heard the liberating diagnosis: "Arrhythmia."

That very afternoon, I left Córdoba. I was through with the

provinces. Despite our mutual promises, our group of friends disbanded and we scattered, losing touch with one another. There were diplomas, marriages, careers embarked on with the eagerness of youth. Years later, in Europe, I learned of Selma's death in childbirth, and Raúl's assassination in Mexico. I still receive a letter now and then from one or another of my old friends; I recognize the handwriting on the envelopes, which I keep in a drawer. Argentines have a characteristic penmanship in which the old-fashioned downstrokes and upstrokes persist like the memory of a time when the legibility of one's writing was an expression of good manners. I seem to be speaking of days gone by, and yet a particular way of forming letters seems to survive all the variations of individual human nature.

I never saw any of my friends from Córdoba again. I remember their faces, their gestures, the way they moved; I can still hear their voices. They all – even those who have died – remain forever young, as do their dreams.

54

THE BUENOS AIRES I REMEMBER IS NOW ONLY A BLACK-and-white version, but one still nuanced with many shades of gray. In the vast chessboard of the city, with its perfectly square blocks of houses stretching from the river to the plain, no colors bloom except Judith's dress of sky blue muslin and the blue-violet of a flowering jacaranda near the cemetery of La Recoleta.

My Buenos Aires is still colored, however, with the fear that reigned there upon my arrival (and even more four years later, when I left the country), a fear that adapts so well, in memory, to a world of shadows.

Whether you were a foreigner or fresh from the provinces, you soon learned not to recognize the countless, anonymous, interchangeable faces of those who constantly insinuated themselves everywhere, but you suspected what they were up to, because they always traveled in pairs, while their felt hats and trench coats – which they wore as late as the season would allow – stamped them as belonging to the servile organization of the unofficial police, which branched out in every direction and whose members sought, at little risk to themselves, to bring in to the police station as many citizens as possible under the pretext of verifying their identification papers. Each new catch brought them a bonus in addition to their salary, a bounty they shared with the police inspector.

Melting by day into a crowd where the slightest deviation from the norms of fashion created a stir (causing passersby to stop in sudden solidarity to register their disapproval), they could be spotted from far off at night, in those hours when you can hear each passing car and every solitary footstep, as they strolled like hunters confidently watching and waiting for their prey.

And the fear grew, and grew, like another person inside of you, on the alert; fear sharpened your hearing and your eyesight, tightened the muscles of your face, quickened your pulse, drawing on the sense of an ever present danger that might be waiting for you that very minute, just around the corner; fear surrounded you, invaded you, possessed you, until there was room in your brain for nothing else.

It was wise to dress conservatively, ignoring fashion trends like the short jackets that were popular at the time, and above all, after nightfall, it was vital to walk with a brisk step and a straight back, to avoid any casual behavior, and never to turn uneasily to see if the shadow glimpsed in a doorway as you passed was now following you, for that alone might lead to your arrest.

There was nothing reassuring left, nothing that did not seem like a sign of danger, and even if you hid yourself away at home, you would be haunted at times by the idea that objects shared your anxiety. You became convinced that the door was ready to betray you and would swing open in welcome all by itself at the first knock. Gradually, without realizing it, you perfected a coded language, and you never telephoned in a public place, except in one of those bars where the phone was next to a mirror, allowing you to keep an eye on the customers.

Were you introduced to someone? You would sniff at each other cautiously, suspiciously, cowed by mutual distrust, and if you should happen to look one another in the eye, you would discover – with shame and chagrin – that each of you was the other's policeman. The small change of denunciation jingled behind doors, passing from hand to hand, pocketed by informers; there was a perpetual bad smell everywhere, but people did not yet fear torture and disappearances. That was coming, however, and they knew it.

When I arrived in Buenos Aires, my entire fortune consisted of my last wages and a few addresses where I might find work. They were generous with their advice in one place; in another, they offered numerous suggestions; elsewhere, they sent me on my way while urging me to stop by again, even recommending me to someone over the telephone then and there. All you have to do to get rid of someone troublesome is show some zeal and interest, lots of interest. I had knocked on quite a few doors by the time I figured out that you obtain nothing, or only very little, by admitting how desperately you need something.

I was still managing to keep up appearances; I had one of those new nylon shirts, with seams that puckered, but it took only a few hours to dry, so I washed it every night in the common bathroom while everyone else in the boarding house was asleep. Each morning I shined my shoes, Italian loafers that were also something new and unusual at the time, and suspicious in the eyes of the police.

For a while the increasing bagginess of my trouser legs and jacket elbows was offset by my polished shoes and a clean collar and cuffs, which gave to my poverty an air of decency much appreciated by people, as it excused them from having to feel any compassion for me.

To my apprenticeship in fear was soon added that of hunger;
I sometimes think that if everyone were to have this experience, the world would be a different place.

Following the advice of Selma, who was fond of the picturesque, I had gone to live in a boarding house on the edge of
the slums down by the docks, which had once been such a thriv-
ing area in this port town that its inhabitants were called
"Porteños." Three blocks away from the harbor, you never would
have suspected its existence had it not been for the bars full of
sailors and the seedy hallways into which they disappeared with
marvelously made-up women. I was too shy and impoverished to
investigate such haunts, but I think back on them with nostalgia.

With shiny cheeks as round as little balloons and a plump double chin, my landlady's face was not unlike a baby's bottom, and
her prominent, lusterless eyes displayed the boundless placidity
of a cow chewing her cud. She was short-waisted but amply
rounded in the bust, which bulged over pudgy hams that fleshed
out this opulent theme on a much larger scale. This impressive
figure was supported by surprisingly tiny feet, on which she trotted busily here and there like a mouse. She wore no lipstick, but
her eyes were so heavily made-up that they looked bruised, her
spit-curls were like scars, and she sported a chestful of curious
glass beads like so many ex-votos in honor of the Sacred Heart of
Jesus, which was tattooed at the base of her throat.

She lived in a vast room that was half ground floor, half basement, where the camphoric scent of a perpetually burning candle did not manage to mask the garlicky kitchen smells. There
were deep scratches on the ceiling from the legs of some folding screens that concealed the stove and the bidet; the screens
had been painted azure blue, and they brought a hint of vaude-
ville to this dismal place.

Doña Sol was a fortune-teller. When I passed by her door,
which she always left ajar, I would often run into ladies dressed
with an elegance that seemed strangely out of place in this sordid building located only a sidewalk away from the slums.

I had paid a month's rent in advance, but that month was

coming to an end, and since I had only enough money to stay on one more week, I decided to confide in my landlady. She hardly ever left her room, where I had glimpsed her a few times through her half-open door as I was going out, and once I watched her for quite a while, my presence concealed by the dim light in the hallway and a noisy delivery truck. Sitting at her table, she was slowly shuffling the cards, moving her lips as if she were praying for divine aid in circumventing her fate. And when she had laid out a few cards, and was reaching to turn over the first one, her hand paused in midair as she stared out into the dark corridor where I was hiding. With a crooked smile, she turned over the card and slapped it down, saying in a mocking voice that dropped an entire octave, "My cards will speak for whoever is watching me. He must stand still, and listen. I have no part in this – I am only a medium, that is all."

Was she inspired by the snowy landscapes of saltpeter traced upon her pink walls by the rising damp? The soul whose fortune she foretold resembled a wall down which water oozed and trickled – tears, or so it seemed. I was a traveler adrift, and only through prolonged and extreme difficulties would I determine my goal. I would plod along, having lost my bearings; she could hardly see me now.... Shuffling the cards more rapidly, with a swipe of her thumb she fanned them out in her hand and snapped them down on the table. Then she continued her allegorical reading, leading me through subterranean darkness as I bent to listen behind the door, hunching my shoulders, tiptoeing into my future; the walls drew in on me, the ceiling dropped, and the ground rolled up behind my feet. I was breathing my last, buried in an endless night of stone.

What had she actually said, up to that point? Her little cry of relief seemed sincere to me: now misfortune had exploded with a great dark noise, and many paths lay before me. But watch out, it would be easy to make a mistake: although all the paths looked alike, only one was truly mine.

When I drew back against the door to let some of the other boarders rush noisily past, the fortune-teller looked up, listening to the creaking stairs with an ear doubtless capable of distinguishing the unfamiliar step that would betray an illicit rendezvous. After adjusting her hairdo and adopting a severe but nevertheless concerned expression by raising her eyebrows pensively and setting her mouth in a line that turned down at the corners, she ordered her unknown observer to enter. I hurried in, tripped on a step, and fell flat on my face at her feet. She shrieked with laughter. As I got to my feet, I pulled out the last of my money, amounting to a week's rent. She invited me to be seated, and we chatted, or rather, she heard my confession; I hid nothing from her, even admitting to her that my prospects were slim at the moment, believing that this extra touch of frankness would win her protection. She read my cards once more, and the darkness paled to gray: there was light at the end of the tunnel, but the tunnel had not grown any shorter. "Artists," she said.... "Artists," she repeated, taking my money and slipping it inside her blouse with the skill of a conjuror.... "Artists always manage to find their own way, and those who have wings are meant to fly."

Then her smile snapped shut like a jackknife as she announced the imminent arrival of her son, who lived in Patagonia, which meant that I would have to vacate my room.

Did I think I must have misheard her? I had understood her perfectly. I was sitting there, too stunned to get up, when the sound of fingernails scratching at the door made me start: a blonde popped her head in the door, lifting her dark glasses to peer at the steps as though she knew and mistrusted their every last defect. Doña Sol welcomed her visitor with honeyed words, simpering and fluttering her chubby fingers to express her delight.

I helped the unknown woman take off her coat, which she shrugged from her shoulders with a wriggle that coursed through her entire body. Her perfume was exquisite; her girlish affectations aged her touchingly, and she seemed to be one of those people who place all their hopes of seduction in the intensity of their gaze – nothing else about her was so brazenly provocative.

I blushed – I had been mistaken: she was only interested in seducing the poet in me, so often praised by doña Sol. She was such a sentimental thing and absolutely adored poetry; she was a singer and insisted that I drop everything else and come hear her that very evening at Le Petit Bar d'Alice. "In French," she added. She batted her lashes at me; there was a maternal gleam in her eyes, and her nearsightedness only added to their charm.

Buenos Aires was calling to me; I dashed up the half-flight of steps to the hall and turned around in her doorway just in time to catch doña Sol's grimace of contempt. I shut the door as quietly as a thief trying to sneak it open.

For a few seconds, I hesitated between the stairs and the street; Buenos Aires lay shimmering just outside the front door.

55

BECAUSE OF WHAT IS PROBABLY AN INCURABLE NEED for affection, I have often trusted complete strangers, some of whom rise to the occasion by displaying the kindness thus expected of them.

In Le Petit Bar d'Alice, where the walls were covered with garnet plush like a box at the opera, an experienced nose would have quickly discerned among the mingled aromas the musty nuance characteristic of night-clubs at opening time.

Patrons slumping in their seats looked up when the entertainer scraped the microphone with her fingernail to make sure it was working and to get everyone's attention, just as she had scratched at doña Sol's door; the full skirt of her dress (Dior's "New Look") stuck out over the edge of the stage, which was so cramped that the pianist was forced to play with his elbows pressed against his body. Only his legs and forearms could be seen, and sometimes his head would bob into view.

To the sound of a Glenn Miller tune, the audience relaxed

again into their languid poses, heads tipped back, mouths slack with boredom, while Alicia sang of the sadness of lost happiness; no one seemed to hear her gracefully sugarcoating the bitterness of past loves, and yet judging from the dreamy expressions on some listeners' faces and the sudden greediness of their caresses, they found Alicia's purring tones sensually arousing. It was as though something inside her wanted to give everything to anybody at all, and be treated in return like nothing; there was something almost macabre about the way her sighs trembled on the edge of tears and her eyelids went up and down so regularly, as though synchronized with her breathing.

Huddled at the end of the banquette, near the checkroom, I was the only person to applaud when the pianist held the last chord under the breathy voice of the chanteuse, who, sweeping her gaze out over the heads of the couples at their tables and across a vast imaginary public, bowed very low, like a diva.

As I write these lines, forty years have slipped away into the past, and yet I see the pink light that bathed Alicia; I see her hands arranging the accordion pleats of her skirt before she gripped the microphone imploringly; I see the sorrowful sweetness of her expression, which I suspect I found sublime.

She had many lovers, I was to learn; she always pretended to miss the last one while living in anticipation of the next. As for me, I offered her poetry, preferably in rhyme, so that she might forget all her troubles and continue being kindly disposed toward me. That very first night, one of her benefactors, who came to pick her up after her performance, hired me on the spot to work in his real estate office. I would start out as a receptionist, but if I was willing and able, there was no telling how far I might go in the business. My new employer was not much older than I was. He was quick to smile, his gestures were graceful, his Spanish was softened by his Brazilian accent, and the look in his eye was hard as iron.

I would have done better to go back to the boarding house, but a surfeit of happiness made me feel adventurous. I felt saved, invulnerable.

I crossed the esplanade in front of the railroad station; the scent of the nearby river was in the air. Driven by euphoria to spend my last pesos, I pushed open the doors of a legendary brasserie where the night owls of Buenos Aires could make their last stand. I remember its bay windows with panes of red, blue, and yellow glass; the tangy aroma of sauerkraut; a woman's laughter floating high above the hubbub; puffs of smoke from invisible cigarettes rising into the air over the high panels separating the booths. The gentleman is alone? The place is full; I am turned away.

As I went to leave, someone stopped me: two patrons raised their steins and invited me to sit at their table. When I hesitated, one of them spoke to me rudely, but the other (who was wearing a tie pin with the red and white insignia of a local soccer team) simply brought his companion to heel with a look. He clearly had some influence on him, and I had the immediate impression that the two of them knew each other so well that they no longer had need of words. On the other hand, I might just mention that at first glance – as in the case of many literary characters bound by a great friendship – there was nothing about these two that revealed any affinity between them, beginning with their clothing and physical appearance. We introduced ourselves by our first names, and something about his easy way of striking childish poses (which did not quite fit with his too-tightly knotted tie) made me peg Hermes, the one who took my arm to get me to sit down, as a dubious artistic type, whereas everything about Aníbal – his reserve, his wariness, his massive calm that went far beyond what is meant by self-control – bespoke an official on good terms with the authorities.

Sometimes he seemed vulgar, and sometimes, when he moved his face out of the circle of light shining on the table, he seemed afraid to reveal a more sensitive nature, but in the end he could not disguise the air of lonely, wounded pride that clung to him despite his composure, his broad shoulders, and the bad taste displayed by that wretched tie pin, as though by drawing attention to his chest he hoped to shield his face from scrutiny.

I was hungry and could have afforded some frankfurters and potato salad, but my embarrassment at the thought of ordering such a cheap meal led me to shake my head when the waiter began to set a place for me at the table. He was already turning to leave when Aníbal signaled to him to set the place anyway.

Hermes imitated my accent, remarking that people from Córdoba managed to drawl even on a monosyllable, so that a simple yes or no was enough to reveal their origins. He ate with such voracity that his knife, plied with sudden bursts of speed, seemed to threaten his companion, who chewed his food calmly and methodically, and I remember that when he had cleaned his plate, Aníbal set his knife and fork down on either side of it, a gesture in keeping with the wearing of the soccer club tie pin. As for me, I had forced myself to eat slowly and had taken only a small serving because I was afraid I did not have enough money to pay a third share in the bill. Luckily, Hermes insisted on serving me a second helping so that he might take some more himself, and I realized that he was trying to justify his constant drinking to Aníbal.

I cannot recall exactly what happened after that; one of us remarked that our first names, which were rather common in our country at the time, had been popularized by magazines publishing serializations of Homer and Latin classics. One thing led to another, and we began chatting about shared interests; Aníbal announced that Hermes was a painter, and when asked about my tastes in this department, I confidently, fatuously pronounced the fatal phrase (banal and insignificant, of course, but not there, not in front of those strangers who had taken up with me for motives I could not even begin to suspect, the one a taciturn and common man, the other with the tired look of a disillusioned dreamer – not there, not those words that I must have read in an article, in the caption to a reproduction of one of the artist's works): "The purity of line of Matisse."

I could feel the phrase floating in the air above our heads like an inscription, and as I was about to repeat it I noticed that Aníbal and Hermes were exchanging a long look of complicity,

with just the flicker of a smile in their eyes, and the waves of
irony flowing out in ever-widening circles from their stunned
amazement washed away the appearance of stability I strove so
desperately to maintain, leaving me alone with my weakness
and pretension. And Aníbal laughed at me by teasing Hermes:
Was he capable of drawing my portrait with the purity of line of
Matisse?

While Hermes stared at me, all those little twitches and gri-
maces that sometimes hovered about his face were smoothed
away; his features grew calm as he studied mine, but he seemed
to be trying to see behind them as well. He pushed plates and
glasses away to clear a space, wiped his lips with the back of his
hand, and his forehead with his sleeve, loosened his tie, produced a pencil, crooked his left arm around a section of the
paper tablecloth to make a shield, and studied me with the deep
concentration that precedes an all-or-nothing effort: once he
began drawing, his hand never faltered or left the paper, as if his
pencil were following an invisible outline instead of the dictates
of his eye. Stopping abruptly, he tore off a good quarter of the
paper sheet and held it out to me. My heart quailed: I felt such
an overwhelming rush of nausea that I feared I might vomit, and
I clung to the edge of the table as though I were hanging on for
dear life over a gaping void. I seemed to see the spider that fell
on my eldest brother's back while he was making love to his
mattress, and his sudden nakedness, and my face watching him
in the narrow mirror – and when I crumpled up the obscene
drawing, Hermes slapped me squarely in the face.

Blood ran from my nose; I leaned forward to avoid staining
my jacket. I had the feeling that the very violence of the other
man's gesture had placed me under Aníbal's protection. After
he had smoothed out the drawing, he rolled it into a little ball
and tossed it over his shoulder – and the only sign of the smile
hidden behind his bushy mustache was a faint crinkling
around his eyes.

As though the painter's slap had been a signal, a fight broke
out at the far end of the room between two women who began

screaming their heads off at each other. People stood up, climbing on the banquettes to get a better view; suddenly surrounded by an attentive silence, the women put on a show, angrily vying for the sympathy of the spectators who were reflected over and over again in the mirrors running the entire length of the room, while the vaulted ceiling echoed with insults and the smack of blows. Their men seemed almost like old cronies watching a cockfight with a critical eye, but when the women (whom Hermes described as a pair of sluts) began to move down the aisle between the booths, one moving backward in retreat, the other waving her arms like a tragic heroine, the men leaped at each other brandishing revolvers. Now the soundtrack exploded with shrieks as people tried to fight their way to the door, with the waiters at their heels, clambering over the tables with the customers' checks in their hands.

Finally, a third man, whose size and broad shoulders marked him as the bouncer, dove expertly between the legs of the adversaries and reared up immediately to seize their wrists in a grip of steel, forcing the weapons from their benumbed fingers. The two rivals then congratulated each other, joined in their reciprocal applause by what was left of the audience.

Facing each other like hissing cobras, the women paused for a moment, and one of them was preening in the mirror, adjusting her expression and coiffure, when the other spat so skillfully at her opponent's image that the spittle dribbled like a huge tear from a reflected eye wide with shock, which set the victim to crying in earnest.

My "friends" had barely noticed this spectacle, which the antagonists decided to break off for lack of an appreciative audience. As for me, safely seated with my companions, I had quite enjoyed the show, and even the slap Hermes had dealt me when I crumpled his drawing now seemed no more than a somewhat over-hasty reaction, for which he was perhaps even a little sorry.

When Aníbal called for the check, which he prevented me from seeing, the waiter glanced toward the two quiescent

Furies and, lowering his voice mysteriously, as if he were denouncing someone, he whispered behind his hand that they were both lousy actresses, but that What's-Her-Name belonged to the Athenaeum Eva Perón and was not only working but even enjoying some success, while her ex–best friend was treading not the boards but the sidewalk, proud of her loyalty to the opposition. And then, after a moment's reflection, he asked Aníbal if it was true, as he had heard, that if kids wanted to do well on their exams, they should belong to the associations founded by the president's wife.

We left the table and stopped at the checkroom. Was I surprised to see them claim the familiar trench coats and felt hats? Aníbal clapped his hat on straight across his forehead; Hermes gave his a rakish tilt, drawn down over one eyebrow. We left, and I felt as though they were escorting me. It was dawn; the brasserie's sign paled in the early morning light. If anyone had seen us, he would have thought – quickening his step – that I was being taken to the police station. Perhaps I wondered about this at the time.... They insisted on seeing me home, saying that they went off duty only at eight o'clock.

We arrived in front of doña Sol's door. Would we ever meet again? They smiled, both of them together this time: we would run into one another, sooner or later.

Aníbal touched two fingers to the brim of his hat in farewell, but Hermes grabbed the back of my neck and then let his hand slip down my spine a bit more slowly than is usual in a parting between strangers.

When they walked off along the empty pavement, they seemed unreal, like ghosts: that was when I noticed that not only were they wearing the policeman's trench coat and hat, but their footsteps were absolutely silent.

It was then that the mechanism of fear began to work, blindly, irreversibly, and inescapably.

56

THERE ARE SOME PEOPLE AND EVENTS YOU WAIT FOR
without realizing it, and it is only when they finally appear or
occur that you understand how long and how impatiently you
have waited for them. That is how it was with Judith. But before
I met her, I had still to lose my way a few more times on the
treacherous chessboard of the city, where every street was tire-
lessly stalked by fear.

My job did not prevent me from going hungry now and then, but
it did allow me to hang on, to avoid having to return to Córdoba – a
defeat from which I would never have recovered. In addition, my
employer, Alicia's young Brazilian, allowed me to sleep in the
shed housing the boiler for the central heating in the office build-
ing.This shed was up on a flat concrete roof edged by a raised border barely a foot high, with a view of other similarly windswept
roofs and a horizon where huge flowers of smoke blossomed on
factory chimney stems. The wind was gritty, like the wind of my
childhood, and so gusty that I was forced to stretch a line between
my "room" and the door to the stairs so that I would have something to cling to on stormy days, since there was no balustrade.
Luckily, my employer had entrusted the office keys to me, and I
had the use of a very fine bathroom. It consoled me for almost
everything. The enameled bathtub with its clawed feet, the floor
paved with large square flags of marble, the walls covered to head
height with lozenge-shaped ceramic tiles, the medicine chest with
its oval mirror – all these things still bring me a kind of happiness.
And I remember that, toward the end of the month, I sharpened
razor blades in the way my father had taught me, which had so irri-

tated me at the time. Although it might seem like a pompous thing to say, this bathroom helped me keep smiling through those first months in Buenos Aires. Of course, I was still in that phase when it was hard to tell whether my life was tragic or ridiculous, for I considered myself a poet through and through, and so felt inclined to believe that everything a poet experiences – especially suffering – will somehow nourish his art.

Some people are convinced they have ruined their lives through carelessness at the crossroads; others, satisfied with their position in life, lay claim to infallible wisdom and virtues so praiseworthy that they take it upon themselves to try and force them upon everyone around them. I personally think that we all have secret missions to accomplish, that life relieves us of them as the years go by, and that there is nothing we can do about it.

Buenos Aires was so many things to me, and so few of them remain, but I am glad to have forgotten them. Has memory been unjust? Not at all. Except for Judith – who is perhaps even now picking out the sky blue dress she will be wearing when we meet by chance for the first time – my only distinct memories of Buenos Aires (where a third of the country's population lives, as if in hope of returning to their roots) are linked to fear, or are the prelude to fear. A dirty fog has seeped into streets that lead nowhere. Aníbal and Hermes would haunt almost all of the four years I spent in the capital, and I would never discover exactly what part I played in their "work."

Did they use me as bait to draw close to their victims or lure them into their nets? They always came and went with the night. I must admit, I would truly like to know whatever became of those two.

They would tell me when to meet them, either in real dives or in those fancy nightclubs where the soft, golden lighting helps middle-aged women relive the grace and beauty of their youth. Besides already established couples and those still in formation, there were single men in these places, men who betrayed themselves by their direct, piercing way of looking, as though they were spying through a keyhole but at the same time revealing everything about themselves, including their recognition of you as one of them, one of their kind.

For a long time I thought my shabby clothes were what so often made me the center of attention for these men, and I would pull back out of the way, into my shell, as though avoiding temptation; my "friends" were always late, so I would sit alone, seemingly dogged by some misfortune, especially when one or another of these men would try to strike up a conversation, and particularly when they spoke to me under their breath, with a private urgency.

I cannot remember when I realized that Aníbal and Hermes were late on purpose, and that even if I ignored the propositions of these strangers, the fact that they had approached me at all singled them out to the attention of someone – a waiter, the checkroom attendant – who would report back to the policemen when they arrived; for despite the care they took to blend in with the other patrons, there was something about the two of them that aroused suspicion and made people cautious. I began to understand this, although without being able to think about it explicitly, when I caught myself growing more and more uneasy whenever I had to wait for them, as well as unhappy – and twice as lonely – when a week went by without my seeing them. It is not difficult to become a Judas out of complaisance, or out of a need for protection. In the imminence of betrayal, is there not something like the belated justice that might have been dispensed by another's hand? I had no vocation for it. But I knew that this situation and my reaction to the obscure bond I felt with Aníbal were proof enough that a part of me was like a dog trembling in adoration before its master, inviting him to play but also to command, asking the impossible of him: love, and devotion, and enslavement. There is in all of us a mad desire to give of ourselves that can lead just as well to triumph as to disaster.

And if I did not try to avoid their company, insofar as that would have been possible, it was because – despite the fact that I knew them and that they introduced me to many of their colleagues we happened to meet, so that these agents would leave me alone (so I thought, but perhaps it was in order that they might recognize and keep track of me) – I was occasionally taken to the police station to spend the night in cells that continued to welcome new guests until dawn. Once, when I was being released the following morning and the police inspector was examining my dossier (he had just arrived for work – I remember that his hair was still damp and that he gave off a pleasant smell of shaving soap), a policeman eager to show his zeal grabbed me by the hair and cut off a handful with some scissors. I can still hear everyone's hearty laughter; I hope that they are all alive today and that life has treated them as they so richly deserve.

If I think back on my increasing boldness when my desire, overruling my fear, would send me off in pursuit of some phantom disappearing down a street or strolling near a park, I realize that I was never arrested in cruising spots but in the business neighborhood, in that part of downtown that shuts up tight at night and where almost no one lives. I have no idea how many times, when I was on my way home, two trench coats lurking in a doorway – betrayed, but too late, by the firefly glow of a cigarette – loomed up suddenly before me to bar my way.

I did not give up: I met all sorts of people, gained entry to the world of the theater, and (thanks to a sonnet containing the words *windmill* and *moon,* published in *La Nación*) I mingled with "society." The photographs in *Rosalinda* and what I had read in other glossy magazines and novels had led me to believe the upper classes lived exclusively in houses invulnerable to wind and dust, contributing to civilization through their respect for good taste, but I soon found their culture and education somewhat superficial. Actually, I envied them only the confident ease with which they spoke of Europe, which to them meant Paris and London. I have not forgotten Noemí Robirosa, back from a trip to the Old World, reciting St.-John Perse's "Anabase" to us after a game of tennis, standing at the edge of the court, her forehead dewy with perspiration, gently tapping out the rhythm of the

poem on her knee with her racquet, and then going into rhap-
sodies over the dazzling performance of Gérard Philipe in
Kleist's *Prince de Hombourg*. She was in love with him; I remember the passion in her voice, and the lengthening shadows of the
poplars falling across the still-sunny lawn.

Sometime that afternoon, or on another one very like it, a feeling of antipathy at first sight turned out to be the beginning of my
friendship with Matías, whom we often missed at those Sunday
matches and who became the object of one of those typical
crushes of mine, in which the body participates only from the
waist up – or rather, from head to waist, as in the old days of the
seminary visiting room – along with some phantom itching of the
hands. I cannot *see* Matías anymore, but I remember a host of
things about him: his relaxed, confident, limber way of moving;
his mocking, uncouth joviality; his habit of half-closing his eyes
when he drank and raising his eyebrows when he listened to you;
and, above all, the scar on his cheek that gave him an air of mystery and a certain influence among his peers as well as with me. I
still remember how he listened and kept a discreet eye on me
whenever I took part in the conversation, the way an orchestra
conductor might watch over the contributions of a novice instru-
mentalist, and I concluded that he had the same feelings for me
as I had for him. I remember so many things about him, and yet,
he fell into a kind of limbo, like a glove shed by a hand – real, but
empty – on the day I realized he was a traitor.

Matías belonged to a family whose reverses of fortune (not to
say complete collapse), while leaving intact the prestige of a past
inextricably bound up with that of the nation, had disturbed the
balance of his mother's mind, which had already been impaired
in her youth, people said, when her parents had prevented her
from devoting her life to singing, forcing her to give up all hope
of a wider audience than her own family and friends.

Matías's very modest means placed our relationship on an
easy footing; as for his social milieu, neither poverty nor the
taint of insanity would ever require the exclusion of someone
boasting an ancestor prominent in the Wars of Independence.

High society thus continued to frequent the dilapidated mansion, and Matías would laughingly tell his friends that the family was locking the doors forever, one after another, on those rooms where the ceiling threatened to fall or the cracks in the walls were growing too large.

Although she wore too much makeup and affected that haughty disdain so characteristic of divas, Matías's mother still had an air of distinction about her, and on Sundays, her flowing gown and the coiffure bristling with hairpins were enough to warn any newcomer that a recital would take place after tea. Her son accompanied her on the piano, which he tuned himself, and when the moment arrived, he would attract the guests' attention with delicate arpeggios, soon followed by a few chords struck with great authority. Then he would rise, ask his mother to join him, sit at the piano again, and wait for the silent signal of readiness from the singer, who would cast her eyes down demurely before suddenly opening them wide like a startled cockatoo, or someone waking in a fright from a bad dream. She had a trained voice with a lovely timbre and knew the art of trills and roulades, which she sometimes broke off gently on a high note, as though she were a nightingale pausing to listen to her own melody. Her audience almost smiled when she would vanish between songs to change her coiffure or to wrap herself in a cape, or when she would brace herself with a hand on the piano at the approach of a difficult note, and bend backwards with the suppleness of a panther. But in the midst of all that, there was a soulful quality to her singing – a longing once buried deep in her heart that now burst from her throat – that kept her audience on their solemn best behavior, and so she exercised through her singing the power of persuasion that ordinarily fell victim to her extravagant appearance and eccentric conversation.

One Sunday, we were applauding one of those "mad scenes" she so favored, and as she slowly nodded her head in gracious thanks, her tiara caught the rays of the setting sun filtering through the windows, scattering them around the audience.

Birds chirped out in the sadly neglected garden, and the late-afternoon sunshine was slanting across the columns of the gallery when Judith appeared at the far end, in a sky blue dress, a small, hieratic figure who somehow seemed to dance with every step, dappled with shadows and reflections from the arcades through which she passed, oblivious to their play of light and darkness upon her face, as I stood transfixed, seized with the insane desire to rush through all the time and space that had separated us until that moment. With each step she drew nearer, but she had already walked into my life.

57

AT THE VERY BEGINNING OF THE MONTH OF AUGUST in 1952, Matías and I were braving an icy wind; every now and then, sudden freezing showers drove us to crowd beneath the awning of some closed café with everyone else who periodically took shelter there, dashing over from the massive, silent, almost paralyzed column of people that nevertheless crept along, as it had for several days, toward the glass coffin of Eva Perón.

We moved farther away from the Avenida de Mayo, which was black with the endless throngs pouring in by train and bus from all corners of the nation like an unstoppable tide that would flood our streets forever, reminding me of the army of locusts that had swarmed through our wheat fields and garden with such disciplined voracity.

In obedience to a tacit injunction, we would pause for a few seconds before the improvised altars on the sidewalks, usually set in a niche in a building, on a street corner, or in the recess of a blind window: a cluster of candles, sometimes a few flowers placed around a photograph of the dead woman in an ornate bronze-gilt frame draped with black crepe, like the public clocks that had all been stopped at 8:25, the official time of her death.

These altars generally displayed a photo of Evita dating from the transition period of her life, when the former actress was still decking herself out in her theatrical finery: showy drop earrings and a picture hat worn over a hairdo that no longer bore any resemblance to hair, as though it were imitating a shell twisting around in a spiral, widening, hollowing itself out, then suddenly drawing in tightly – stiff, metallic, untouchable.

It was a far cry from these photographs, which were only five or six years old, to the woman who, in a startling metamorphosis, had refined her taste by frequenting the great Parisian fashion houses of the Avenue Montaigne and acquired that diaphanous beauty bestowed only by the secret approach of death.

Putting on a face of mournful gravity in front of the weeping men and women on their knees praying not for her, but to her for themselves, as though she were the Madonna, Matías fearlessly mumbled a string of sarcastic comments, any one of which, if overheard by the faithful, would have gotten us lynched, and whenever I felt I might burst out laughing, I managed to disguise the rebellious impulse as a sob.

Did I think back on the days when she fed her ambition by commissioning scripts for radio serials in which she portrayed Elizabeth of England, Sarah Bernhardt, Catherine of Russia, Eugénie de Montijo? Did I remember the performer who, when brought to heel by military censorship prohibiting tragic endings and the depiction of love outside the bonds of marriage, was forced to give up playing Lola Montès and – more painful still – Isadora Duncan, because this last, according to persistent legend, had danced "La Marseillaise" at the Teatro Colón, her ample charms draped only in the Argentine flag?

Like the knight of La Mancha befuddled by his fondness for marvelous tales of chivalry, Eva Duarte – from the Virgin Queen to Catherine the Great, from the Empress Carlotta to Madame Curie, abandoning the microphones of the radio for

those of the speaker's platform and the presidential balcony –
had ended by playing the role of Eva Perón, and never more so
than at the moment when, defeated by reality, she died like an
actress who has rehearsed a scene to death.

Ever since I had met Judith, my crush on Matías had subsided, the way a bright color fades in the sun, and now that he
no longer feared my timid attempts to draw close to him (the
furtive touches, my brushing against him), he did not hesitate
to show affection for me. Sometimes he took my arm in the
street, which bold behavior I attributed to his aristocratic background and which made me fear spending not one night in jail
but a long time in prison. Had he not informed me himself, in a
bantering tone, that it is only in the third generation that the
wearing of formal attire becomes natural to a family?

And noblesse oblige: since the driving rain was making me
shiver more and more, he calmly took off his raincoat and made
me slip it on. It hung down to my ankles. We finally came to a
deserted avenue, and I remember how our laughter rang out so
scandalously in that time of national mourning, and how it
stopped so abruptly when a car pulled slowly over to the curb
next to us. I remember the softness of the felt hat Matías shoved
all the way down to my ears; it had been his father's hat.

Today, it all seems to come out of nowhere: the long arm that
wrapped around my shoulders and hugged me to the slender
body, now shivering in turn.

But the two shadows that clapped their hands heavily on our
shoulders from behind at an intersection – the same unforgiv-
able gesture a friend might make, catching up with you in the
street, like the tip-off of thugs who peddled such small treach-
eries to the police for a bit of extra money – definitely belonged
to that time when slinking was a way of walking, and all eyes
seemed permanently on the watch.

Matías was coolly gracious, the way he was at home for one of
his mother's Sunday afternoon receptions, and showed the
playful irreverence one reserves for idiots or children, but
when he was impertinent enough to ask to see the gentlemen's

actually his friends, not mine (the tennis players, the admirer of St.-John Perse who adored Gérard Philipe), but after a few days, I did denounce him.

I learned later that they had continued to see him anyway, and I even learned that he had stopped inconveniently backing out of tennis matches at the last minute. Had they thanked me for telling them what I knew? I never heard from them again. And although their attitude was hard to bear, I understood why it was necessary.

Such was the chaos, the moral confusion, the abasement provoked by a fear that was pervasive and well founded, and that really had nothing to do, after all, with a lack of courage. Not so long ago, I happened to see the last photograph taken of Eva Perón before she died. She is wearing slacks and a knitted top; her hair is pulled away from her face into a long braid that hangs down her back. She is sitting, somewhat hunched over, in an armchair, and the chairs on either side of her are empty. She is holding an invitation or a program in her hands, which are clasped between her knees. She is wearing no makeup. There is a wan smile on her lips, her nose has become pinched and sharp, and she has the eyes of an orphan waiting listlessly in a visiting room. Her body has wasted away.

58

WE SHOULD LEARN TO BE SILENT, TO LET GO OF THOSE superfluous things that memory fetishizes and treasures so piously, but our reason does not discourage us from this soon enough, and so we never lose hope of keeping alive what has moved us until it has completed its mysterious journey through our being. Is it possible that the world has a memory? Each one identity papers, he was suddenly bent double by a blow to his stomach. One man held him by the hair while the other hit him again, and again, with a kind of voluptuous rage, and when Matías fell full length upon the sidewalk, they began kicking him. Finally I was able to let out the cry that had been choking me from the moment I had recognized Aníbal and Hermes, who then recognized me as well. One of them, probably Hermes, lifted the hat from my head and let it fall again with a wry little laugh. Taking advantage of their surprise, Matías had jumped up, and huddled over like a runner on the starting line, his arms stretched out behind as if he were bracing himself against an imaginary wall, he leaped at Aníbal, who simply laid him out again with one open-handed push. Then, beaten, Matías flipped over the lapel of his jacket to reveal a gleaming badge: Aníbal and Hermes flinched backward, almost as if they were drawing themselves up to salute him.

I remember that when he stood up, Matías made a gesture that seemed to express helpless regret. Was he trying to make me understand what he would have liked to admit to me? He changed his mind, but before he turned away, we looked into each other's eyes with equal despair. And I had the impression he was collapsing inside, being expelled from reality.

The three of them stared at one another without moving, absolutely stupefied. Then, to make sure that they were all indeed on the same side, they began cautiously to mumble passwords, names, places where the police often went to round up victims. And suddenly I exploded in fury, cursing, trembling. I tore off the raincoat and hat, holding them stiffly out to their owner. He would not take them? I threw them in his face, emboldened by my familiarity with his colleagues.

I would have liked so much to leave with Aníbal and Hermes, but that was not an option: Matías had some kind of authority over them, and judging from his off-hand manner and their obsequiousness, he must have occupied a higher position than theirs in the hierarchy of darkness.

I was hesitant to warn our common acquaintances, who were

of us keeps a piece of it and is sole witness to what it safe-
guards: the lamp a mother pushes across the table toward her
child; a landscape suddenly etched by lightning; tears trickling
down a cheek; the geometric figure revealed in an agate held up
against the light; a wounded bird; abandoned graves – all
things that death will hasten to scatter, the way the belongings
of a dead person are dispersed.

Why all these delays and excuses when I cannot go forward until I evoke Judith as she was over there, in a time and
place long gone, with her smooth, stubborn brow and her
throaty laughter that revealed the bright pink festoon of the
gums delicately edging her teeth? Because words will have
nothing to do anymore, among themselves, with the word *love*?
Because they think that love is worth making, but not worth living and still less praising?

Love is a stranger passing through life; life assigns specific
goals to love, and love must reach them, whereas we – we fail,
because the intensity of emotion we experience through love is
independent of its mission. What would be needed is a new
perception of ourselves, of space; we would have to arrest the
process of change and muffle the ticking of the passing hours to
seize love and abandon ourselves to it. At first, we are blinded
by the obvious; then, when we realize that the other's very presence affects the passage of time, it seems like music to us. But
where does the music go when it sets silence free? It continues
to exist, of that we are sure – but where? and will it return? Of
that we are less certain. That is the nature of love, the star that
dances lightly over the heaviness of our lives. And when love
has ended, we still love it as we would a heavenly music after
the last note has died away.

There are so many barriers between someone who writes and
those he commemorates or betrays; reality eludes the grasp of
words, and years go by, and for me there is always the ocean,
like a wall of oblivion.

My later images of Judith bar my way back to the first
absolute image, which they spoil and conceal.

I have never met anyone more convinced than Judith was that the struggles we wage are what make life worthwhile. And how alone the two of us seem to be when I look back, how powerfully her presence eclipses all others! She stands out, and everything else that must have surrounded us, furnishing those moments, has dwindled down to a few scattered elements: a tree, a street, a bench, several beds.

Neither of us had any money; we met every day after that first Sunday, but we had nowhere to go, no room to be alone in, and not for anything in the world would I have dragged her up to my shack on the roof, nor would she have taken me to the boarding house where she was staying with a girlfriend. We knew instinctively that love is easily shocked and offended. On my way to meet her one day, I could see her triumphant and conspiratorial smile from a distance, and her eyes twinkled mischievously: she had hoodwinked her father, who was in the capital for a brief visit, and we would be going to the Tigre for our honeymoon.

I had never been to the delta of the Tigre, and I never went back. The wooden houses of the region are of English or Scandinavian inspiration, and the memory of their peaked roofs emerging jauntily from the lush greenery makes it hard for me to picture the delta over there, at the junction of the Paraná and the Uruguay, the two mighty brothers – one with its headwaters deep in Brazil, the other forming the border between that country and Argentina – that run parallel to each other over a great distance before mingling amid a tangle of islands and spreading out together in the watery plain of the Río de la Plata, flowing with its imperceptible current the color of dust along banks that soon move farther and farther apart, as though each of the rivers that had come together between them was striving to return to its own bed.

In the delta, vegetation springing from the spongy ground and its millennial decay runs riot after so much sky and dry land, shooting up into towering tree ferns on islands trapped by bedrock thrown up from the depths of the planet, while tiny islets float through a labyrinth of channels, drifting lazily along until they dissolve at the mouth of the river.

The train let us off in the middle of the afternoon near the dock, where we climbed aboard an old rowboat that nevertheless came equipped with a lantern at the bow and a smaller light at the stern. I cannot remember the face of the man at the oars. We passed from sunlight to shadow, entering this nomadic landscape; as we passed, curtains of vines and willow branches parted only to close immediately behind us. Myriad soft buzzing sounds followed us, like the scattered notes of a faint melody, and quickly died away.

Patches of fog drifted on all sides, coiling along the surface of the water, enveloping the rare poplars that reared their heads amid the gloomy mist.

And then it was as if doors had opened in the undergrowth: the slanting light fell upon houses with well-kept lawns of a particular green that seemed almost artificial in those surroundings. We had arrived. On the outside of the house, the gray paint was peeling, allowing glimpses of the previous coat, a delicate old rose; the trees as well as the shutter fittings seemed rusty, but when we stepped into the parlor, the odor of floor wax, the parquet (slightly warped in places), the artful arrangement of the rugs, and the hostess, who put down her book and arose in greeting from the divan set by the bow window, gave us an impression of genteel poverty that was entirely to our taste, and happily within our means. There was an air of cleanliness about our little room, with its double beds of blond wood – just for appearances – made up with eiderdowns and big, soft pillows.

And now, how can I describe Judith's nakedness, and myself seeking to enter her, and the sensation of the sweet and terrible rending that her body, all gathered in a single place, transmits to mine? I feel I am more Judith than myself. And yet I can feel my entire body for the first time, with no denial between love and desire, with no barrier at the waist, no division between the upper and lower halves, finally all of a piece. Happy are those who caress their loves without a second thought....

The intensity of the consummation in that room in the Tigre was like suffering to us, both deliverance and captivity: a god had pierced us through and through but was already abandoning us.

We believe we are moving endlessly beyond the reach of time; but, without our realizing it, we all return to earth at the last moment of our love, and then everything begins to resemble a dream that has cast us upon the shore of morning, with nothing but the small change of words clutched in our hands. And these words ask questions, they demand to know if we are "really" loved, as if it rested with us to "really" do something, when the words themselves fragment us, keeping us from being truly where we are.

Since we both cherished rituals and little ceremonies, even if they were just simple ones or only half serious, we dressed for dinner, exchanging those foolish sweet nothings that come to mind only in the play of a dialogue between oneself and one's self. And we would break off abruptly to gaze at each other: each of us a shoulder for the other to lean upon, a head bent to listen to the other's thoughts.

I remember the pile of pillows and eiderdowns on one of the beds, the ray of green light in the dim room, myself opening the window and pushing back the shutters. Our room looked out over a canal; on the opposite bank, lights shone through the foliage, softening and blurring its outlines. Night spread across the sky. And, suddenly, a floating island the size of a barge passed before our eyes, bearing at its center an aspen that saluted us, with the help of the breeze, in a flurry of quaking leaves. Our eyes followed it; a fern slipped from its shrinking banks, swirling for a moment in its wake. And we held each other tightly: we would not be going down to the dining room.

One day we would remember the room and our love, each in his own way, but we would share at least one pristine memory: the islet gliding by with its straight little tree, rooted in a disintegrating clump of earth. Actually, even that image would become somewhat different, because today, when I remember the steadfastness of the haughty aspen, I think of Judith: proud, resolute, and on the verge of sinking. Although she had chosen to be free, Judith was nevertheless often governed by a sense of sexual modesty I could not fathom, and there were feelings she did not allow me to arouse in her. Like every man who doubts his own virility and desires most urgently to prove himself in his own eyes, I was appallingly clumsy, but I knew how to imagine, to devise, to think out a body, because the little hunchback with flaxen hair had taught me to invent my own, on those nights in Villa del Rosario. Some friends lent us a cramped apartment in a well-to-do suburb for a few months; there was not much furniture, but luckily we had a big bed, a night table, a lamp, and two chairs. Judith looked for work but could find none. In the evening, she went to dance classes, while I took a course in theater.

One morning it was almost dawn when I returned. I had been chatting with my teacher, who enjoyed talking with me, and who knew the city so well that in crossing from one end of it to the other, after midnight, he took only streets not frequented by the police. I no longer recall whether it was during our walk that night or during a class workshop that he mentioned one of his own precepts on the art of acting, which so impressed me that I think of it almost every day: he said that an actor must know how to draw his body in space, and that to do this he must imagine it from all points of view, reflected in a circular mirror.

I came into the bedroom without turning on any lights and slipped into bed; my foot felt under the covers for Judith's feet, but she jerked them away.

That day she seemed gloomy and withdrawn. And as time went by, I saw a thin vertical line appear between her eyebrows, disfiguring her smooth forehead with a frown; then the wrinkle deepened, and sometimes I wondered if she was working herself up to a complete break rather than a simple quarrel. If I spoke to her, she would retreat into silence. When she refused to make love, I tried to bully her; she stopped me, but gently, by stroking my face. Her caresses were so thoughtful they seemed like farewells. She turned out the lamp, and in a crisp, clear voice, she said, "We are going to have a baby." My lips barely brushed against her cheek. She stifled a sob and swallowed hard. I placed my hand on her belly, and I suddenly thought of a tombstone. She took away my hand. There was no need to worry: she would do what had to be done. It was an emotional scene, driven by the confused and antic energy of two bodies seeking each other – and then she let go of me, and I did not press her. We respected the virtual presence of the being we had just condemned to nonexistence. I think she acted in my interest, for me; and so did I.

As I left for work one morning, she gave me the address of a café, in a neighborhood where we hardly ever went, and asked me to wait for her there at the end of the day.

She walked in, taking care to make her usual entrance in a public place, raising her chin as though to settle her features in their proper position. Her face seemed calm but had lost some of its radiance. She sat down and said quietly, "It's over." She had a cup of coffee, a swallow of cognac, and we left.

We walked to the subway, so close to each other that our clothing touched, and yet a chasm was growing between us. Had we shared responsibility for a murder? All complicity between us had vanished. Something had become firmly fixed behind that clear, stubborn brow, a kind of patient hatred; her thoughts had caught on a nail, and the words would not come. Beneath the familiar surface, something mysterious and foreign to our consciousness circulated under the skin, plotting, planning battles, taking stock of defeats, bringing struggles to a close.

When she returned to herself, and to me, Judith found me gone. Of course, I believed I still loved the woman I no longer desired in the same way as before. We went on with our lives, and by simulating passion, I almost wound up feeling it again; I was imitating myself. But in the ebb and flow of these nights, our love withered before it had a chance to flower, and we slipped into silence as though slipping into a grave. Our words were like explosions; when the shattering noise died away, they slunk back into the shadows, leaving behind a brief victory or defeat, but no illusions. Love, and even tenderness, were giving way to hostility.

Here is one scene in a little public square. A young couple appears. It is impossible to hear what they are quarreling about; sometimes they both speak at once, and the argument has probably been going on for a long while. He seems angry at times; at others, tired and discouraged. She, on the other hand, appears bitter and determined. She sits down on a bench, her back as straight as a poker, her head high, her expression scornful. He slumps dejectedly.

The words come more distinctly now: she seems to be repeating a question already asked several times before, judging from the way she carefully pronounces the syllables, emphasizing them. She wants to know why such a decision was made, even though she had wanted it just as much as he had, if not more. Just that, the reason why, the logical explanation, from the beginning.

He looks away, smiling wanly at passersby, who are listening in. The light is fading; they begin to feel chilly. I remember the shadows creeping across the lawn, but I no longer recall what answer I gave or how the tension mounted until I heard the sob I hear now, right here, in front of this page, a sob that must have both relieved and angered me there in that little park. Other people's tears, even those of strangers, upset me terribly, but tears shed for me, or because of me, turn me to stone – worse yet, they set me free. There is nothing I can do about this, and whoever weeps in front of me has lost his case for good and all.

He dashes from the park, slamming the low gate behind him, and rushes away as though hurrying to make up for lost time. He hears the gate bang closed again, and the swift clacking of Judith's high heels; she quickens her pace, trying to catch up with him, but then the staccato noise fades and is gone. Breathing deeply, he strides off. I must not have realized yet that life inveterately leads to all sorts of repetitions, prolongations, encores.

The curtain falls. When it rises again on the same actors, a quarter of a century will have passed. In order not to confuse the spectator with this leap in time, the master of ceremonies will bring the audience up to date, while the scenery is being changed, on the other two encounters life has allotted our protagonists: a few minutes, the first time, after they had not seen each other for more than six years, and an hour or two – but not alone together – fifteen years after he had gone abroad for the first time.

We are in Buenos Aires, at the end of the summer of 1961. Through the open windows of the bar drifts a confused hum from the old pedestrian passage where, toward evening, people would gather to talk and window-shop in a kind of no man's land of idle relaxation.

Judith and he had loved that place; they used to go there at the beginning of the month, when they might permit themselves the illusion of feeling flush. He chooses their favorite table, from which one might see who was entering without being seen. He waits for her. Why had he contacted her upon his return? He would have liked to learn that she was happy, for her happiness would relieve him of a great weight, free him from remorse. Then, so far away in the past, he hears the only noise he is listening for, the sound of Judith's steps as she comes nearer, hesitates, hurries forward when she sees him, preceded by her swelling belly. She smiles, seemingly satisfied at his astonishment. The delicate precision of the features has not changed in that bright, peaceful face, and her skin seems to glow from within with the radiance that pregnant women have, for they are no longer alone in their bodies.

He cannot remember now what they talked about, but he knows that her expression would sometimes stiffen and that her former obstinacy was still evident in her brow. His last image of her, however, is indelible: Judith crossing the street as the passing crowd parts to let her through; and, above all, the pang of distress he feels when, just as he is admiring the way she carries herself so proudly, he notices how scuffed her navy blue shoes are, with a wrinkled little strip of leather flapping from the middle of one heel.

I next returned to my native country nine years later, to Córdoba, where my parents were living. I was welcomed festively, imprisoned in the situation from which I had fled – that of being loved – but I tried not to be difficult about it. My visit wore on and began drawing to a close. I had long conversations with my father, knowing that he realized we would never see each other again.

One day, some of my nephews insisted on taking me to a nightclub not too far from the city but already out in the sierra. As the lights of Córdoba dropped away behind us, the road grew dark; we drove along for a while before spotting faint glimmerings up in the mountains ahead.

Lamps with opaque shades gleam in the semidarkness of the empty room, and one of them casts its glow on the profile of a woman raising a glass to her lips. It is Judith.

She recognizes me, stands up – she cannot believe her eyes, just can't get over it.... I am glad to hear her throaty laugh, but I feel immediately like an intruder; I imagine how embarrassed Judith must feel to be surprised like this, sitting alone in a bar like a dance hostess.Then I notice a slight flaw in her smile, a perplexing little something I cannot quite figure out but which suddenly becomes clear: her gum line is much too pink and shiny, and there is an unnatural slant to the way it cuts up over the incisors. Has she noticed me staring? I propose toast after toast, urging the young people to dance, and Judith leans closer to tell me that her son is eight years old, and would I have believed it? The two of us are as alike as two drops of water.

The next day, when my mother asks me for news of Judith, I realize that the expedition of the previous night had been set up by my entire family. It is not curiosity that I detect in her question, but something much worse: the accent of hope. She has been expecting a happy reunion that might have induced me to stay, keeping her vagabond son at home. It hurts me to disappoint her. I remember the way her smile lingered vaguely and the little toss of her head she made to hide her regret. The pain

I caused her is still with me, and even grows deeper, so many years after her death.

Finally, a quarter century after the scene in the park, the curtain rises on a Parisian café where the actor is waiting for Judith. There are many extras about; some are seated at tables nearby, reading newspapers. When she enters and comes toward him, the rustle of pages being shaken into place should be heard. She has aged well: she is still slim and carries herself with the same determination. The fine wrinkles around her eyes and the slight blotchiness at the wings of her nose have not touched her beauty, which he quickly tells her is unchanged. In reply, she looks him up and down and remarks, reproachfully, that he looked better when he was thinner. She informs him that her son is eighteen years old, lives in Paris, and has just married a Frenchwoman. She raises her glass of whiskey with assurance, drinks, lights a cigarette. He looks at her hands and hears himself say, as though the words have come all by themselves, that there is something about her fingers, with their blunt tips, that is... he tries to find another word, as he looks into her eyes, but the word drops from his lips like a pebble into a placid pool: stubborn. She doesn't understand; he assures her that he doesn't, either, and they are both silent once more. They seem to be standing on a threshold they do not dare cross. He fiddles with the knot of his tie. She draws herself up, and he senses all her old obstinacy focused behind that broad forehead. He makes some kind of gesture but stops in midair. And there they are, ready to tear each other apart.

Her voice is carefully modulated, as if a judge has given her the right to speak. She would like, once and for all, to understand, to untangle the skein of their relationship, to have it out with him. She urges him to be explicit, to analyze things in detail, so that the facts of the case could all be set in order. From the beginning? Yes, that's right, from the beginning.

He leans back in his chair, watching a revolving door as it swallows and disgorges a steady stream of extras in the background. And, suddenly, he plants his elbows on the table, crosses his hands beneath his chin: he is going to speak. Her expression hardens; he begins. He says he can no longer clearly recall what happened, for the past has its own way of muddling events that imagination is constantly transforming, since words change these events every time memory or anxiety calls them to mind. He says that syntax – yes, syntax – is stronger than life and subdues it, disposing of life by formalizing it, and that this form either embalms life or saves it, depending on the way you look at it. And when he thinks about his own journey and its drifting course, his memory projects only shadows. However curious he may be about the farthest reaches of his soul, can she understand his inability to talk about the full significance of some gesture or action? Can she not see that this disaffection, this free-floating way of life – one lived, above all, without "examining his conscience" – are what has allowed him to survive?

She smiles wickedly. He sees the same strikingly pink and uneven gum line of her dentures and looks away. She flares up bitterly, reproaching him for his indifference to others, to injustice, to the ruination and collapse of his own country, while he hides safely in his ivory tower far from everything, no strings attached, nowhere; as for her, she knows what she is talking about: the wretched poverty, the people's helplessness, the impotence of an entire continent, and the struggle, and the need for an upheaval that is constantly repressed, thanks to the indifference of privileged people like him.... Does he dare interrupt her sermon? Is he naive enough, impudent enough to try and shut her up by slipping in, when she pauses for breath, this shocking, outrageous word? One of the all-purpose words of its time: *gulag*.... She shouts out her answer amid the hubbub of customers who have set aside their newspapers: "We need even more of that: sixty years of revolution are not enough to finish off the..."

He is not listening anymore. He pays the check, gets up, and leaves. Startled, she empties her glass and stands up, but he is already going out the door. She puts on her coat and follows him.

The icy winter wind sweeping down the boulevard is fiercer than the stream of cars. The audience can still hear, however, the faint clicking of Judith's heel, and her shouts directed at the man up ahead, but the wind quickly beats down her voice, carrying it away – while I stride on without looking back, no longer sure, for a dizzying moment, if I am walking along a sidewalk in Paris, or if I am that young man rushing down a street in Buenos Aires while the same voice dies away behind him and the same step falters and stops in resignation. Like the mistress of the house who makes certain that the candlesticks are placed in perfect symmetry upon the mantel, life took care to repeat, without any precise significance, the end of an affair.

Years later – last summer, in fact, seven or eight months ago – while I was simply walking along in my neighborhood, or so I thought, a young man in his thirties with a boyish smile on his full lips, his manner all adolescent eagerness, called out to me by name. He seemed pleasant, ingratiating, and I was won over by his poise and gangling elegance. There was something familiar about his eyes; they were Judith's eyes, and he was Judith's son. He lived nearby. We exchanged addresses; we'd call one another we each promised, impulsively. And as we were saying goodby, I noticed a faint, jagged scar along the bridge of his nose. When I raised my hand as if to touch him, he told me, probably to ward off the caress, "A motorcycle accident." I asked him to be more careful in the future and his smile broadened, to hide his irritation. And I thought of Judith, surrounded by poverty, standing sturdily on her own two feet, her shoulders squared, incapable of asking for mercy, and still fighting on.

We parted, the young man and I; as he crossed the street, he turned to wave. Our son would have been eight years older.

59

THE DEATH OF EVA PERÓN, ON JULY 26, 1952, REVIVED hope among the various opponents of the regime; some wished for more freedom, while others desired a more effective dictatorship. It was said that the general, who affected the grave demeanor of an elephant about to fall on its knees, was only pretending to be bereaved. The army – which had acted in concert with Perón to keep the Madonna of *los descamisados* from assuming the office of vice president, because the woman was not yet born who could give orders to an Argentine soldier – was growing restive.

In its haste to reassert itself when the wife of the president was rumored to be at death's door, hadn't the army suffered a stinging setback, inflicted by the dying woman in person, who from her deathbed ordered the purchase of thousands of machine guns for distribution to the most seasoned and loyal of her "troops," the workers?

This woman who had once portrayed Marie Antoinette and the Empress Carlotta was perfectly aware that the military's hostility toward her candidacy would enrich her legend, offering one more example of misfortune, an injustice of the kind that brightens the glory of heroes. She had an obligation not just to her own people, but to the public of the entire nation, which had become her theater. As it happened, history would prove generous in those incidents that nourish a myth, incidents that might have seemed concocted by a screenwriter gone mad, if you consider the theft of the corpse and the wanderings of the coffin from one hiding place to another until it finally came to rest in an anonymous grave in the vast cemetery in Milan, from which it would be disinterred many years later so that the mummy might be installed in the Exile's mansion in Madrid. There is a photograph showing the body in profile, clothed in a white tunic, the hands clasped over a rosary of large beads with the cross hanging down facing the photographer, who has arranged carnations in the foreground. Behind the catafalque, by the head of the dead woman, sits a bald man, wearing glasses with very heavy frames, whose hand rests on the Idol's wrist as though to assess her state of conservation. He wears an expression of satisfied solemnity. He is the embalmer. A small picture that seems to be painted on a metal plaque hangs on the wall, twinkling in the half-light: the Virgin appears to be supervising the photo session, while arrangements are being made to return Eva's remains to her native country, unless the body is only a dummy intended to stir up the masses in preparation for the Old Man's return in the role of Savior of the Fatherland.

The fog of oppression thickened over the city after the death of Eva Perón, and the tall bronze statue of Christopher Columbus that dominates the port, turning its back upon the country, seemed to strain harder than ever to see its native shore once again.

Were the authorities receiving information about conspiracies, seditious plots, a palace revolution? As the indications of subversion became more plausible, the network of undercover police relentlessly combed the endless grid of Buenos Aires, but at times they seemed almost subdued, as if they themselves shared in the fear they were helping to instill in others. Their superiors must have been suspicious of their activities, pressuring them for more results, and so they had to redouble their zeal and make more arrests, keeping busy enough to avoid becoming involved in the growing practice of police torture. They no longer traveled always in pairs, and some of them displayed a vague uneasiness that alerted me several times to the fact that these watchers were being watched. There were some who disguised themselves even from the others, and at the beginning of each month, moreover, their numbers always increased. One of them stopped me to check on my papers, and there was something about the way he peered into my wallet that tipped me off: the corner of a choice bill was sticking up, and I arranged to drop it to the ground. His shoe (battered, but quick) promptly pinned the money to the sidewalk. I remember him holding my identity card, his obsequious manner when he returned it to me, and then the hard look and the menace in his voice when he ordered me to beat it – while his shoe inched forward to completely cover the bill lying on the ground.

This incident taught me a useful skill, so that in the future (albeit for a less exorbitant price) I avoided spending any more nights in the police station.

Sycophancy, denunciation, perjury, villainy, idiocy, all the evils encouraged by dictatorship spread and grew worse with each passing day, and while a few of us were dismayed to belong to a people capable of creating and fostering such routine abjection, we did not suspect, perhaps, that our lack of protest was feeding a complete disregard for the most basic ethical standards, which the future would make appallingly clear. In those days, did we think of the future? We saw it as a wall, coming closer and closer, and closing in around us. What did we think of the friend who went over to the other side and admitted why he was now supporting that regime? He would tell us, by way of justification, that such and such a benefit or favor helped to shield a number of people, that he didn't really take the government seriously, and then to prove it, he would whisper in your ear the latest joke about the Widower.

Whenever I came home and heard the heavy front door with its bars entwined with copper ivy clang solidly shut behind me, relief would flood my entire body, which was always on the qui vive, but this happy, fleeting sensation of lightness would drain away as the elevator climbed to the top of the building. When I arrived at the emergency exit door opening onto the roof, when I stealthily inserted the key into the lock (which I carefully oiled every Sunday), I was once again on guard, my heart pounding.

It was the end of January, the middle of summertime for us; a new moon bleached the rough concrete surface of the roof. As usual, I double-locked the little door; the one on my shack did not even have a bolt: I felt secure barricading myself up on the roof, under the open sky. It was not hard to imagine that the air, although quite humid, was fresher up there than down in the street.

I remember the unreal brightness of the moonlight upon the neighboring buildings, and my feeling of mindless lassitude, a calm despair that was something like a deep peace of the soul. Then I was startled to see a shadow move, very slowly, over by the shack. The man took a step and struck a match: its tiny flame illuminated a face that became pitted with dark hollows, like a skull, when he pulled on the cigarette until the tip glowed red. One more step and he was in the moonlight. It was Hermes.

I had not seen either him or his partner for weeks. Did Hermes feel free, for once, of the influence Aníbal exercised on him? He ventured a bland smile, and his voice adopted a distant, nostalgic tone: it was a pity we had never had a chance to talk in private, but he could not stay long that evening. He had brought me a message, and perhaps something more. Before giving me the long envelope he pulled from his hip pocket, he made me swear that I would never, ever, reveal that he had been there. He looked around, and we both tried not to laugh.

He went over to the edge of the roof, on the side facing the street, and we leaned over to look straight down: far below, the asphalt had a dirty, oily gleam to it. Hermes mumbled something melodramatic, calculating the number of seconds a body would take to plummet to the sidewalk. As the moon sank lower in the sky, it stretched out the shadows of the chimneys. Hermes hummed a tango under his breath. I loathed him.

Was I hoping he would let himself fall? He was silent now, and his breathing was shallow, irregular; he seemed to hesitate…. I did not make the slightest move to hold him back, since I did not believe he would do anything. He straightened up abruptly, ordering me in a threatening voice to look down at the street, off to the left. I took a step away from him before I leaned over to look: hands crossed behind his back, Aníbal was walking along the opposite sidewalk with measured tread. In spite of the heat, he was wearing his felt hat. He stopped short; when he looked up, I moved back out of sight.

Meanwhile, Hermes had forced the lock again with a hook, which he showed me, and leaning casually against the door jamb, he waved his hand limply, the way a traveler does as his train picks up speed, as long as those left behind on the platform might still see him. Then backed through the emergency exit door, disappearing into darkness.

The thick envelope bore only my initials and the warning, "Do not bend." It contained a boat ticket in my name for a passage to Naples. With it was a letter, in which I was invited to leave. The word "invited" made me smile. I was to go as soon as possible to the police station, where I was to see so-and-so about obtaining my passport, presenting him on the spot with the following necessary documents, and so on. I was to proceed to the travel agency, and I was not to forget to pass the hat around among my friends.

After these formal instructions, carefully numbered in the margins, Matías's writing opened up, spread out, and his four words of farewell slanted across the bottom of the page. The exclamation point, surrounded by a constellation of tiny splatters, had scratched the notepaper.

You can never know what to expect in life. Comforted by the illusion of choice and the virtues of patience, we spend our time trying to predict the future, and all for nothing.

One day, impelled by mutual attraction, or curiosity, you strike up a conversation, discover shared interests, and a friendship is born. You try to live the same hopes and dreams, feeling at ease, even happy; the friendship becomes part of your life. Then treachery strikes, and a great desolate wind sweeps away those castles in the sand. Wounded, despairing, angry, disoriented, you wish you were dead – you'd even like to kill your former friend. Then other mirages appear on the horizon, and one fine day, all that is left is a tiny scar on your heart, no bigger than a fingernail scratch. You no longer care anymore.

Once you have forgotten all about it, the person who hurt you might feel a deep need to make amends, and might compensate for his offense a hundredfold.

It was only a boat ticket, but I clutched it to my breast as though I had caught destiny in full flight.

Like a spider waiting out a storm in a crevice of tree bark, I had spent four years in that miserable shack. Now I was going to leave. I was so afraid I might be dreaming that I never closed my eyes all night, and I watched the neighboring rooftops reemerge at first light and the sky swell with the rising sun.

Matías: at this moment, I remember his disheveled black hair, the pallor of his face, and his right eye – or rather, the eyelid – which seems just about to wink at me.

60

FORTUNE WAS SMILING ON ME, AND I EAGERLY FOLLOWED her lead: How good it was to fling off fear, to forget those modest hopes dribbling on unfulfilled day after day, to feel at one – at last – with adventure!

I followed Matías's careful instructions successfully, and Alicia organized an evening of entertainment at her Petit Bar to raise money for my expenses. I no longer recall anything about this jolly soirée except that doña Sol, making her reappearance in my life after many years, arrived armed with her tarot cards and triumphed over the singers and comics: her predictions were a hit with the customers, who made a great fuss over her.

Late that night, I accompanied her home, and I will never forget the mysterious expression that came over her face when she turned as she was already crossing the threshold, and placing a chubby hand on my wrist, she whispered straight into my face, as though she had just received the message that instant from another dimension, that I was not leaving for the Old World but returning there.

Next, I took a quick trip out to Córdoba, where Cecilia now lived in a huge house with a garden, out in some distant suburb. Over the years, my brothers and sisters had gone to live near her, and then my parents had joined them all. Their house was in every respect similar to the one in Villa del Rosario and contained the same furniture. The top of the mahogany sideboard, where we had kept dishes at the farm, now seemed like a shrine where objects that had taken on a sacred character were exhibited behind glass. The duty of remembrance had governed my parents' enterprise, just as it commands this book. And so, to my amazement, I saw once more the skin of the "leopardina" tanned years ago by La Pinotta and hung from a nail at the head of her bed, between Christ and the Madonna. The yellow color seemed less bright, and the spots not quite as black as before, but the absolute terror of my first snake was still there, intact. They also had the photograph of Umberto of Savoy, my mother's wedding wreath of wax flowers, a rosary of olive-wood beads, a palm branch – blessed, no doubt – and a rock lobster's carapace, of an orange that stood out sharply against the faded colors of the other things. Tomasito Carrara had once brought this crustacean's shell to my father from Chile, where he spent his vacations.

On the day of my departure, my father summoned my mother and me into the dining room. He sat down at the end of the table, folding his hands on top of a thick register bound in maroon sheepskin in which he kept the accounts of his debtors up to date. My parents did not possess any assets other than their own savings, which they loaned to others, living on the monthly interest they received. At the time, over there, most people who were a little wealthier than their neighbors had made a respectable profession out of this practice, and as a result, usury was no longer a problem in the country. As if on purpose, the register in my father's hands opened to the page where my debt was recorded. Since I could not repay the sum due before my departure, nor even pay off the interest, he warned me against allowing the back-interest to accumulate. It was simply not in his character to forgive any delay whatsoever or to be pleased by anything other than the meticulousness of his bookkeeping, so there was no point in trying to win his confidence, either through a gesture of affection, which was unheard-of between us, or by a promise. But I did promise, firmly, to heed his advice.

My mother watched all this in silence, and it seemed to me that the look of severity in her eyes – in those eyes that had never let themselves betray terror or sorrow in front of her children – was only pretense.

Were there farewells? I cannot recall any of my brothers and sisters, or my father, or even my mother when the time comes for me to say good-bye. But when I leave, anxious to disappear from her sight around the first corner, I hear a sob that contracts, shrinks, drops into a low moan, and this stifled cry draws me back to her: my arms are around her shoulders, and I am holding my mother – who belongs to me, just for a second – so tightly that she is almost bent backward, and I do believe that in her solemn, childlike gaze I now see reflected the loving trust she has resolved to put in me. Her lips quiver, and she dares not smile for fear the tears she has been holding back will overflow.

In the bus, which seems to skim along the road, I do not tell myself that I am crossing the invincible plain for the last time, but that by going farther and ever farther away, I will get out. And mile after mile, I stare straight ahead, as though I were going to punch through the horizon.

After I had written the above lines, two small incidents occurred, a few hours apart, both involving photographs. I could not resist the temptation to consider these events as signs: silent, transient, infinitesimal signs, without any other consequence besides their evocation here, but signs nevertheless.

Between the pages of a book he must have lent me about fifteen years ago, a friend found a photo of my mother, the last one she had ever sent me. She is not looking at the camera but outside the frame, at the invisible person who was probably trying to make her laugh when the picture was taken. I never heard her laughter, and this image, bringing me a trace of it across the years, makes me jealous in a strange way. On the back, in quavery handwriting, she has noted the date, 3-14-75, thus continuing the intimate memorial she had begun by recording on a piece of paper the day and hour of birth, accurate to the minute, of all her children.

She was to die four years later. Since then, we have been absent from one another, scattered, wandering, lost, and yet it seems to me that we are constantly drawing close to one another, for we would like so much to soothe our feelings of remorse.

And then, on the same day, as I rummaged through the papers in a drawer, I came across the passport I had obtained through the scheming of Matías; I had forgotten all about it. And I stare in disbelief at my passport photo, spellbound in contemplation: How I would love to be that stranger who knows nothing of me, so sure of his chances, on his own, mysteriously sleek. I discover that I feel drawn to him and ashamed that I have not measured up to the dream he had of me. He has the confident gaze of statues, and there is no way to reach him. Perhaps he did not know his own face any more than I can recognize myself in it. And the more I study him, in that tiny photograph, the more he draws away, and the more I become a stranger to him, when suddenly I look from his head to his neck, and then his chest, and I can hear the whispery sound of the light, faintly rough material of his summer jacket, which becomes a proof of recognition, and the only link between us.

Did he leave me on the pier, trapped in that immense country? I remember the elephantine maneuvers of the ship, which took forever to swing around and head out to sea; I remember the happiness of watching the coast fall away behind us, and the feeling of peace that came over him when that first night at sea began to sweep up from the horizon, spreading its great blue wing across the sky. Why do I now feel that pain in my heart, that retrospective need to warn the traveler about the slow pace of destiny, and the traps it sets for us, when he is still the one who can show me the way and revive my sense of direction at the crossroads of life?

It does not matter to him that his pockets are empty; he is fully alive only to the wind, which is blustering like a grand organ in its loft, and to the intoxication of having left at last, a young man who can do whatever he pleases with the whole wide world.

And most of all, I remember the moment one evening on the promenade deck when a little girl cried out, "Tonight you cannot see the Southern Cross anymore!" She was as delighted as if she herself had erased the constellation from the sky. When the young man looked up at the new stars overhead, his entire existence broke free of time, toppling into the ocean depths and carrying to the bottom of his soul the anguish of the endless plain, the faces he loved and those he hated, his fear in the streets of Buenos Aires, and – without any dimming of his happiness by compassion – the stifled grief of his mother.

Did his conscience awaken, allowing him a glimpse of the dangers he was running? Refusing all self-doubt and hesitation, he banished such thoughts with the confidence of one enjoying at last the power of freedom. He knew that we are not often proud of belonging to the human race, which is blind and without pity. But he told himself – and here is where we leave each other – that whatever happened on the unknown shores where he was bound, be it poverty and failure and even death, it would all be, in the end, and for always, in honor of life.